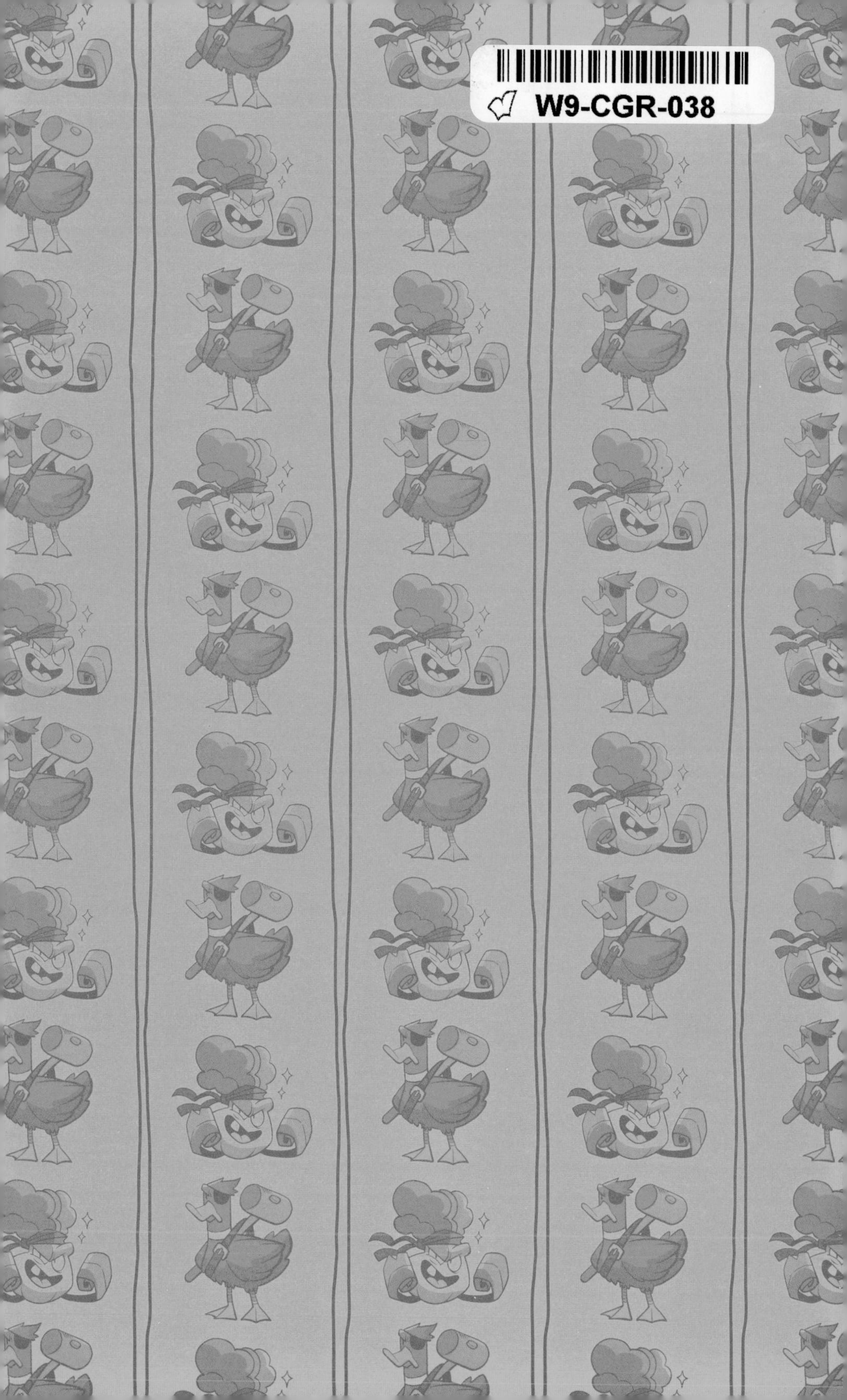

PLANTS VS. ZOMBIES

FAULTY FABLES

Written by PAUL TOBIN
Art by CHRISTIANNE GILLENARDO-GOUDREAU
Colors by HEATHER BRECKEL
Letters by STEVE DUTRO
Cover by CHRISTIANNE GILLENARDO-GOUDREAU

DARK HORSE BOOKS

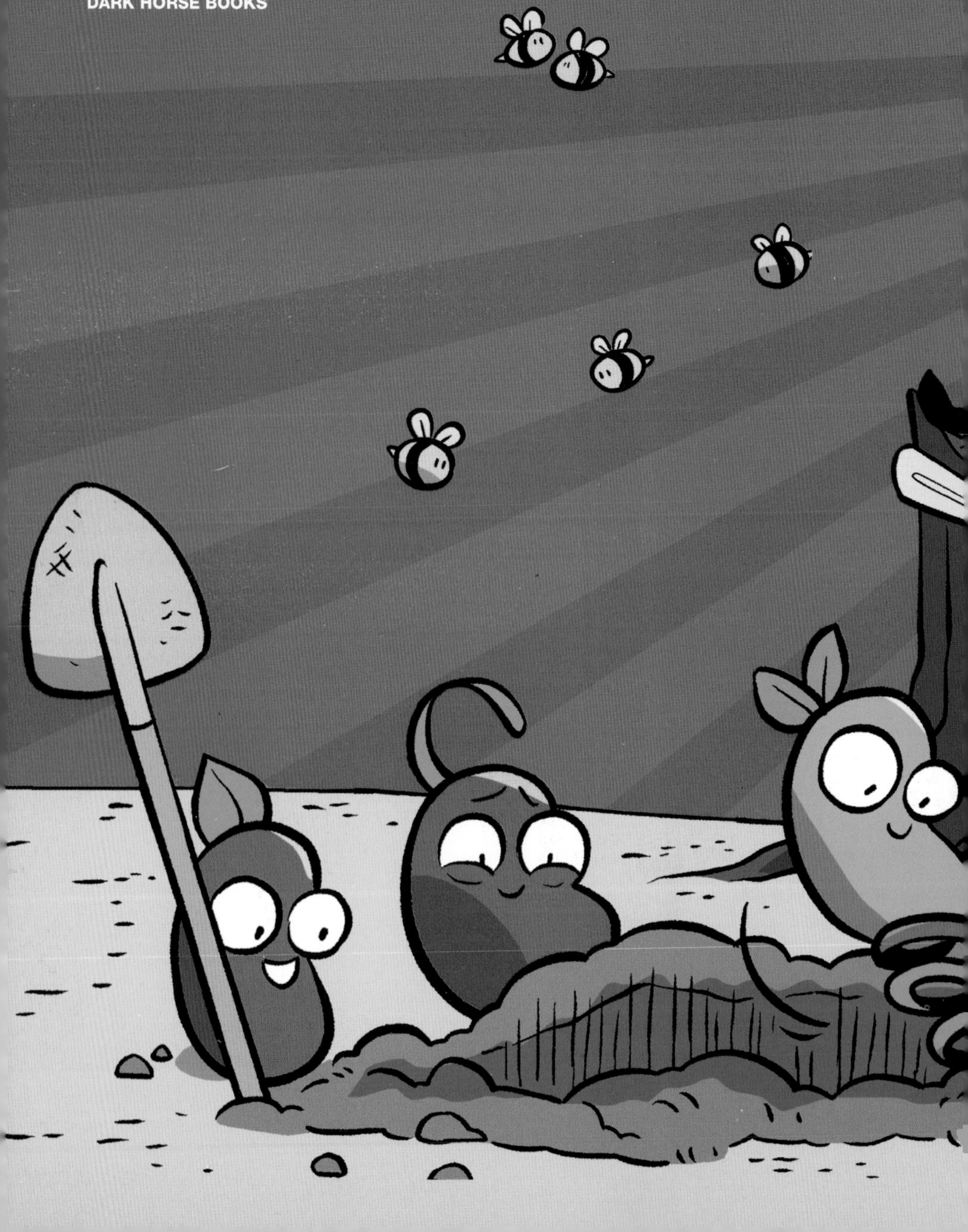

PLANTS VS. ZOMBIES™

FAULTY FABLES

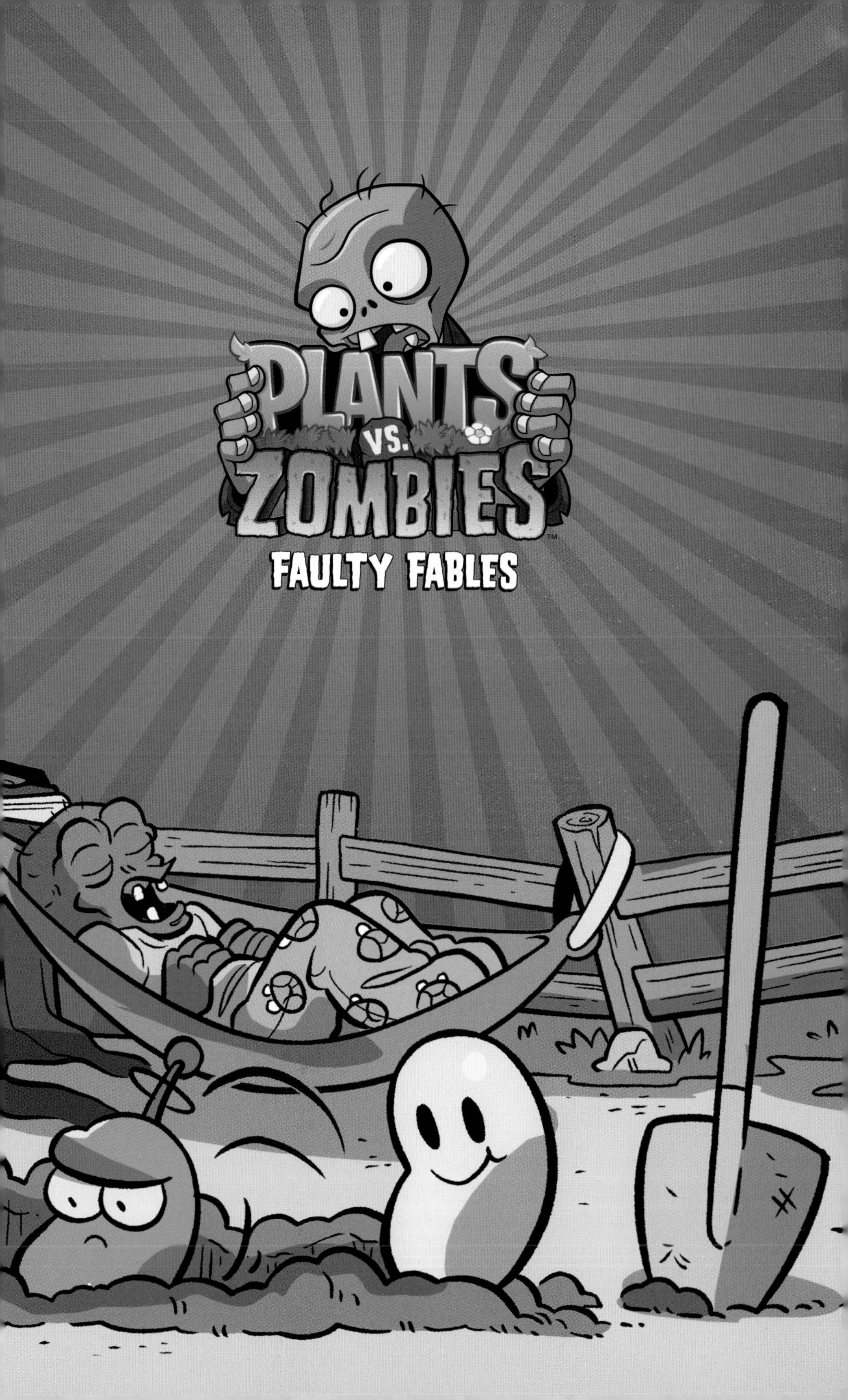

President and Publisher **MIKE RICHARDSON**
Senior Editor **PHILIP R. SIMON**
Associate Editor **JUDY KHUU**
Assistant Editor **ROSE WEITZ**
Designer **KATHLEEN BARNETT**
Digital Art Technician **ALLYSON HALLER**

Special thanks to Joshua Franks, Ryan Jones, Jessica Leung, Christopher Olsen, Kristen Star, Matt Townsend, and everyone at PopCap Games and EA Games.

First Edition: February 2023
Ebook ISBN 978-1-50672-854-4
Hardcover ISBN 978-1-50672-846-9

10 9 8 7 6 5 4 3 2 1
Printed in China

MIX
Paper from responsible sources
FSC® C109093

DarkHorse.com
PopCap.com

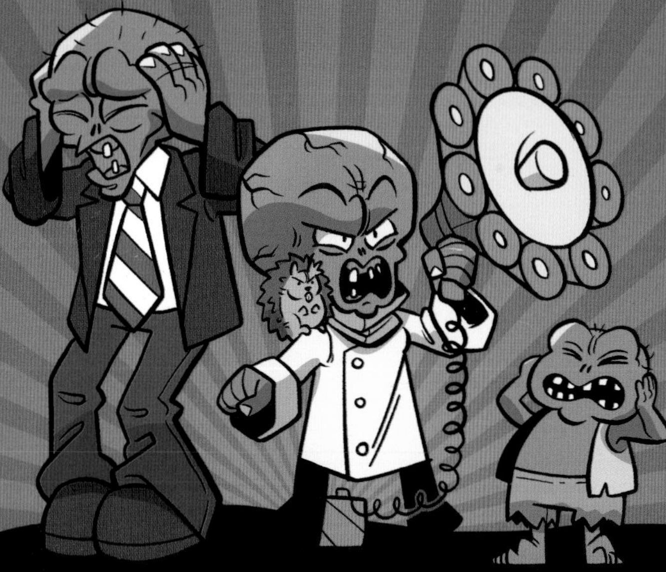

No plants were harmed in the making of this graphic novel. However, the zombie named Frogpants was definitely injured . . . and many zombie imps are now missing.

Library of Congress Cataloging-in-Publication Data

Names: Tobin, Paul, 1965- author. | Breckel, Heather, colourist. | Dutro, Steve, letterer. | Gillenardo-Goudreau, Christianne, cover artist.
Title: Faulty fables / writer, Paul Tobin ; colors, Heather Breckel ; letters, Steve Dutro ; cover art, Christianne Gillenardo-Goudreau.
Description: Milwaukie, OR : Dark Horse Books, [2023] | Series: Plants vs. zombies ; volume 20 | Audience: Ages 8+. | Audience: Grades 2-3.
Identifiers: LCCN 2022040860 (print) | LCCN 2022040861 (ebook) | ISBN 9781506728469 (hardcover) | ISBN 9781506728544 (ebook)
Subjects: CYAC: Graphic novels. | Zombies--Fiction. | Plants--Fiction. | Humorous stories. | LCGFT: Humorous comics. | Graphic novels.
Classification: LCC PZ7.7.T62 Fau 2023 (print) | LCC PZ7.7.T62 (ebook) | DDC 741.5/973--dc23/eng/20220917
LC record available at https://lccn.loc.gov/2022040860
LC ebook record available at https://lccn.loc.gov/2022040861

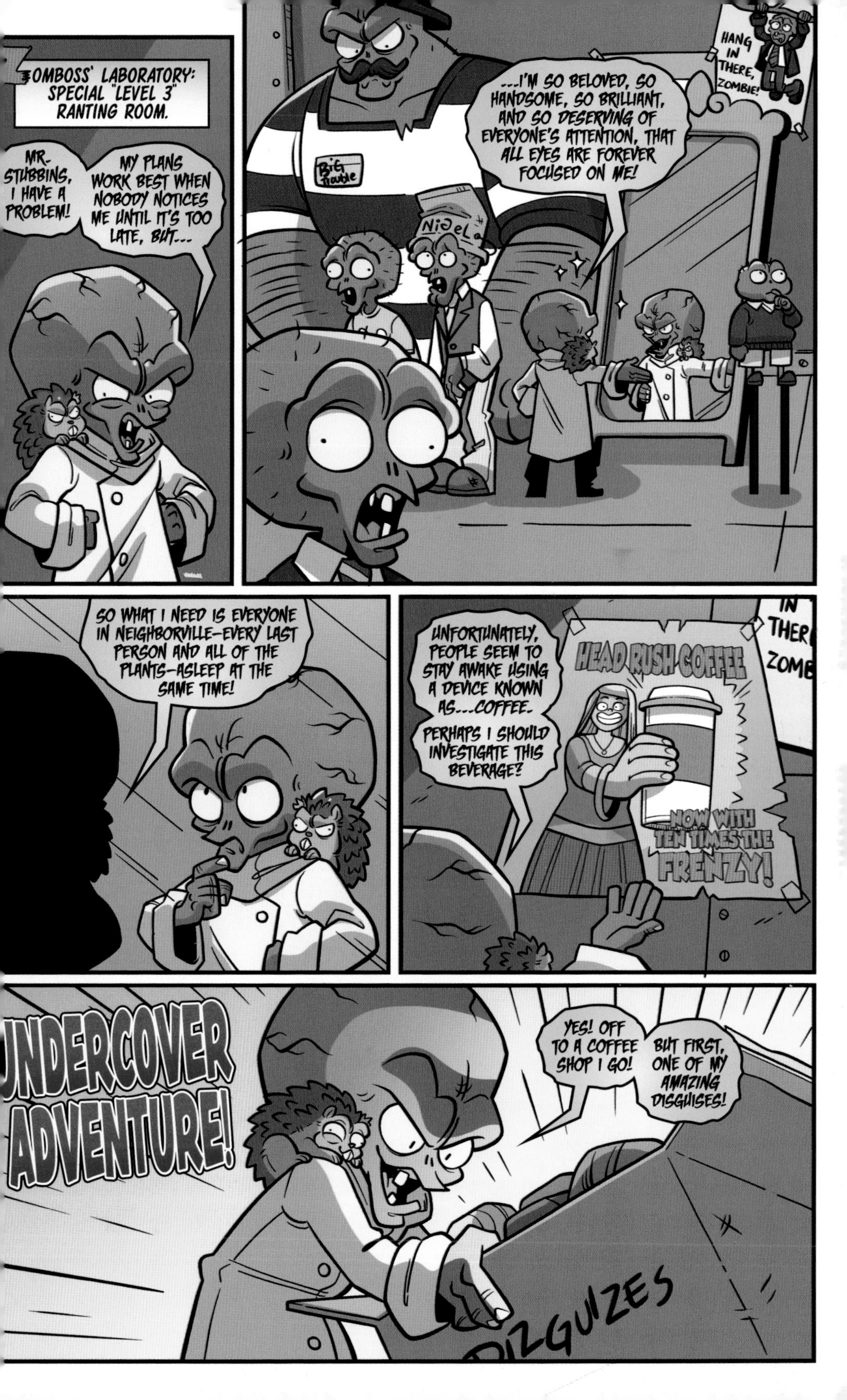
ZOMBOSS' LABORATORY: SPECIAL "LEVEL 3" RANTING ROOM.
MR. STUBBINS, I HAVE A PROBLEM!
MY PLANS WORK BEST WHEN NOBODY NOTICES ME UNTIL IT'S TOO LATE, BUT...
...I'M SO BELOVED, SO HANDSOME, SO BRILLIANT, AND SO DESERVING OF EVERYONE'S ATTENTION, THAT ALL EYES ARE FOREVER FOCUSED ON ME!
HANG IN THERE, ZOMBIE!
BIG TROUBLE
NIGEL
SO WHAT I NEED IS EVERYONE IN NEIGHBORVILLE—EVERY LAST PERSON AND ALL OF THE PLANTS—ASLEEP AT THE SAME TIME!
UNFORTUNATELY, PEOPLE SEEM TO STAY AWAKE USING A DEVICE KNOWN AS...COFFEE.
PERHAPS I SHOULD INVESTIGATE THIS BEVERAGE?
HEAD RUSH COFFEE
NOW WITH TEN TIMES THE FRENZY!
UNDERCOVER ADVENTURE!
YES! OFF TO A COFFEE SHOP I GO!
BUT FIRST, ONE OF MY AMAZING DISGUISES!
DIZGUIZES

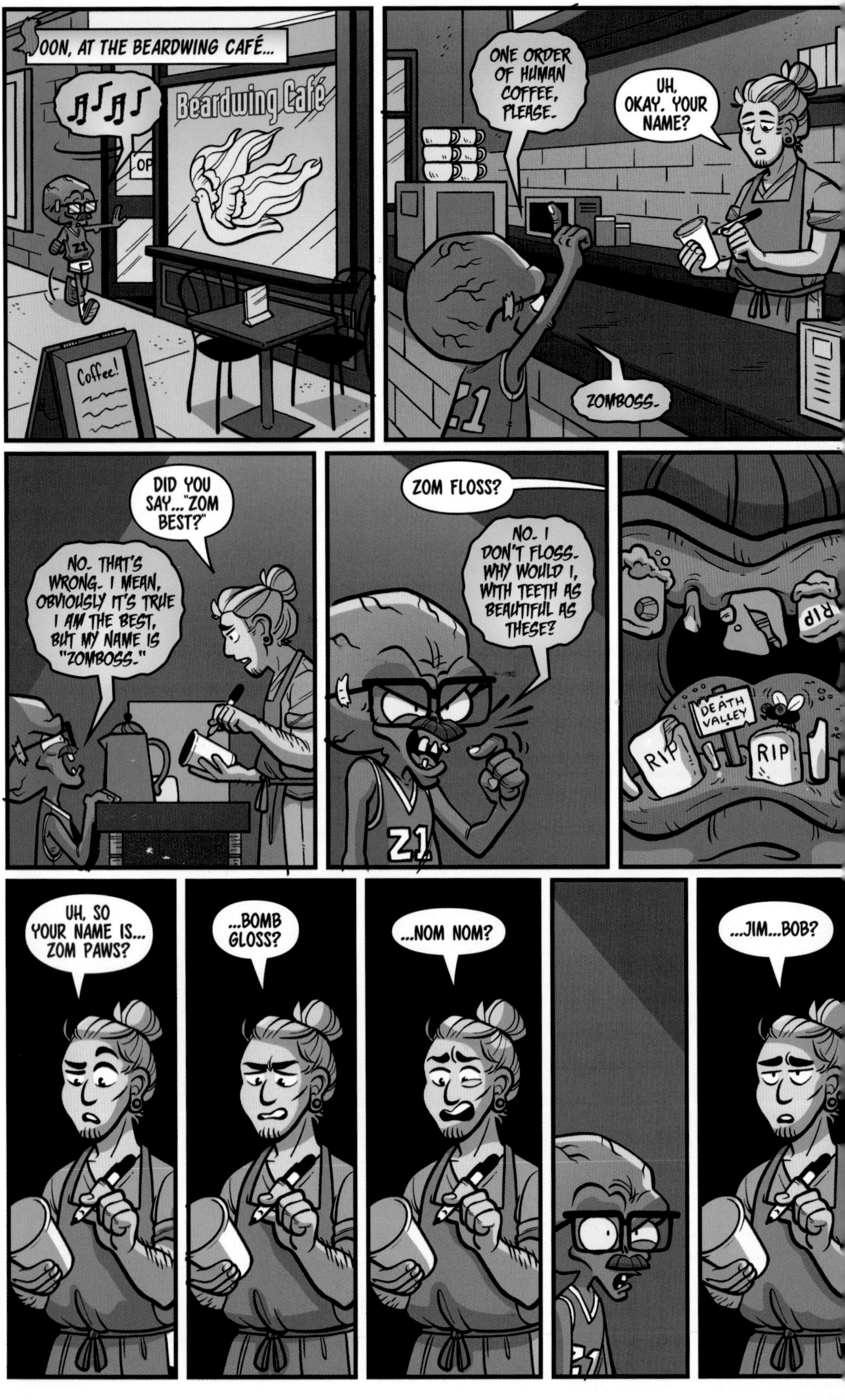
SOON, AT THE BEARDWING CAFÉ...
Beardwing Café
OP
Coffee!
ONE ORDER OF HUMAN COFFEE, PLEASE.
UH, OKAY. YOUR NAME?
ZOMBOSS.
DID YOU SAY..."ZOM BEST?"
NO. THAT'S WRONG. I MEAN, OBVIOUSLY IT'S TRUE I AM THE BEST, BUT MY NAME IS "ZOMBOSS."
ZOM FLOSS?
NO. I DON'T FLOSS. WHY WOULD I, WITH TEETH AS BEAUTIFUL AS THESE?
RIP
DEATH VALLEY
RIP
RIP
UH, SO YOUR NAME IS... ZOM PAWS?
...BOMB GLOSS?
...NOM NOM?
...JIM...BOB?

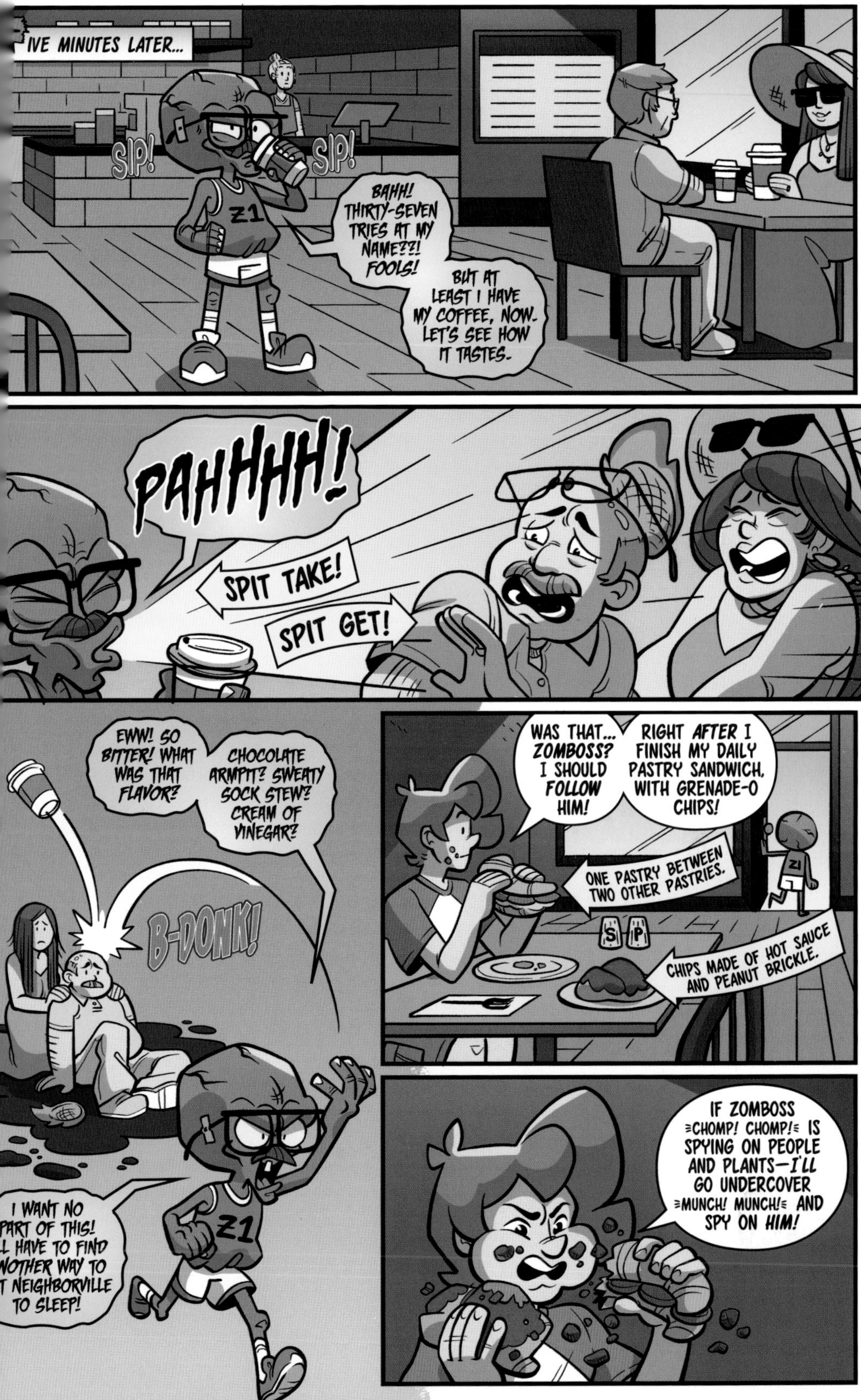
IVE MINUTES LATER...
SIP! SIP!
BAHH! THIRTY-SEVEN TRIES AT MY NAME??! FOOLS!
BUT AT LEAST I HAVE MY COFFEE, NOW. LET'S SEE HOW IT TASTES.
PAHHHH!
SPIT TAKE!
SPIT GET!
EWW! SO BITTER! WHAT WAS THAT FLAVOR?
CHOCOLATE ARMPIT? SWEATY SOCK STEW? CREAM OF VINEGAR?
B-DONK!
I WANT NO PART OF THIS! LL HAVE TO FIND NOTHER WAY TO T NEIGHBORVILLE TO SLEEP!
WAS THAT... ZOMBOSS? I SHOULD FOLLOW HIM!
RIGHT AFTER I FINISH MY DAILY PASTRY SANDWICH, WITH GRENADE-O CHIPS!
ONE PASTRY BETWEEN TWO OTHER PASTRIES.
S P
CHIPS MADE OF HOT SAUCE AND PEANUT BRICKLE.
IF ZOMBOSS CHOMP! CHOMP! IS SPYING ON PEOPLE AND PLANTS—I'LL GO UNDERCOVER MUNCH! MUNCH! AND SPY ON HIM!

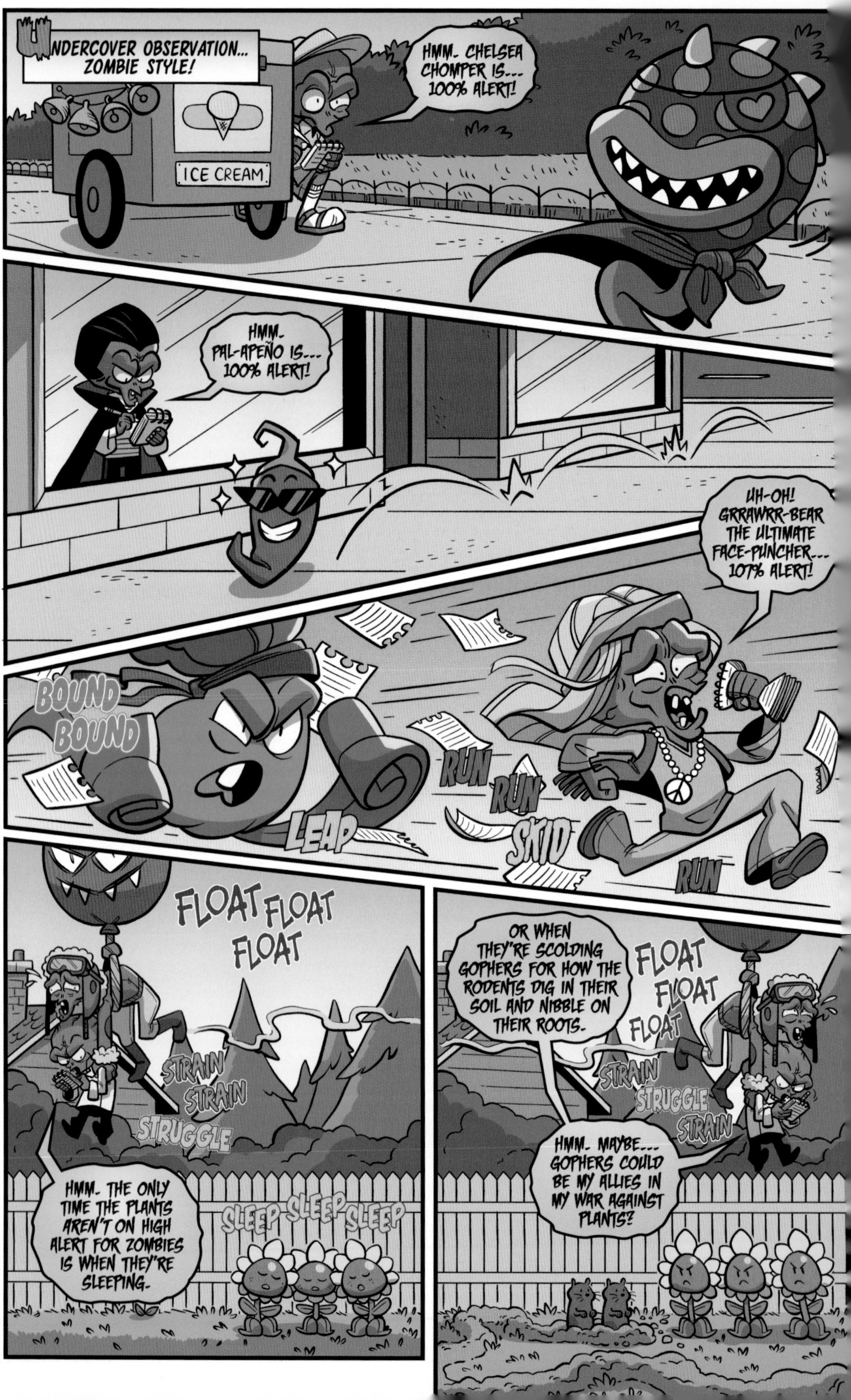

UNDERCOVER OBSERVATION... ZOMBIE STYLE!
ICE CREAM
HMM. CHELSEA CHOMPER IS... 100% ALERT!
HMM. PAL-APEÑO IS... 100% ALERT!
UH-OH! GRRAWRR-BEAR THE ULTIMATE FACE-PUNCHER... 107% ALERT!
BOUND BOUND
LEAP
RUN RUN
SKID
RUN
FLOAT FLOAT FLOAT
STRAIN STRAIN
STRUGGLE
HMM. THE ONLY TIME THE PLANTS AREN'T ON HIGH ALERT FOR ZOMBIES IS WHEN THEY'RE SLEEPING.
SLEEP SLEEP SLEEP
OR WHEN THEY'RE SCOLDING GOPHERS FOR HOW THE RODENTS DIG IN THEIR SOIL AND NIBBLE ON THEIR ROOTS.
FLOAT FLOAT FLOAT
STRAIN
STRUGGLE
STRAIN
HMM. MAYBE... GOPHERS COULD BE MY ALLIES IN MY WAR AGAINST PLANTS?

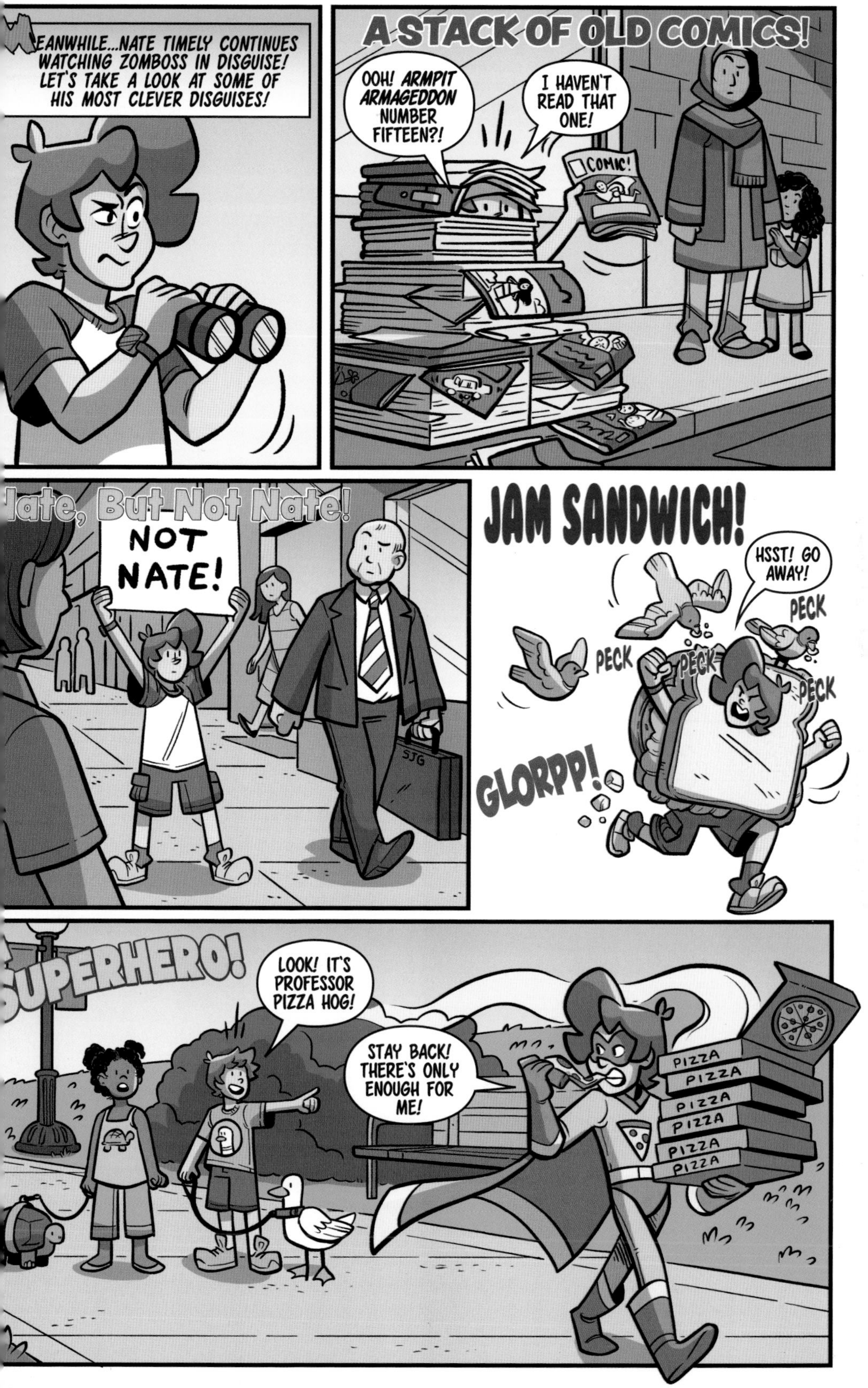
MEANWHILE...NATE TIMELY CONTINUES WATCHING ZOMBOSS IN DISGUISE! LET'S TAKE A LOOK AT SOME OF HIS MOST CLEVER DISGUISES!
A STACK OF OLD COMICS!
OOH! *ARMPIT ARMAGEDDON* NUMBER FIFTEEN?!
I HAVEN'T READ THAT ONE!
COMIC!
Nate, But Not Nate!
NOT NATE!
SJG
JAM SANDWICH!
HSST! GO AWAY!
PECK
PECK
PECK
PECK
GLORPP!
SUPERHERO!
LOOK! IT'S PROFESSOR PIZZA HOG!
STAY BACK! THERE'S ONLY ENOUGH FOR ME!
PIZZA
PIZZA
PIZZA
PIZZA
PIZZA
PIZZA

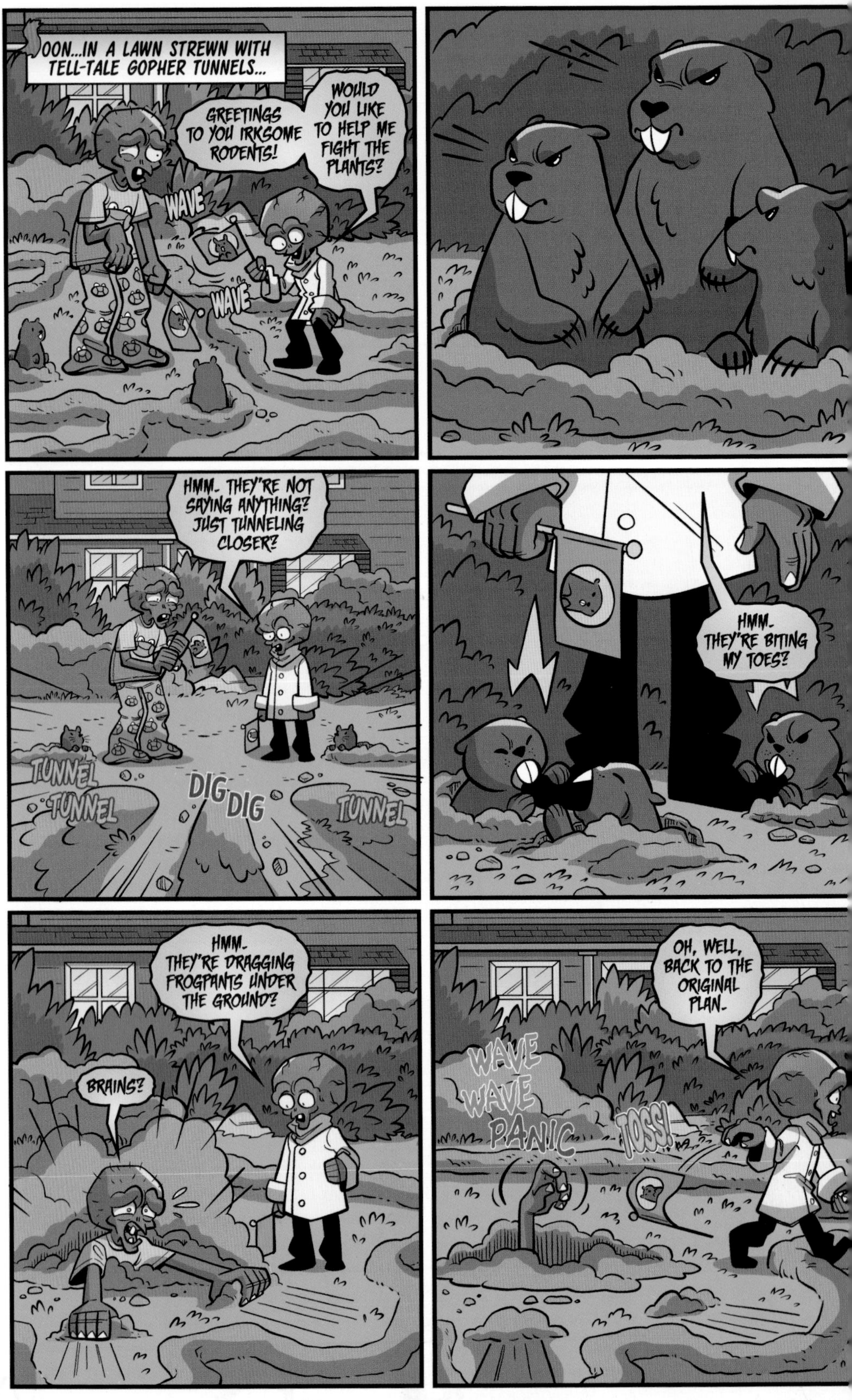
SOON...IN A LAWN STREWN WITH TELL-TALE GOPHER TUNNELS...
GREETINGS TO YOU IRKSOME RODENTS!
WOULD YOU LIKE TO HELP ME FIGHT THE PLANTS?
WAVE
WAVE
HMM. THEY'RE NOT SAYING ANYTHING? JUST TUNNELING CLOSER?
TUNNEL
TUNNEL
DIG
DIG
TUNNEL
HMM. THEY'RE BITING MY TOES?
HMM. THEY'RE DRAGGING FROGPANTS UNDER THE GROUND?
BRAINS?
OH, WELL, BACK TO THE ORIGINAL PLAN.
WAVE
WAVE
PANIC
TOSS!

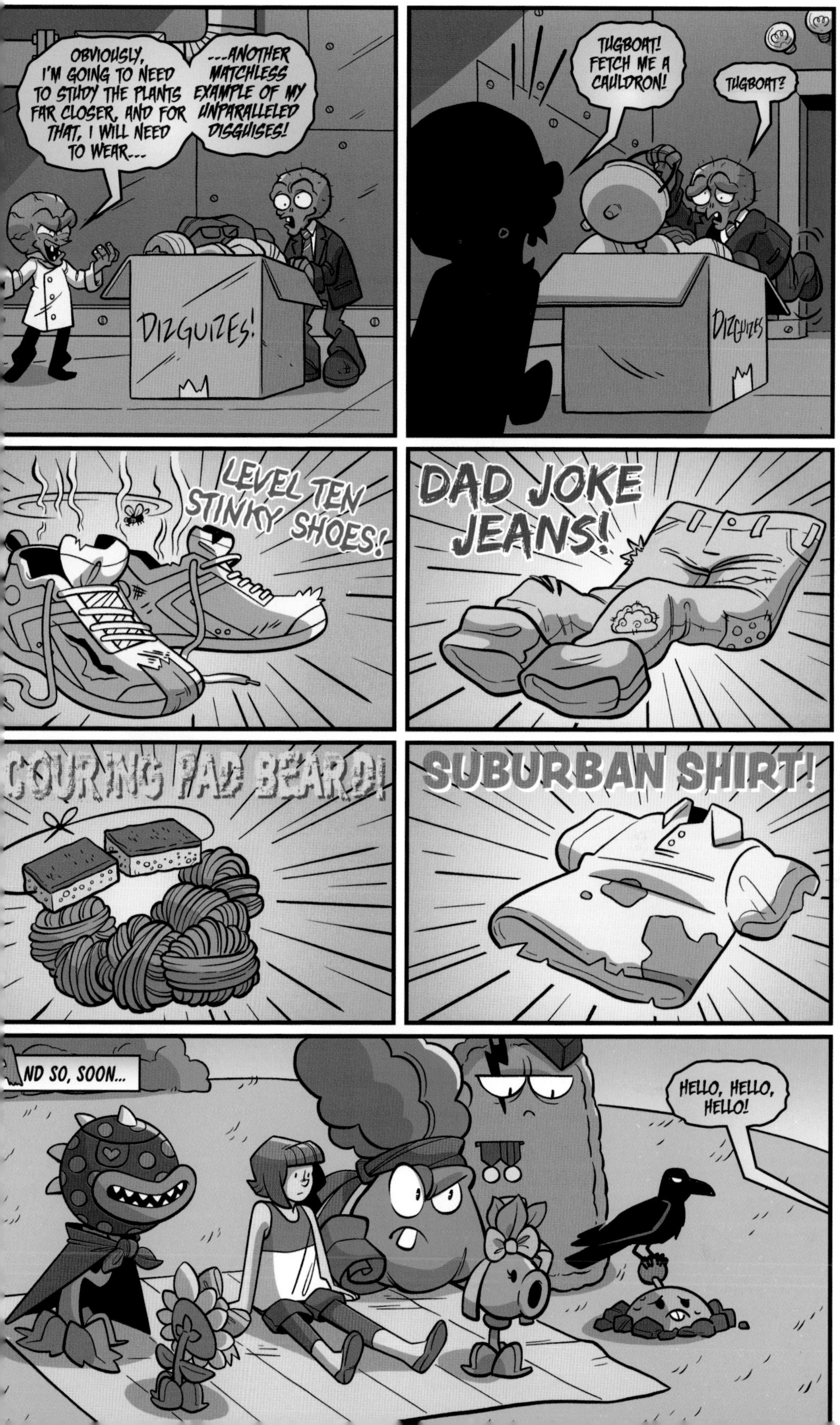
OBVIOUSLY, I'M GOING TO NEED TO STUDY THE PLANTS FAR CLOSER, AND FOR THAT, I WILL NEED TO WEAR...
...ANOTHER MATCHLESS EXAMPLE OF MY UNPARALLELED DISGUISES!
DIZGUIZES!
TUGBOAT! FETCH ME A CAULDRON!
TUGBOAT?
DIZGUIZES
LEVEL TEN STINKY SHOES!
DAD JOKE JEANS!
COURING PAD BEARD!
SUBURBAN SHIRT!
ND SO, SOON...
HELLO, HELLO, HELLO!

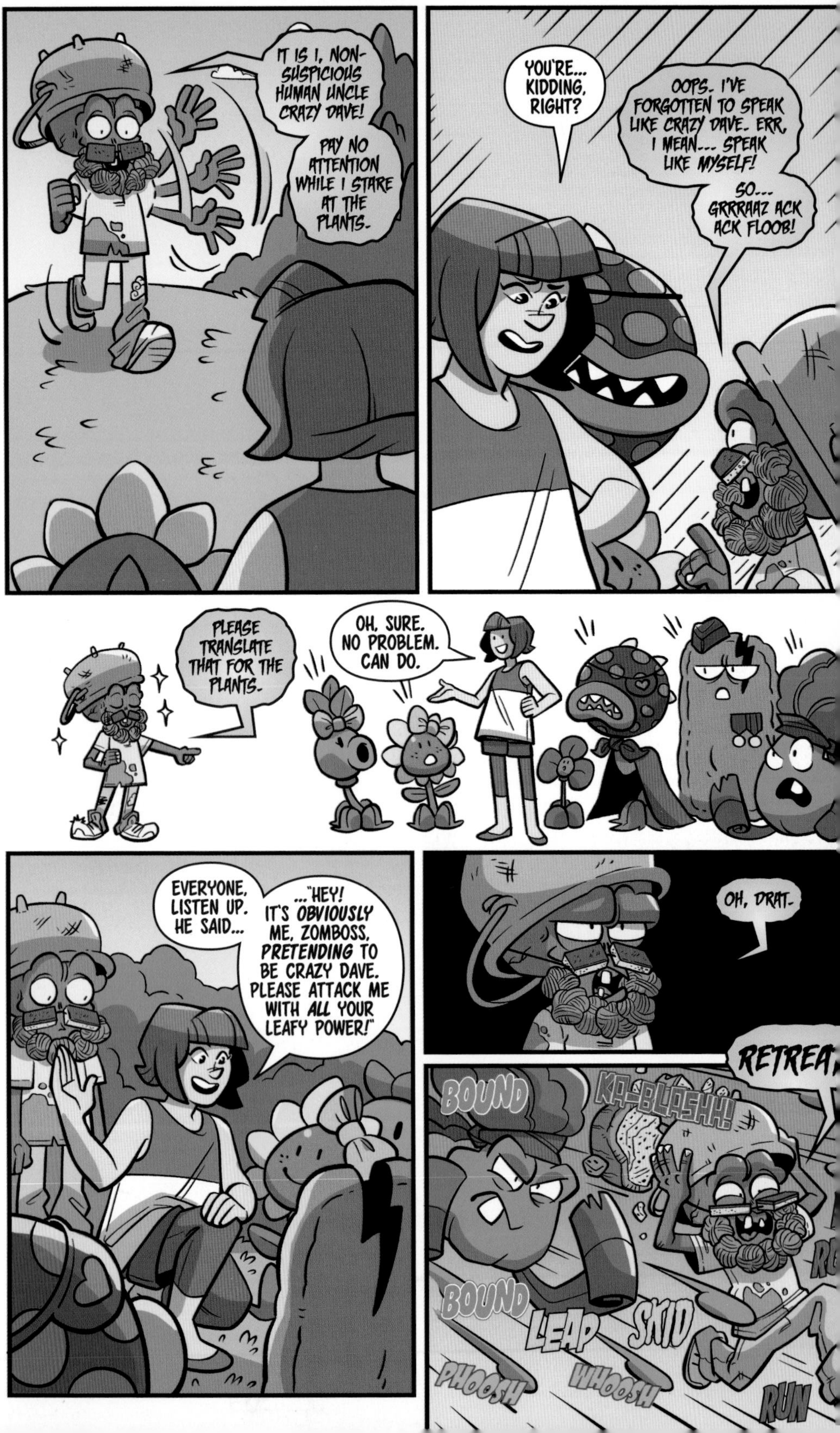

IT IS I, NON-SUSPICIOUS HUMAN UNCLE CRAZY DAVE!
PAY NO ATTENTION WHILE I STARE AT THE PLANTS.
YOU'RE... KIDDING, RIGHT?
OOPS. I'VE FORGOTTEN TO SPEAK LIKE CRAZY DAVE. ERR, I MEAN... SPEAK LIKE MYSELF!
SO... GRRRAAZ ACK ACK FLOOB!
PLEASE TRANSLATE THAT FOR THE PLANTS.
OH, SURE. NO PROBLEM. CAN DO.
EVERYONE, LISTEN UP. HE SAID...
..."HEY! IT'S OBVIOUSLY ME, ZOMBOSS, PRETENDING TO BE CRAZY DAVE. PLEASE ATTACK ME WITH ALL YOUR LEAFY POWER!"
OH, DRAT.
RETREA
BOUND
KA-BLASHH!
BOUND
LEAP
SKID
PHOOSH
WHOOSH
RUN

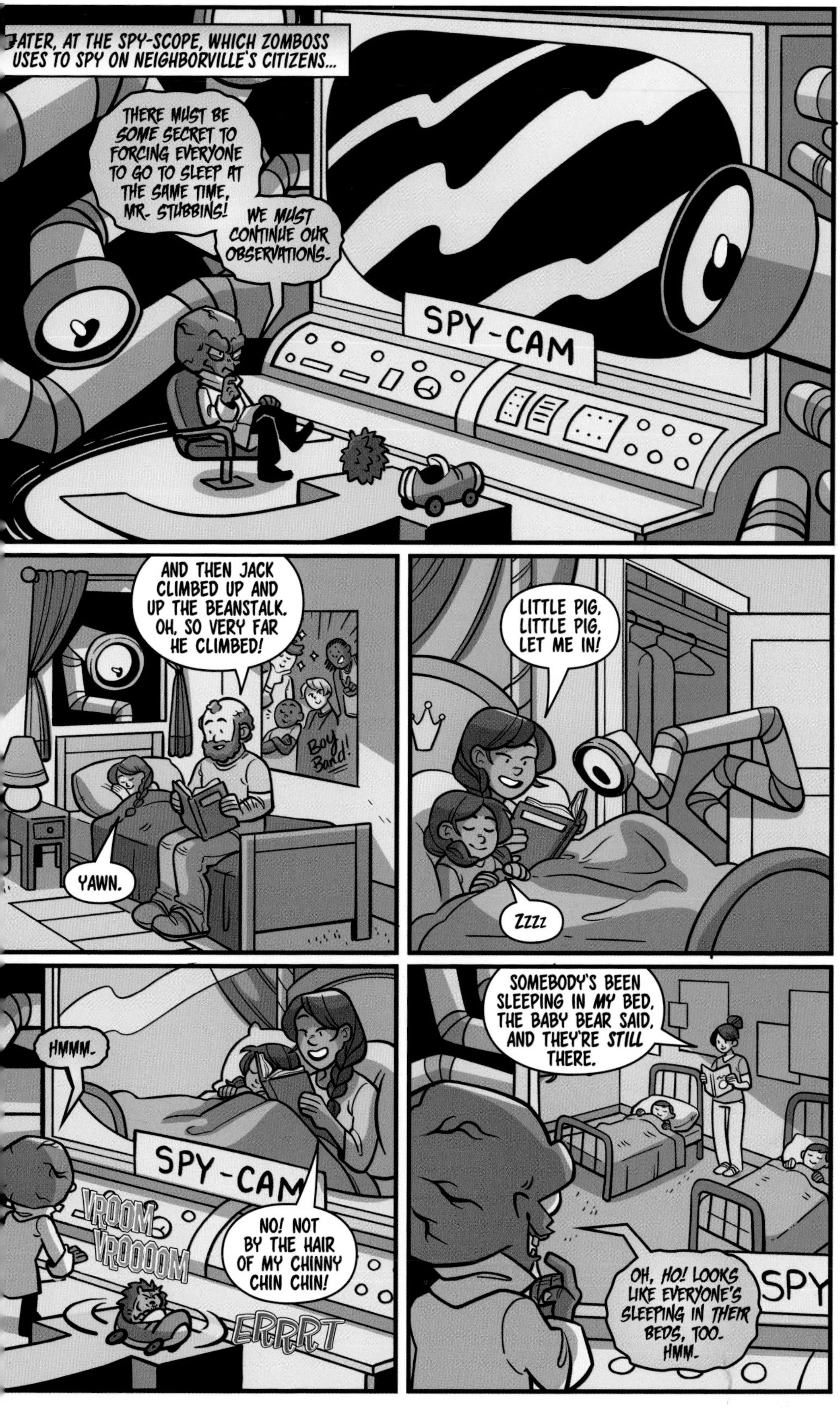
LATER, AT THE SPY-SCOPE, WHICH ZOMBOSS USES TO SPY ON NEIGHBORVILLE'S CITIZENS...
THERE MUST BE SOME SECRET TO FORCING EVERYONE TO GO TO SLEEP AT THE SAME TIME, MR. STUBBINS!
WE MUST CONTINUE OUR OBSERVATIONS.
SPY-CAM
AND THEN JACK CLIMBED UP AND UP THE BEANSTALK. OH, SO VERY FAR HE CLIMBED!
Boy Band!
YAWN.
LITTLE PIG, LITTLE PIG, LET ME IN!
ZZZZ
HMMM.
SPY-CAM
VROOM VROOOOM
NO! NOT BY THE HAIR OF MY CHINNY CHIN CHIN!
ERRRRT
SOMEBODY'S BEEN SLEEPING IN MY BED, THE BABY BEAR SAID, AND THEY'RE STILL THERE.
OH, HO! LOOKS LIKE EVERYONE'S SLEEPING IN THEIR BEDS, TOO. HMM.
SPY

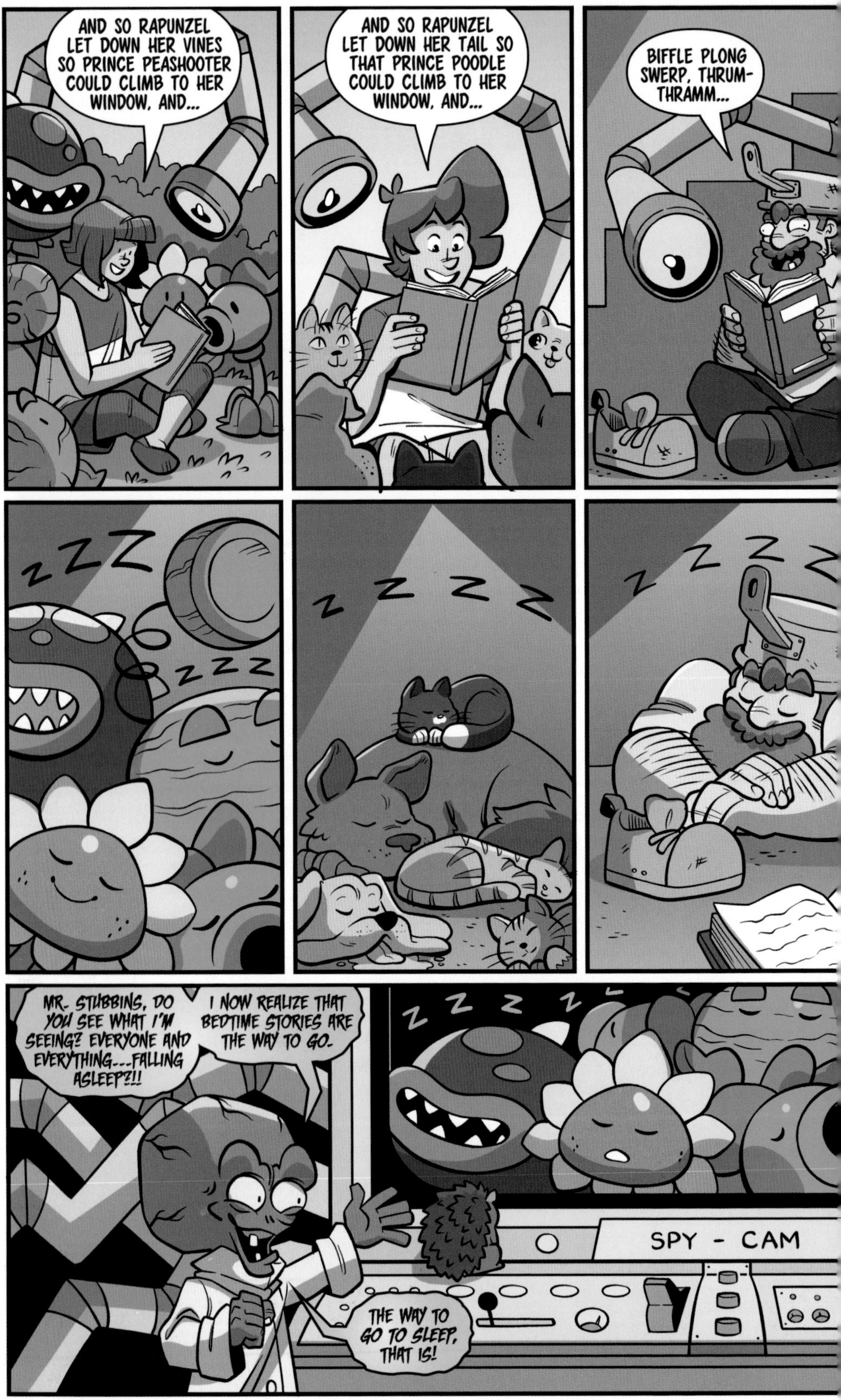
AND SO RAPUNZEL LET DOWN HER VINES SO PRINCE PEASHOOTER COULD CLIMB TO HER WINDOW, AND...
AND SO RAPUNZEL LET DOWN HER TAIL SO THAT PRINCE POODLE COULD CLIMB TO HER WINDOW, AND...
BIFFLE PLONG SWERP, THRUM-THRAMM...
MR. STUBBINS, DO YOU SEE WHAT I'M SEEING? EVERYONE AND EVERYTHING...FALLING ASLEEP?!!
I NOW REALIZE THAT BEDTIME STORIES ARE THE WAY TO GO.
SPY - CAM
THE WAY TO GO TO SLEEP, THAT IS!

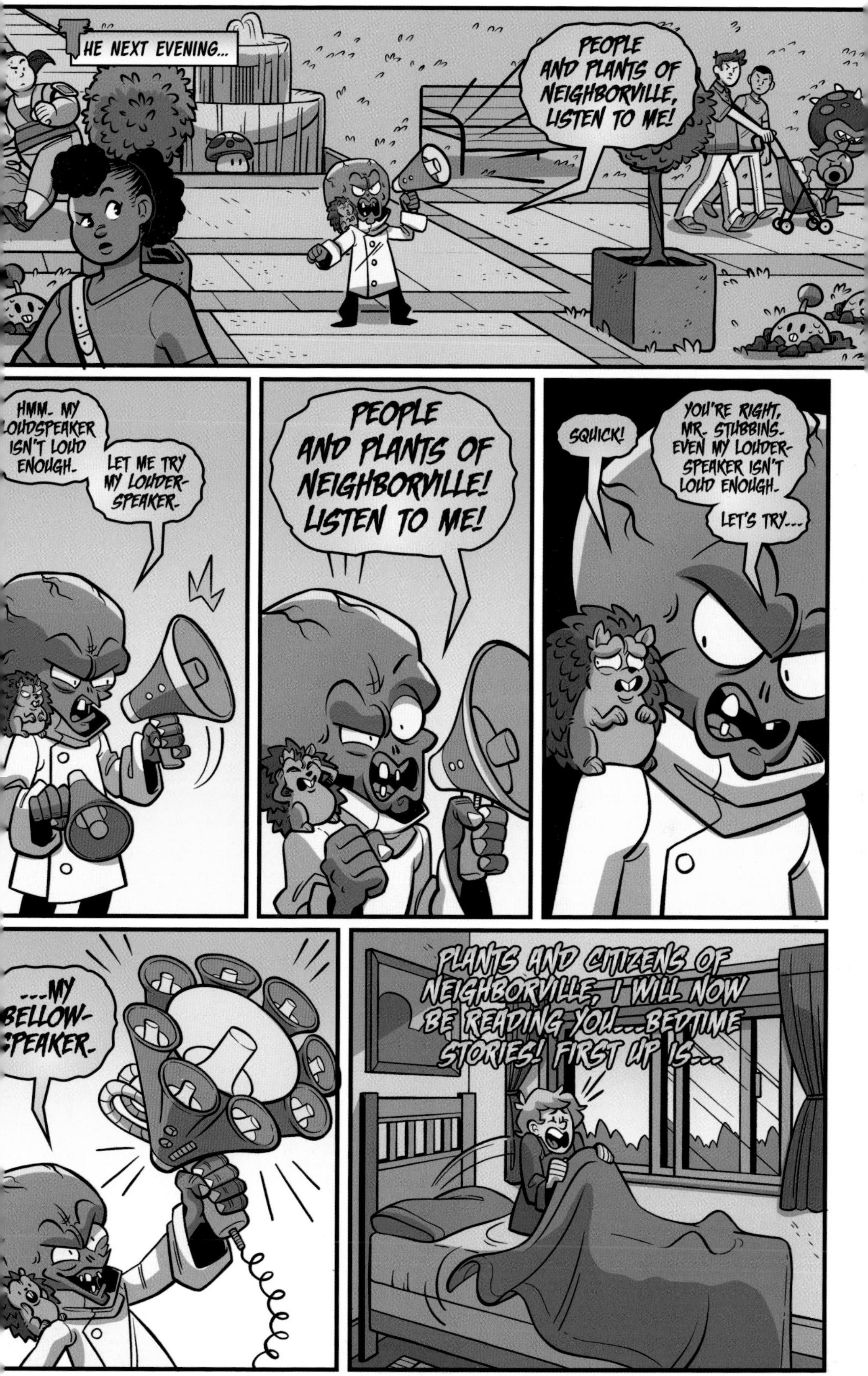

THE NEXT EVENING...
PEOPLE AND PLANTS OF NEIGHBORVILLE, LISTEN TO ME!
HMM. MY LOUDSPEAKER ISN'T LOUD ENOUGH.
LET ME TRY MY LOUDER-SPEAKER.
PEOPLE AND PLANTS OF NEIGHBORVILLE! LISTEN TO ME!
SQUICK!
YOU'RE RIGHT, MR. STUBBINS. EVEN MY LOUDER-SPEAKER ISN'T LOUD ENOUGH.
LET'S TRY...
...MY BELLOW-SPEAKER.
PLANTS AND CITIZENS OF NEIGHBORVILLE, I WILL NOW BE READING YOU...BEDTIME STORIES! FIRST UP IS...

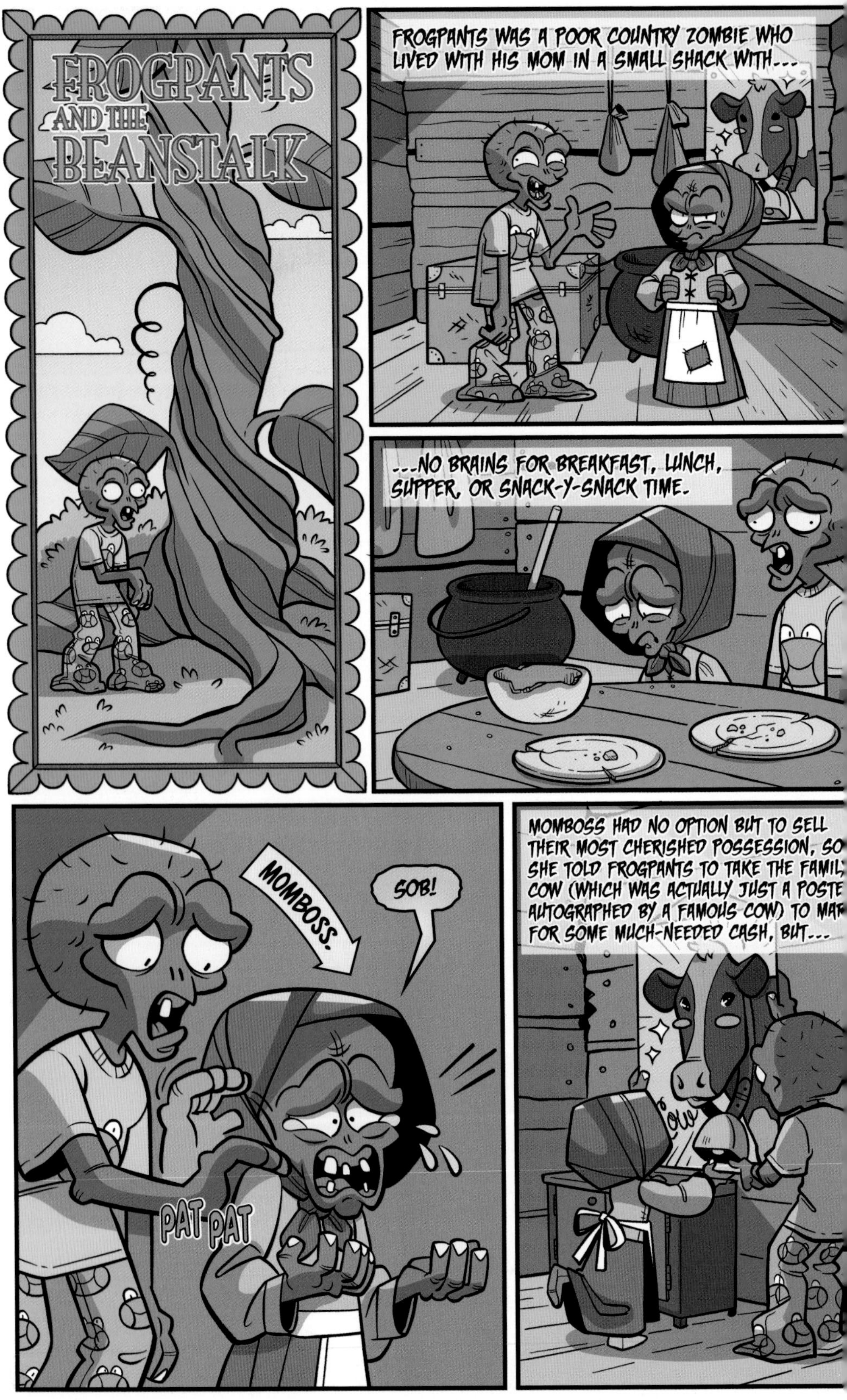
FROGPANTS AND THE BEANSTALK
FROGPANTS WAS A POOR COUNTRY ZOMBIE WHO LIVED WITH HIS MOM IN A SMALL SHACK WITH...
...NO BRAINS FOR BREAKFAST, LUNCH, SUPPER, OR SNACK-Y-SNACK TIME.
MOMBOSS.
SOB!
PAT PAT
MOMBOSS HAD NO OPTION BUT TO SELL THEIR MOST CHERISHED POSSESSION, SO SHE TOLD FROGPANTS TO TAKE THE FAMIL COW (WHICH WAS ACTUALLY JUST A POSTE AUTOGRAPHED BY A FAMOUS COW) TO MA FOR SOME MUCH-NEEDED CASH, BUT...
COW

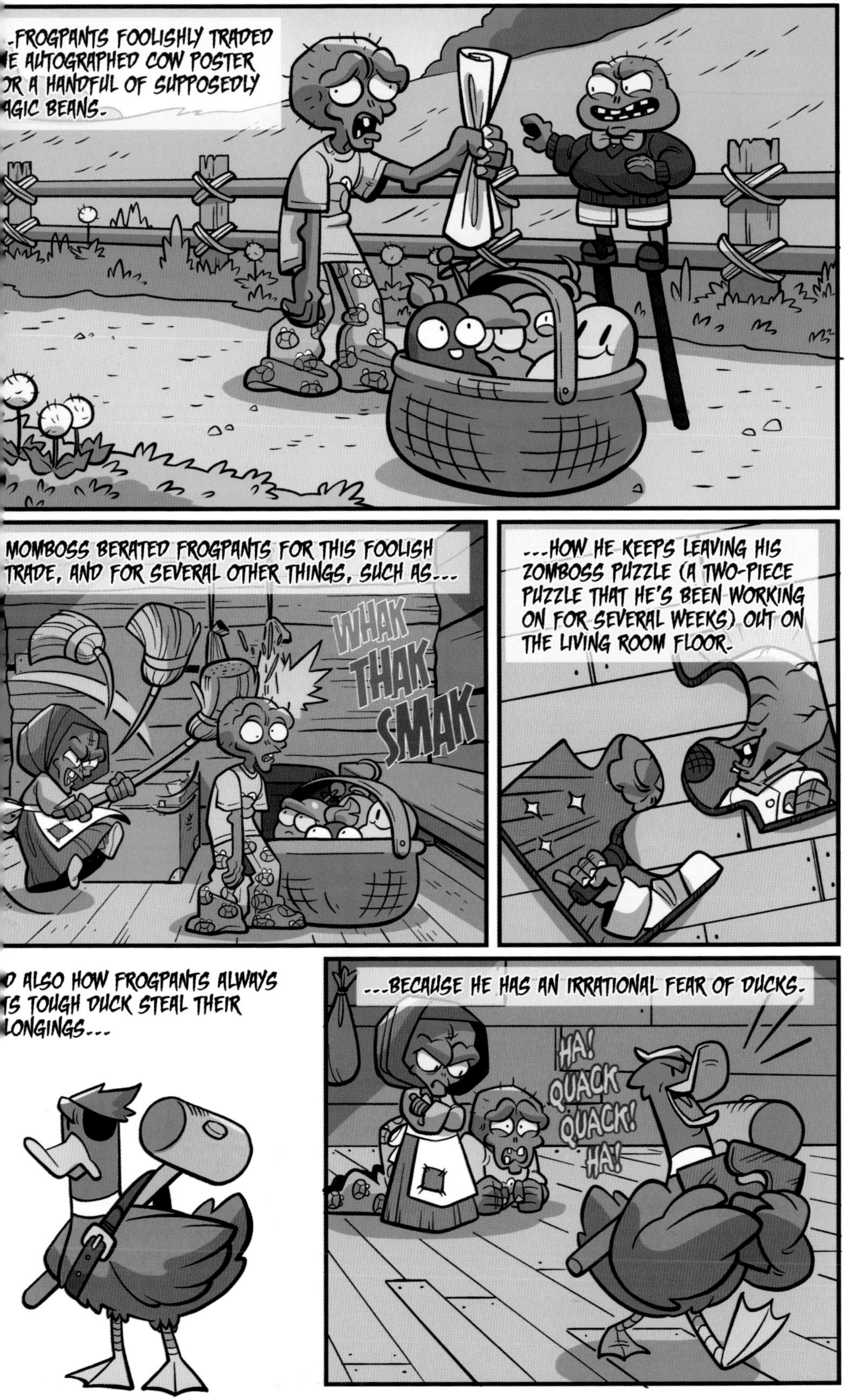
.-FROGPANTS FOOLISHLY TRADED
E AUTOGRAPHED COW POSTER
R A HANDFUL OF SUPPOSEDLY
AGIC BEANS.
MOMBOSS BERATED FROGPANTS FOR THIS FOOLISH TRADE, AND FOR SEVERAL OTHER THINGS, SUCH AS...
WHAK
THAK
SMAK
...HOW HE KEEPS LEAVING HIS ZOMBOSS PUZZLE (A TWO-PIECE PUZZLE THAT HE'S BEEN WORKING ON FOR SEVERAL WEEKS) OUT ON THE LIVING ROOM FLOOR.
D ALSO HOW FROGPANTS ALWAYS
S TOUGH DUCK STEAL THEIR
LONGINGS...
...BECAUSE HE HAS AN IRRATIONAL FEAR OF DUCKS.
HA!
QUACK
QUACK!
HA!

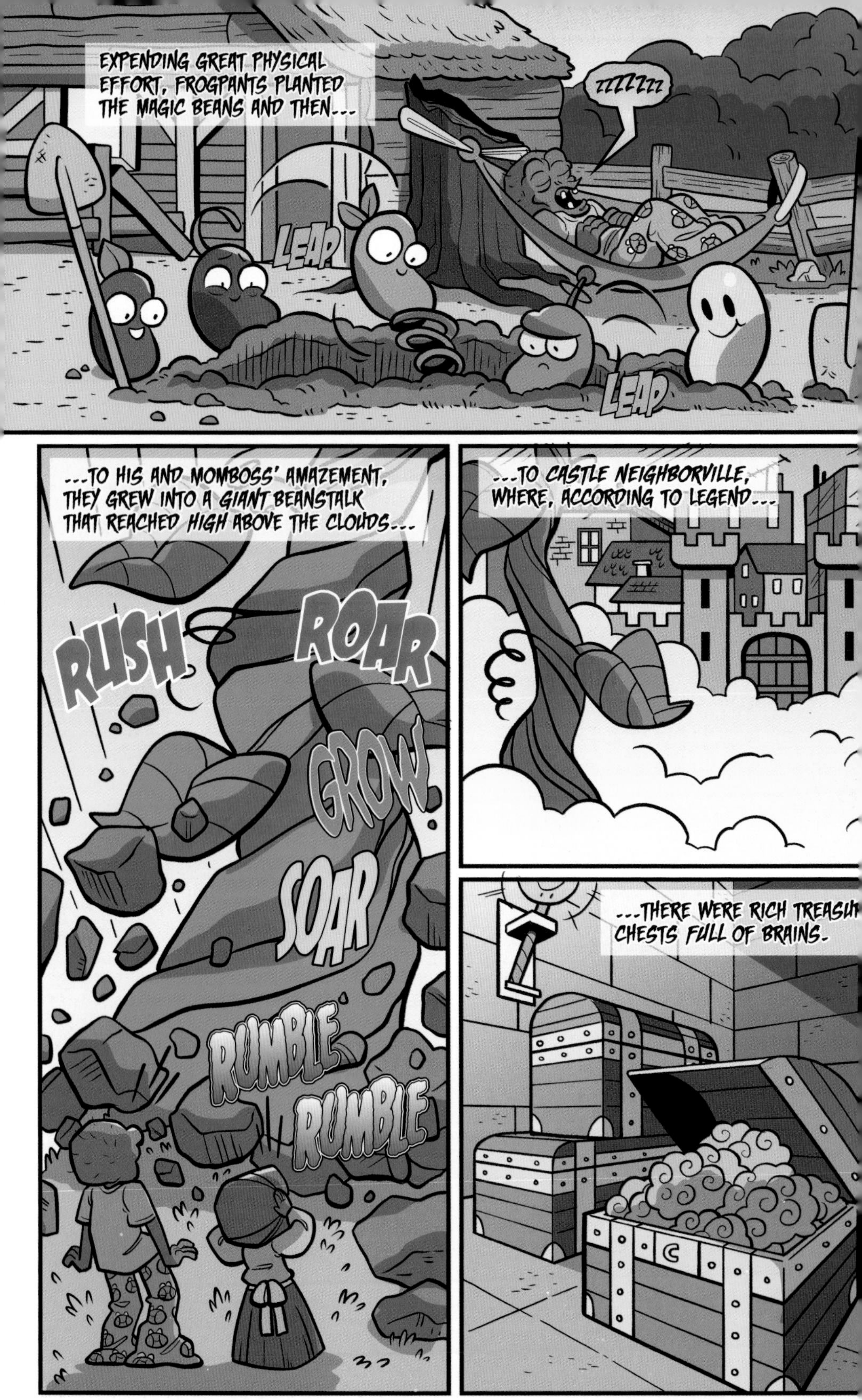
EXPENDING GREAT PHYSICAL EFFORT, FROGPANTS PLANTED THE MAGIC BEANS AND THEN...
ZZZZZZZ
LEAP
LEAP
...TO HIS AND MOMBOSS' AMAZEMENT, THEY GREW INTO A GIANT BEANSTALK THAT REACHED HIGH ABOVE THE CLOUDS...
RUSH
ROAR
GROW
SOAR
RUMBLE
RUMBLE
...TO CASTLE NEIGHBORVILLE, WHERE, ACCORDING TO LEGEND...
...THERE WERE RICH TREASU
CHESTS FULL OF BRAINS.

FROGPANTS TRIED TO CLIMB THE BEANSTALK, BUT...

...LET'S FACE IT, A BEANSTALK IS A PLANT.

!!

WHAPP!

D THE BEANSTALK KICKED HIS BUTT.

WHAPP

THWACK

RUN RUN

SCURRY

WHAPP

SMACK

BRAINS?

WHAPP

WHAPP

THIS LEFT FROGPANTS WITH NO CHOICE BUT TO CLIMB THE NEARBY BEESTALK, WHICH IS KIND OF LIKE A BEANSTALK, EXCEPT...

...IT'S MADE OF BEES.

FROGPANTS?

BUZZ BUZZ BUZZ BUZZ BUZZ BUZZ BUZZ BUZZ BUZZ BUZZ BUZZ BUZZ BUZZ BUZZ

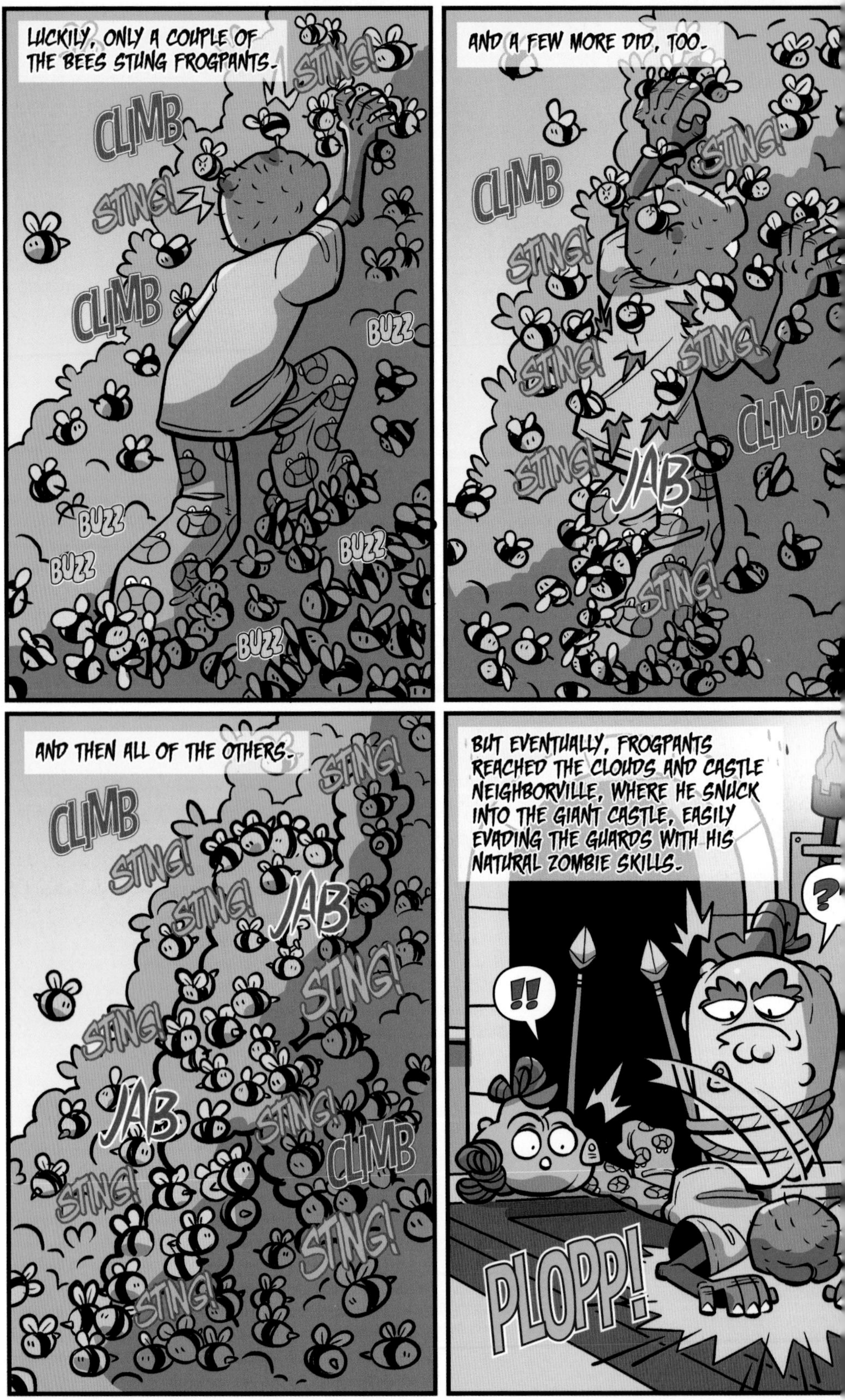
LUCKILY, ONLY A COUPLE OF THE BEES STUNG FROGPANTS.
STING!
CLIMB
STING!
CLIMB
BUZZ
BUZZ
BUZZ
BUZZ
BUZZ
AND A FEW MORE DID, TOO.
STING!
CLIMB
STING!
STING!
STING!
CLIMB
STING!
JAB
STING!
AND THEN ALL OF THE OTHERS.
STING!
CLIMB
STING!
STING!
JAB
STING!
STING!
JAB
STING!
CLIMB
STING!
STING!
STING!
BUT EVENTUALLY, FROGPANTS REACHED THE CLOUDS AND CASTLE NEIGHBORVILLE, WHERE HE SNUCK INTO THE GIANT CASTLE, EASILY EVADING THE GUARDS WITH HIS NATURAL ZOMBIE SKILLS.
?
!!
PLOPP!

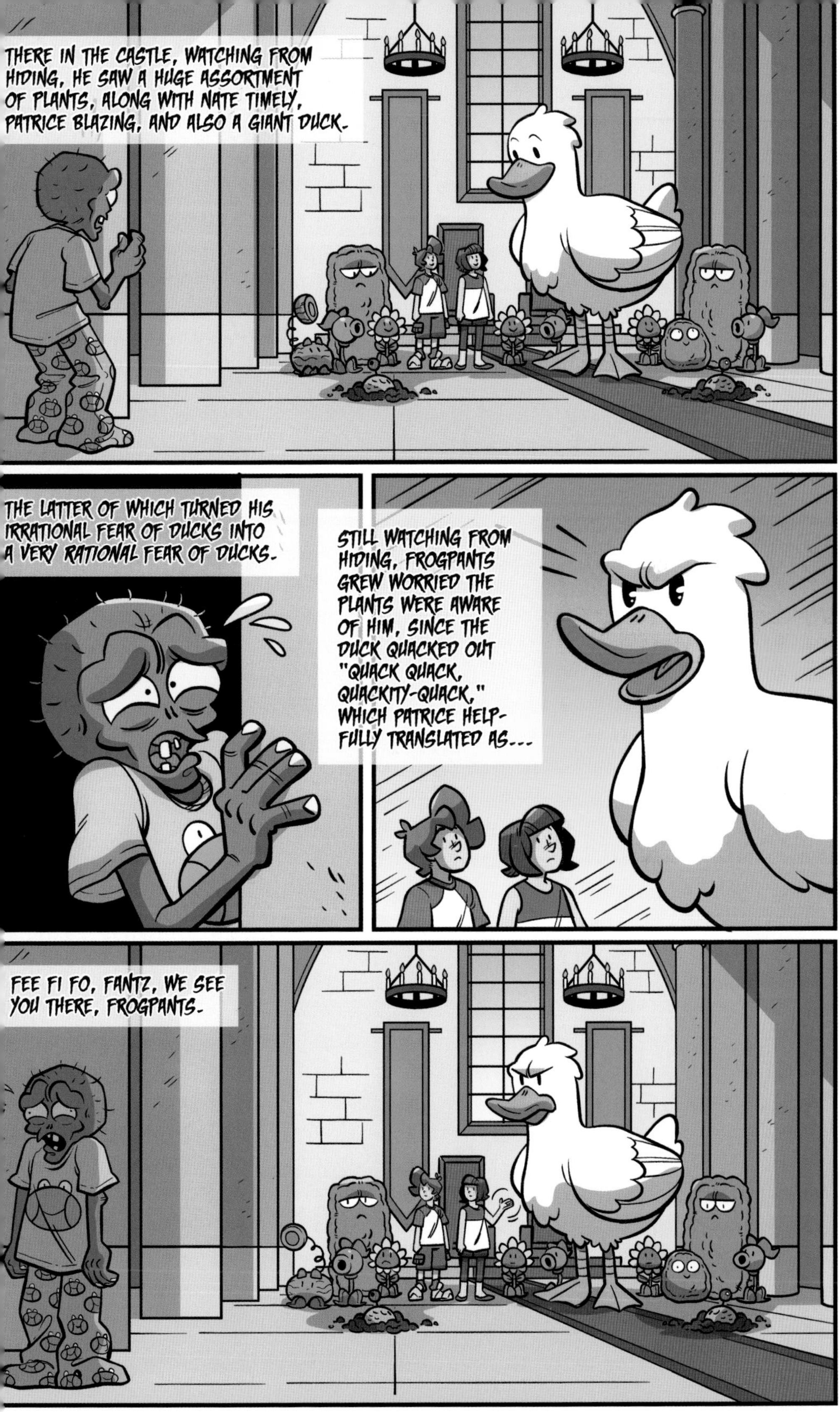
THERE IN THE CASTLE, WATCHING FROM HIDING, HE SAW A HUGE ASSORTMENT OF PLANTS, ALONG WITH NATE TIMELY, PATRICE BLAZING, AND ALSO A GIANT DUCK.
THE LATTER OF WHICH TURNED HIS IRRATIONAL FEAR OF DUCKS INTO A VERY RATIONAL FEAR OF DUCKS.
STILL WATCHING FROM HIDING, FROGPANTS GREW WORRIED THE PLANTS WERE AWARE OF HIM, SINCE THE DUCK QUACKED OUT "QUACK QUACK, QUACKITY-QUACK," WHICH PATRICE HELPFULLY TRANSLATED AS...
FEE FI FO, FANTZ, WE SEE YOU THERE, FROGPANTS.

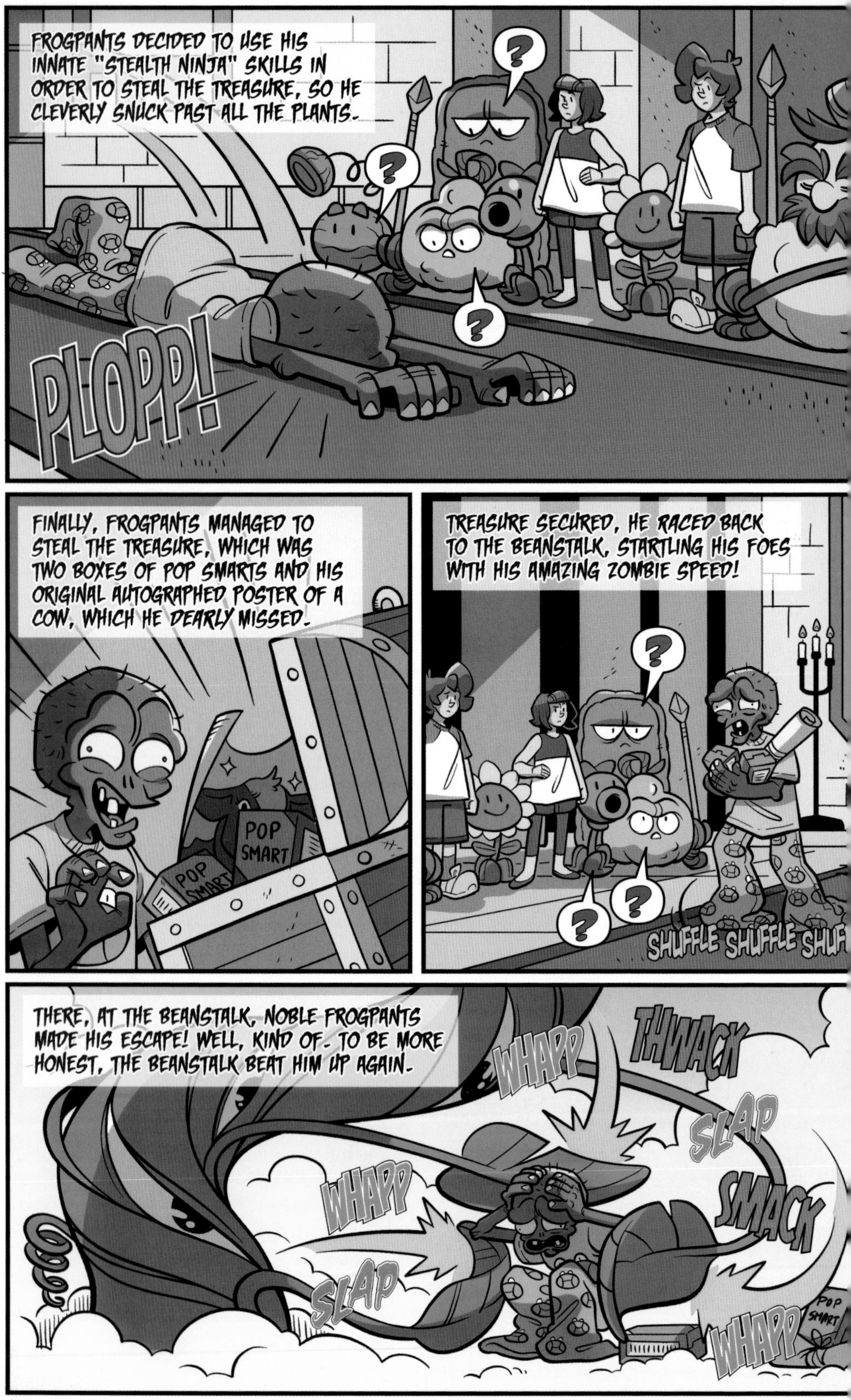
FROGPANTS DECIDED TO USE HIS INNATE "STEALTH NINJA" SKILLS IN ORDER TO STEAL THE TREASURE, SO HE CLEVERLY SNUCK PAST ALL THE PLANTS.
?
?
?
PLOPP!
FINALLY, FROGPANTS MANAGED TO STEAL THE TREASURE, WHICH WAS TWO BOXES OF POP SMARTS AND HIS ORIGINAL AUTOGRAPHED POSTER OF A COW, WHICH HE DEARLY MISSED.
POP SMART
POP SMART
TREASURE SECURED, HE RACED BACK TO THE BEANSTALK, STARTLING HIS FOES WITH HIS AMAZING ZOMBIE SPEED!
?
?
?
SHUFFLE SHUFFLE
THERE, AT THE BEANSTALK, NOBLE FROGPANTS MADE HIS ESCAPE! WELL, KIND OF. TO BE MORE HONEST, THE BEANSTALK BEAT HIM UP AGAIN.
WHAPP
THWACK
SLAP
WHAPP
SMACK
SLAP
WHAPP
POP SMART

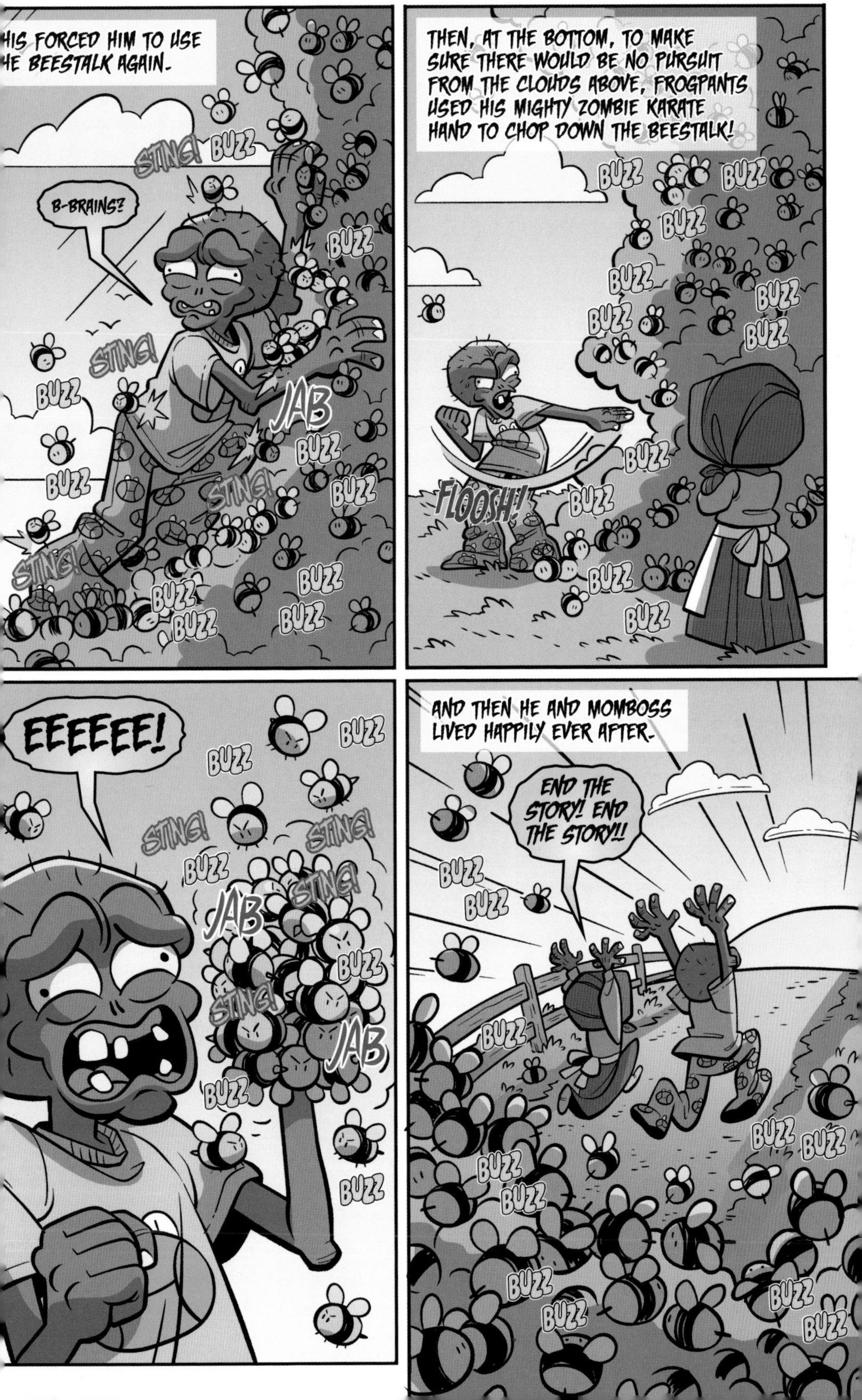
HIS FORCED HIM TO USE
HE BEESTALK AGAIN.
STING! BUZZ
B-BRAINS?
BUZZ
STING!
BUZZ
JAB
BUZZ
BUZZ
STING!
BUZZ
STING!
BUZZ
BUZZ
BUZZ
BUZZ
THEN, AT THE BOTTOM, TO MAKE SURE THERE WOULD BE NO PURSUIT FROM THE CLOUDS ABOVE, FROGPANTS USED HIS MIGHTY ZOMBIE KARATE HAND TO CHOP DOWN THE BEESTALK!
BUZZ
BUZZ
BUZZ
BUZZ
BUZZ
BUZZ
BUZZ
BUZZ
FLOOSH!
BUZZ
BUZZ
BUZZ
EEEEEE!
BUZZ
BUZZ
STING!
STING!
BUZZ
JAB
STING!
BUZZ
STING!
JAB
BUZZ
BUZZ
AND THEN HE AND MOMBOSS LIVED HAPPILY EVER AFTER.
END THE STORY! END THE STORY!!
BUZZ
BUZZ
BUZZ
BUZZ
BUZZ
BUZZ
BUZZ
BUZZ
BUZZ
BUZZ
BUZZ

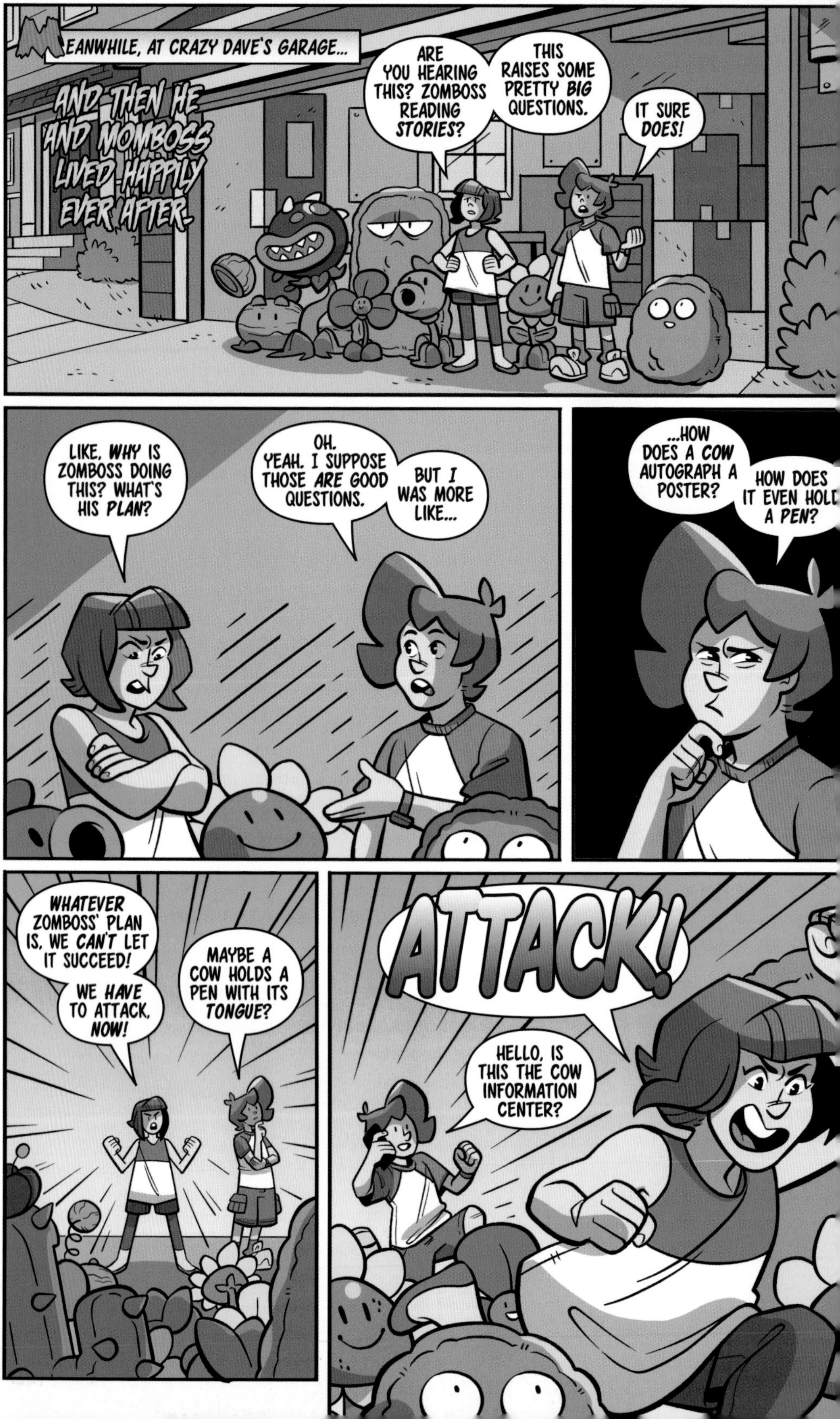
MEANWHILE, AT CRAZY DAVE'S GARAGE...
AND THEN HE AND MOMBOSS LIVED HAPPILY EVER AFTER.
ARE YOU HEARING THIS? ZOMBOSS READING STORIES?
THIS RAISES SOME PRETTY BIG QUESTIONS.
IT SURE DOES!
LIKE, WHY IS ZOMBOSS DOING THIS? WHAT'S HIS PLAN?
OH. YEAH. I SUPPOSE THOSE ARE GOOD QUESTIONS.
BUT I WAS MORE LIKE...
...HOW DOES A COW AUTOGRAPH A POSTER?
HOW DOES IT EVEN HOLD A PEN?
WHATEVER ZOMBOSS' PLAN IS, WE CAN'T LET IT SUCCEED!
WE HAVE TO ATTACK, NOW!
MAYBE A COW HOLDS A PEN WITH ITS TONGUE?
ATTACK!
HELLO, IS THIS THE COW INFORMATION CENTER?

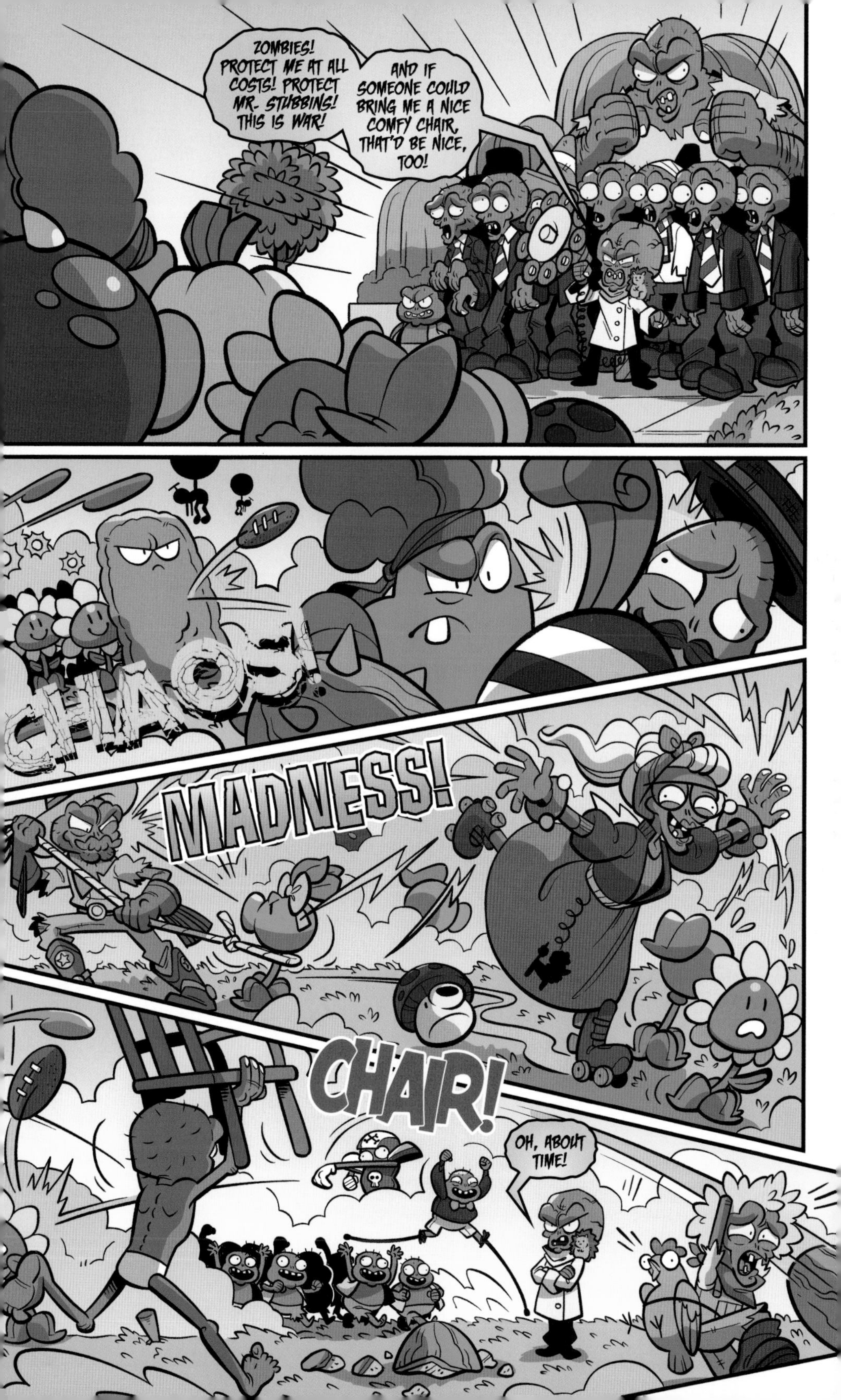

ZOMBIES! PROTECT ME AT ALL COSTS! PROTECT MR. STUBBINS! THIS IS WAR!
AND IF SOMEONE COULD BRING ME A NICE COMFY CHAIR, THAT'D BE NICE, TOO!
CHAOS!
MADNESS!
CHAIR!
OH, ABOUT TIME!

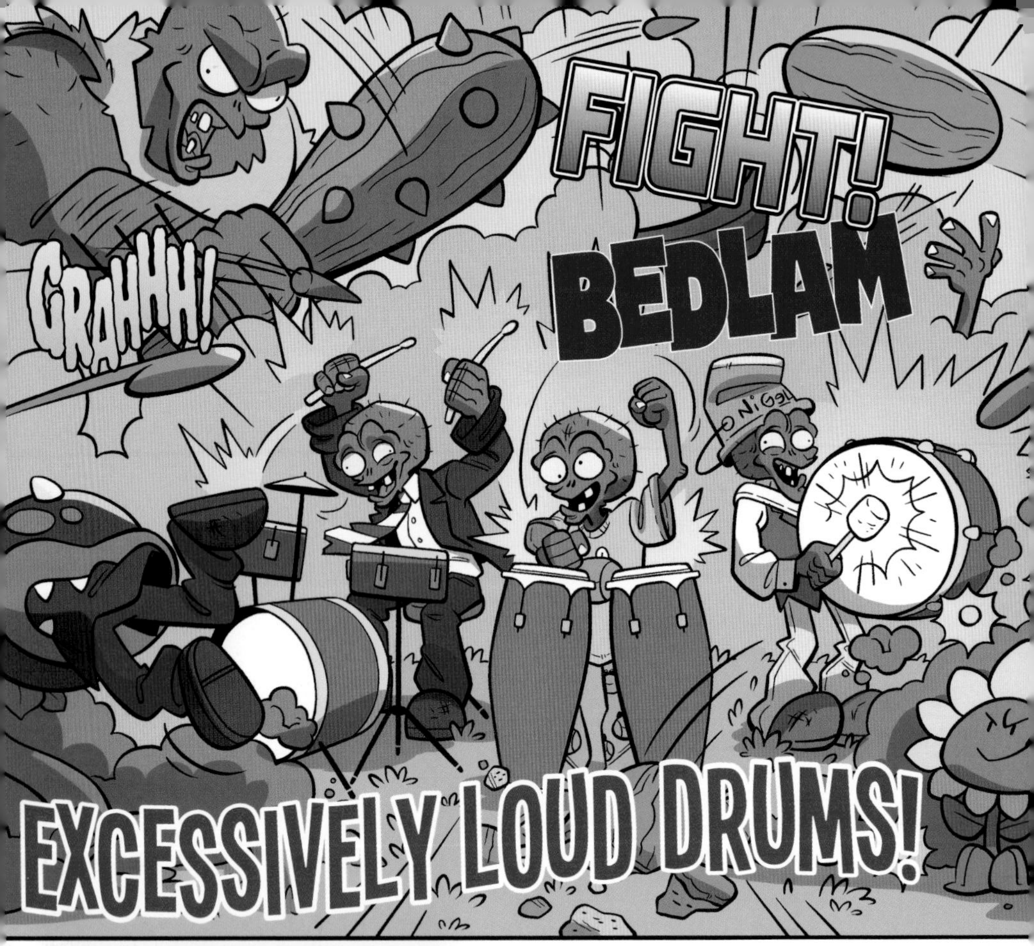

GRAHHH!
FIGHT!
BEDLAM
EXCESSIVELY LOUD DRUMS!

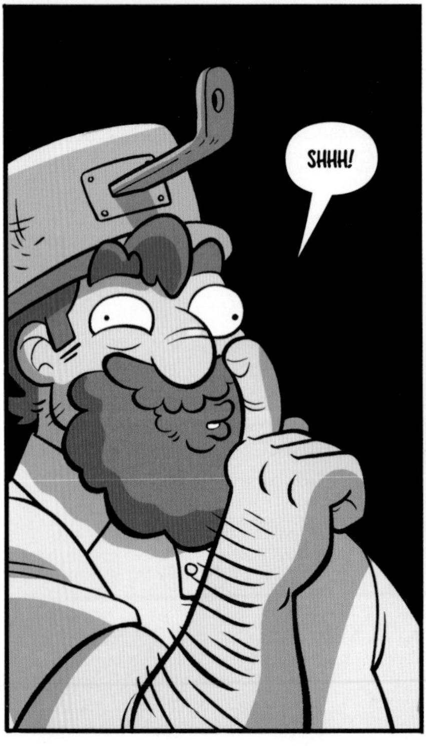

SHHH!

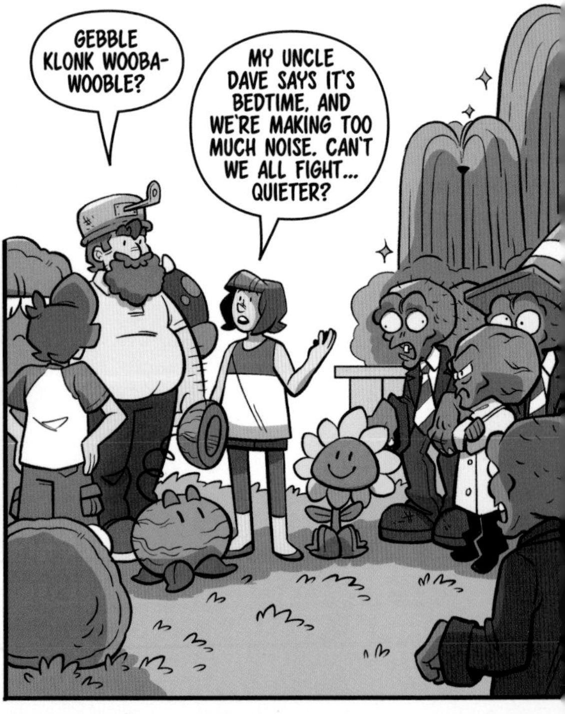

GEBBLE KLONK WOOBA-WOOBLE?
MY UNCLE DAVE SAYS IT'S BEDTIME, AND WE'RE MAKING TOO MUCH NOISE. CAN'T WE ALL FIGHT... QUIETER?

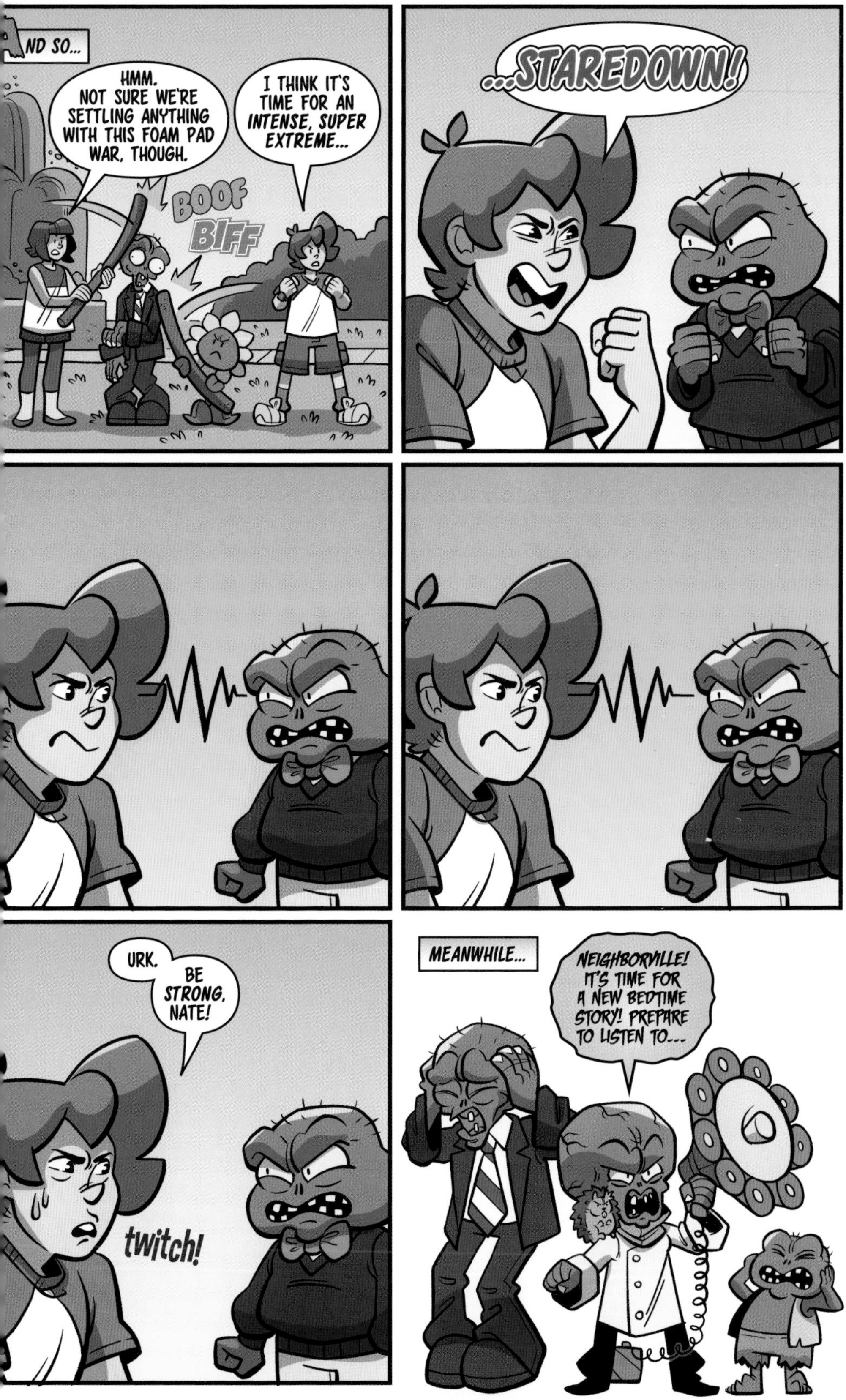
AND SO...
HMM. NOT SURE WE'RE SETTLING ANYTHING WITH THIS FOAM PAD WAR, THOUGH.
BOOF
BIFF
I THINK IT'S TIME FOR AN INTENSE, SUPER EXTREME...
...STAREDOWN!
URK.
BE STRONG, NATE!
twitch!
MEANWHILE...
NEIGHBORVILLE! IT'S TIME FOR A NEW BEDTIME STORY! PREPARE TO LISTEN TO...

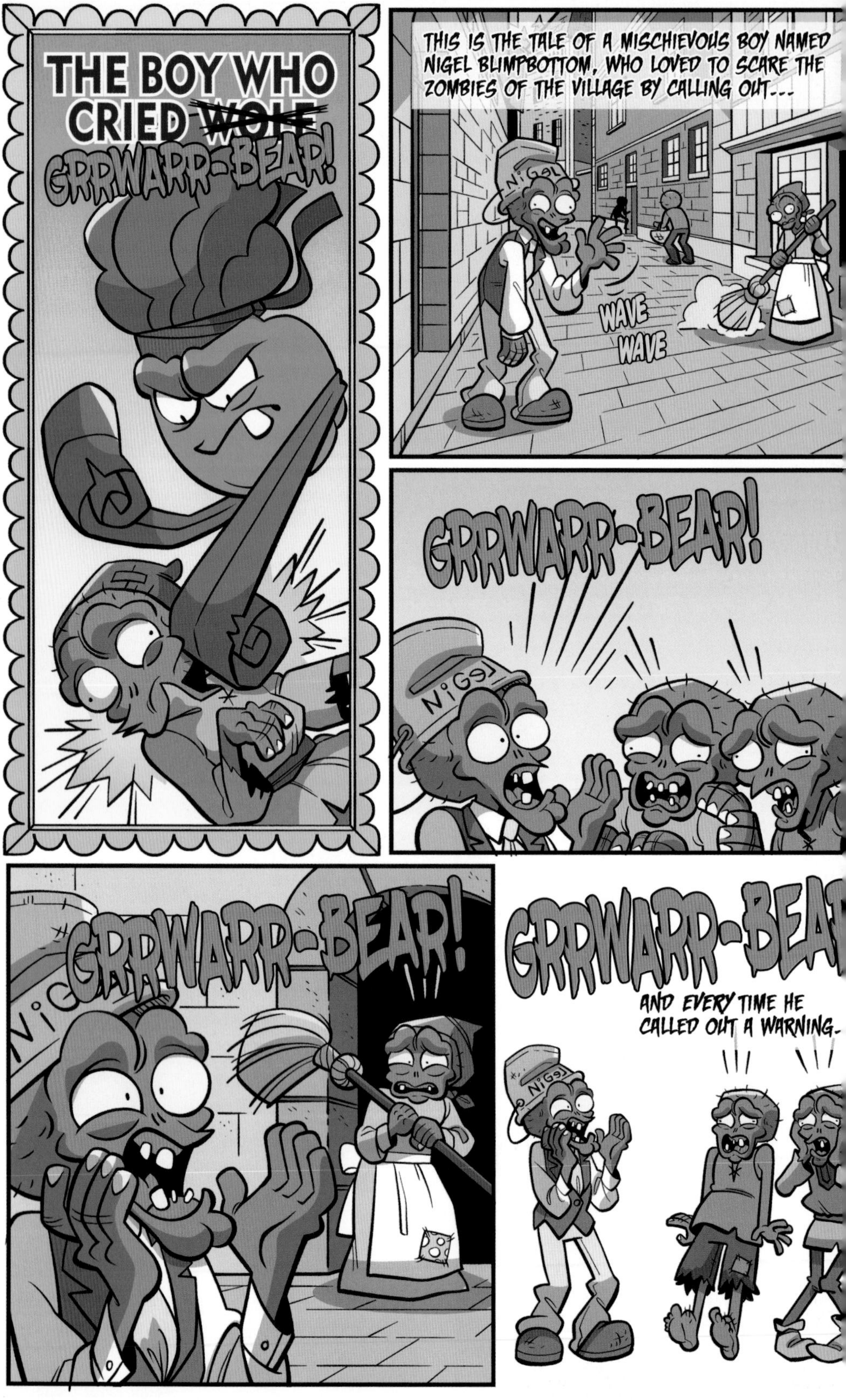
THE BOY WHO CRIED ~~WOLF~~ GRRWARR-BEAR!
THIS IS THE TALE OF A MISCHIEVOUS BOY NAMED NIGEL BLIMPBOTTOM, WHO LOVED TO SCARE THE ZOMBIES OF THE VILLAGE BY CALLING OUT...
NIGEL
WAVE
WAVE
GRRWARR-BEAR!
NIGEL
GRRWARR-BEAR!
GRRWARR-BEA
AND EVERY TIME HE CALLED OUT A WARNING...
NIGEL

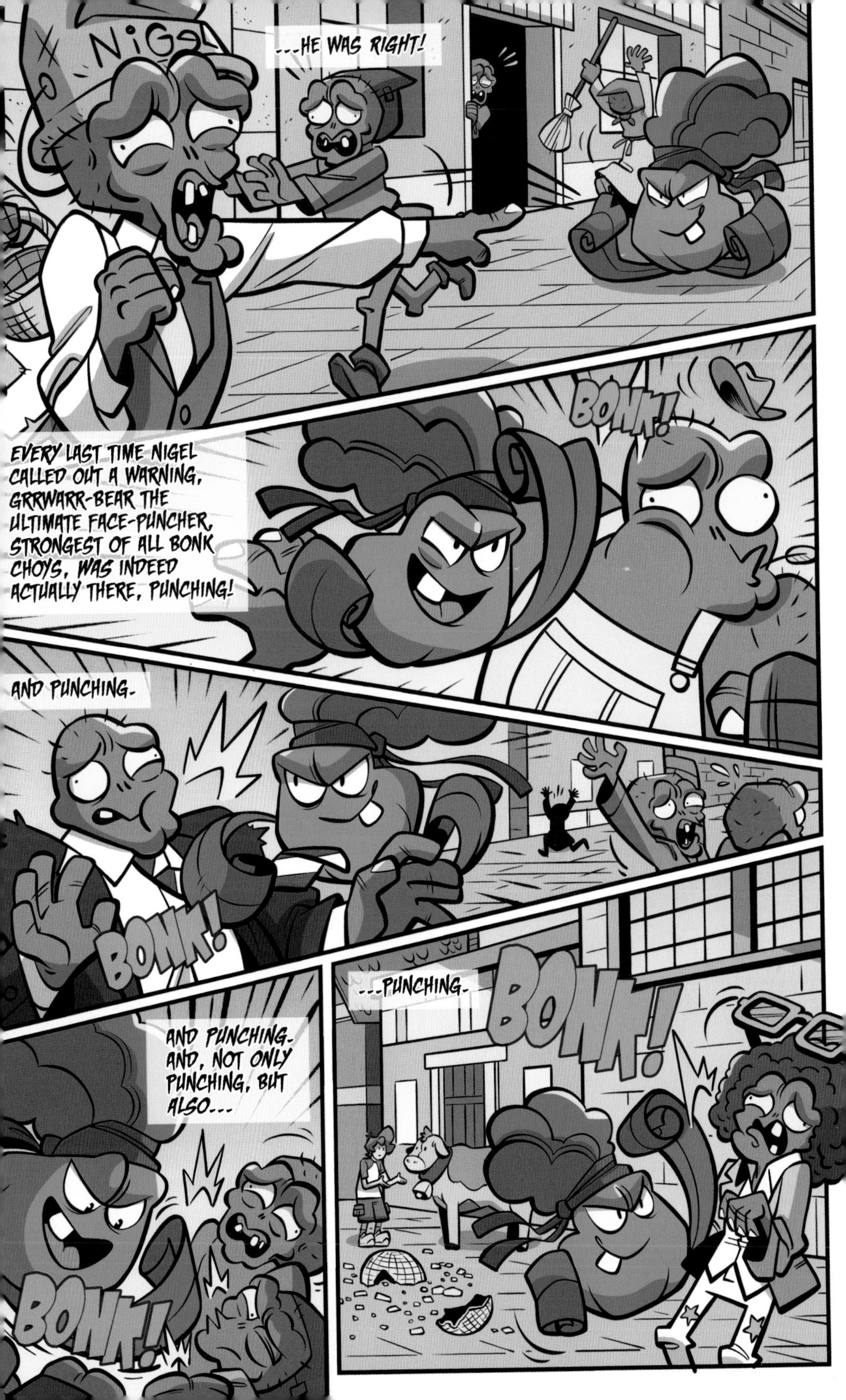
NiGeL
...HE WAS RIGHT!
BONK!
EVERY LAST TIME NIGEL CALLED OUT A WARNING, GRRWARR-BEAR THE ULTIMATE FACE-PUNCHER, STRONGEST OF ALL BONK CHOYS, WAS INDEED ACTUALLY THERE, PUNCHING!
AND PUNCHING.
BONK!
...PUNCHING.
BONK!
AND PUNCHING. AND, NOT ONLY PUNCHING, BUT ALSO...
BONK!

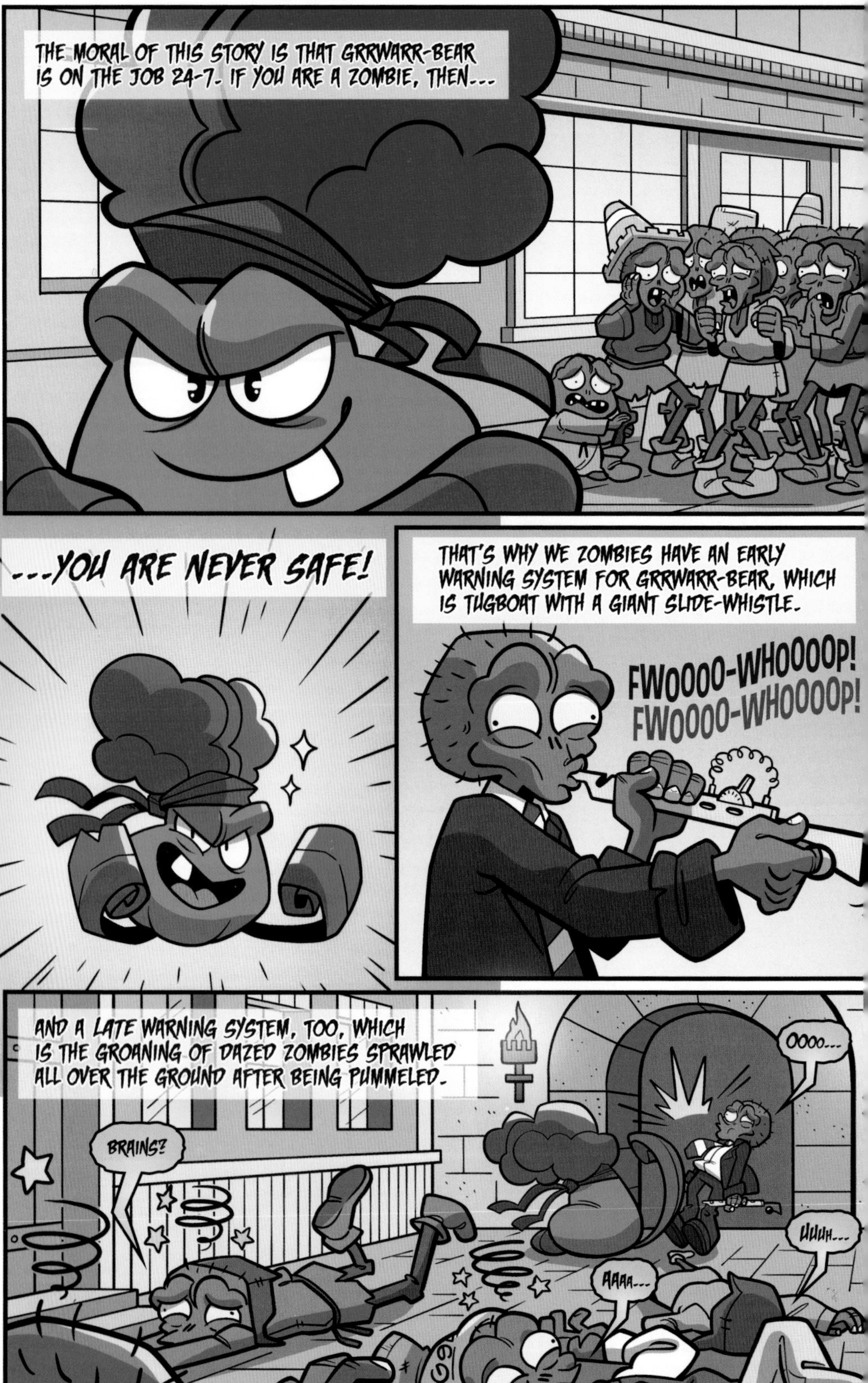
THE MORAL OF THIS STORY IS THAT GRRWARR-BEAR IS ON THE JOB 24-7. IF YOU ARE A ZOMBIE, THEN...
...YOU ARE NEVER SAFE!
THAT'S WHY WE ZOMBIES HAVE AN EARLY WARNING SYSTEM FOR GRRWARR-BEAR, WHICH IS TUGBOAT WITH A GIANT SLIDE-WHISTLE.
FWOOOO-WHOOOOP!
FWOOOO-WHOOOOP!
AND A LATE WARNING SYSTEM, TOO, WHICH IS THE GROANING OF DAZED ZOMBIES SPRAWLED ALL OVER THE GROUND AFTER BEING PUMMELED.
OOOO...
BRAINS?
UUUH...
AAAA...

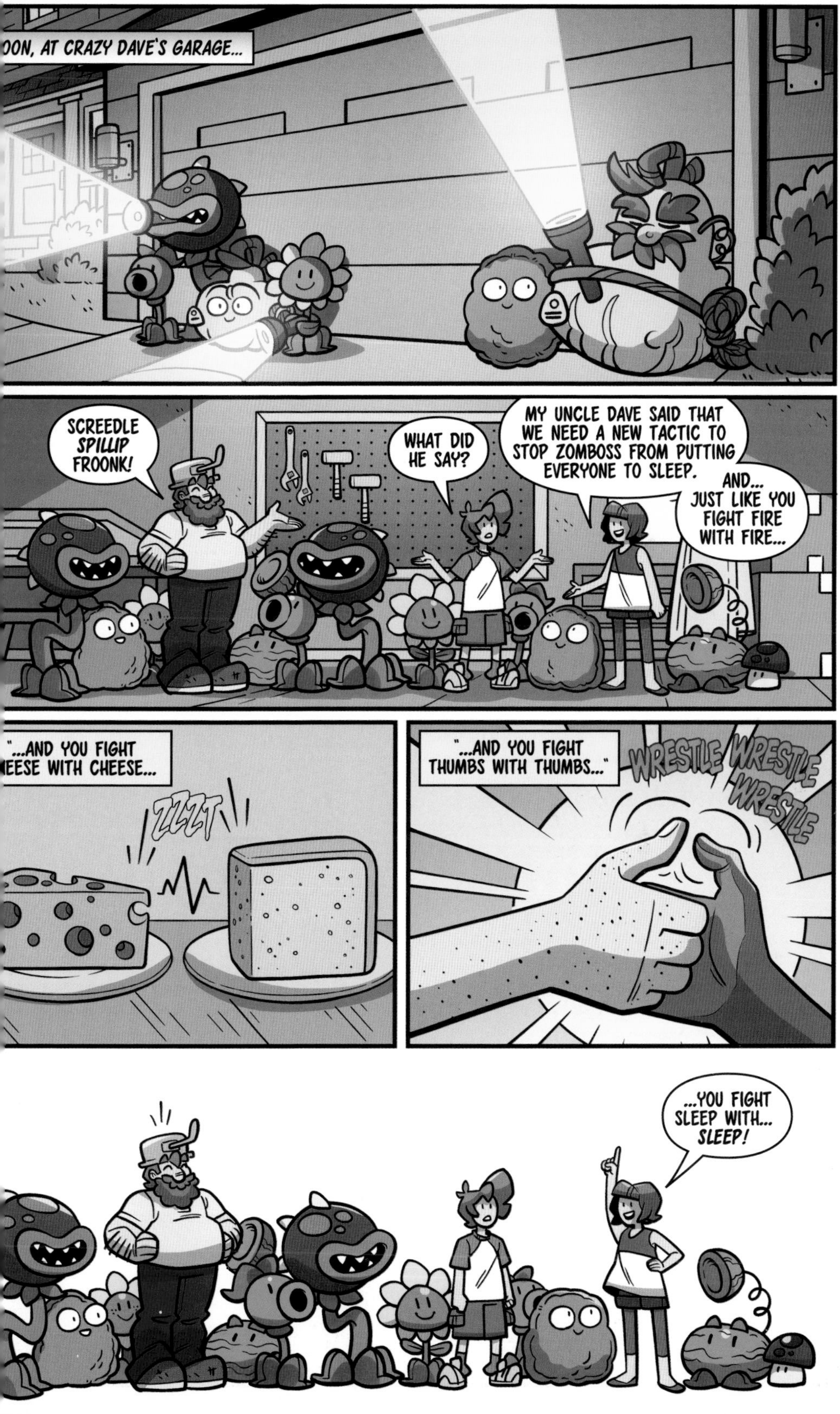
OON, AT CRAZY DAVE'S GARAGE...
SCREEDLE SPILLIP FROONK!
WHAT DID HE SAY?
MY UNCLE DAVE SAID THAT WE NEED A NEW TACTIC TO STOP ZOMBOSS FROM PUTTING EVERYONE TO SLEEP.
AND... JUST LIKE YOU FIGHT FIRE WITH FIRE...
"...AND YOU FIGHT
EESE WITH CHEESE...
ZZZT
"...AND YOU FIGHT THUMBS WITH THUMBS..."
WRESTLE WRESTLE WRESTLE
...YOU FIGHT SLEEP WITH... SLEEP!

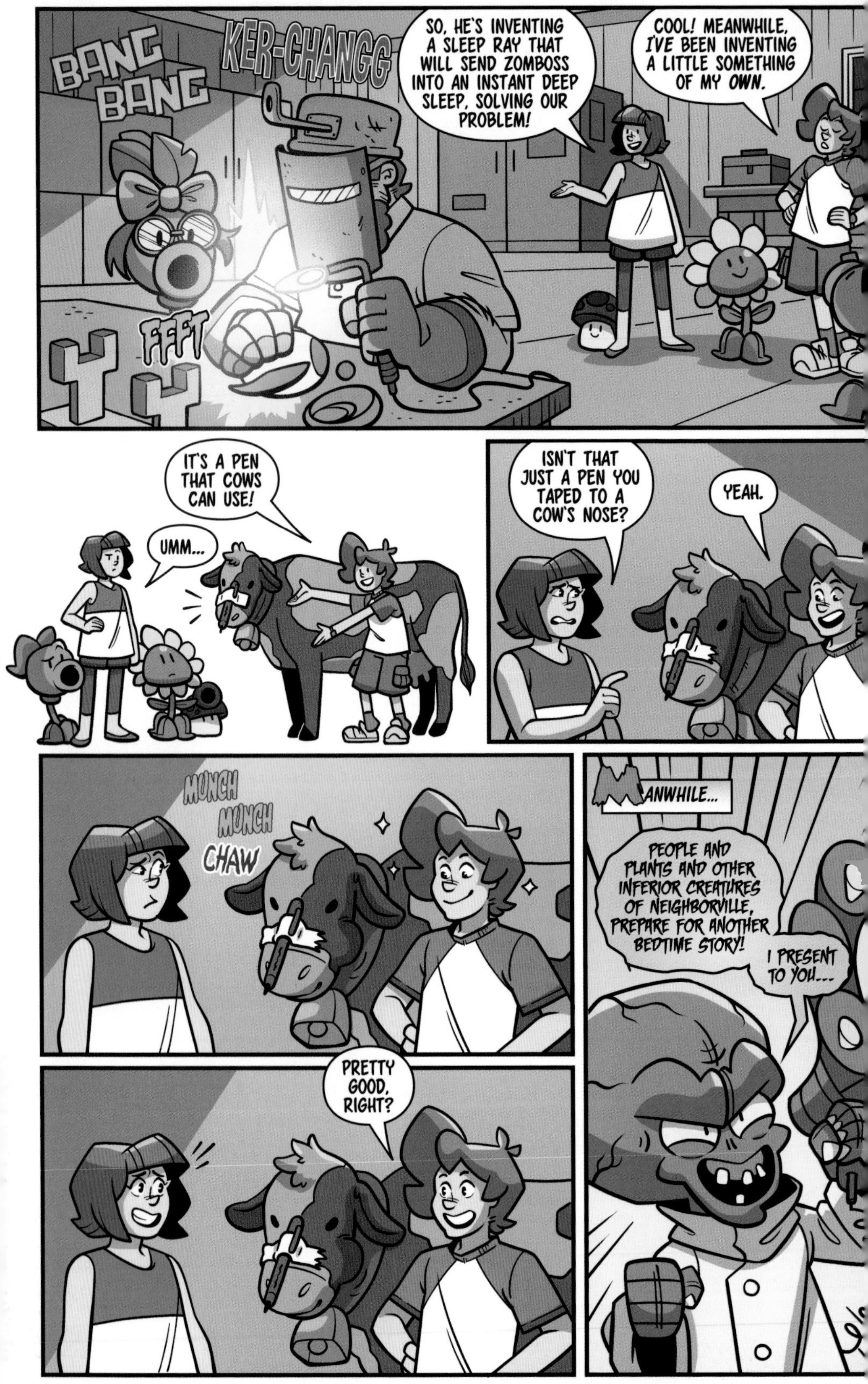
BANG
BANG
KER-CHANGG
SO, HE'S INVENTING A SLEEP RAY THAT WILL SEND ZOMBOSS INTO AN INSTANT DEEP SLEEP, SOLVING OUR PROBLEM!
COOL! MEANWHILE, I'VE BEEN INVENTING A LITTLE SOMETHING OF MY OWN.
FFFT
IT'S A PEN THAT COWS CAN USE!
UMM...
ISN'T THAT JUST A PEN YOU TAPED TO A COW'S NOSE?
YEAH.
MUNCH
MUNCH
CHAW
PRETTY GOOD, RIGHT?
MEANWHILE...
PEOPLE AND PLANTS AND OTHER INFERIOR CREATURES OF NEIGHBORVILLE, PREPARE FOR ANOTHER BEDTIME STORY!
I PRESENT TO YOU...

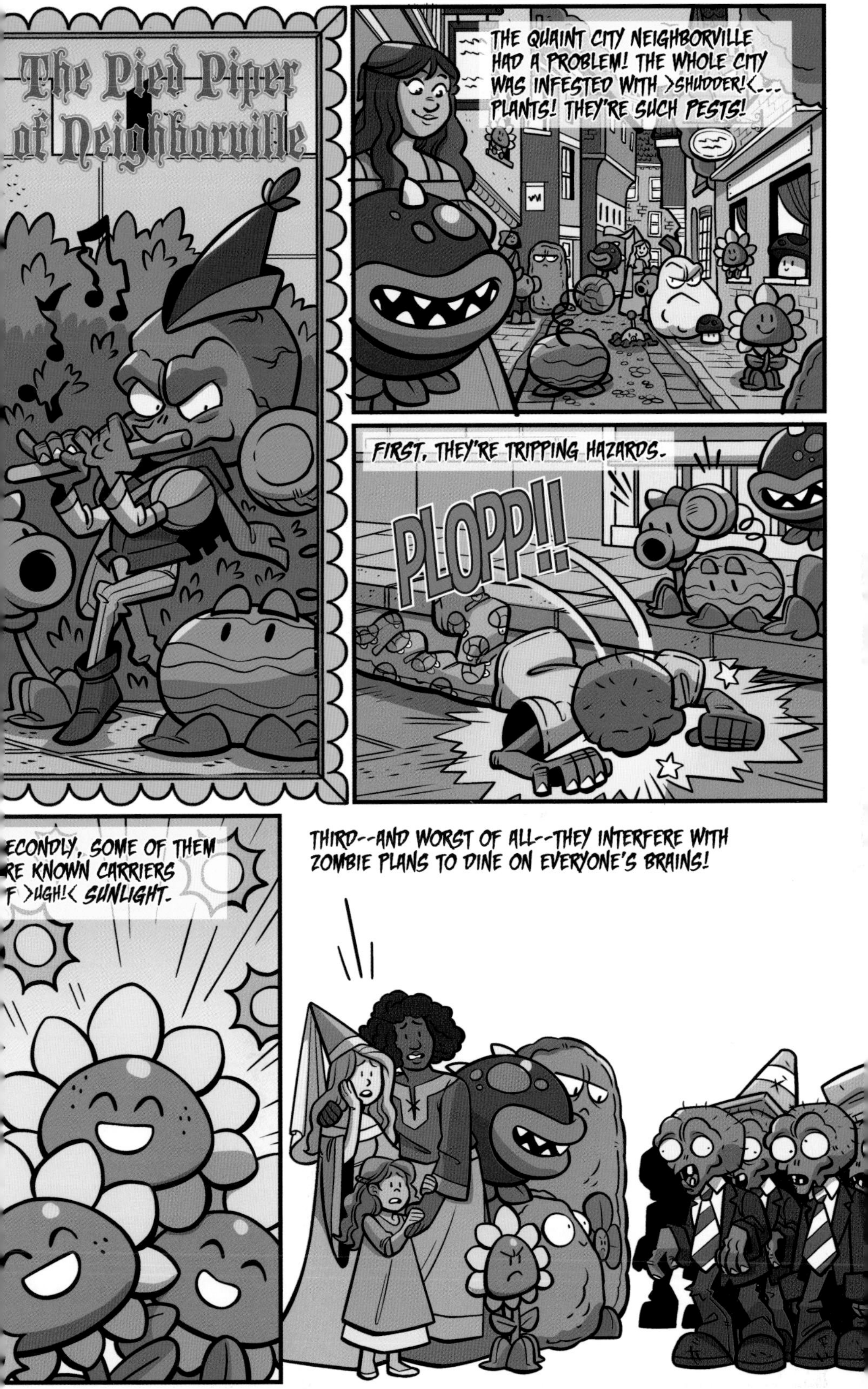

The Pied Piper of Neighborville
THE QUAINT CITY NEIGHBORVILLE HAD A PROBLEM! THE WHOLE CITY WAS INFESTED WITH >SHUDDER!<... PLANTS! THEY'RE SUCH PESTS!
FIRST, THEY'RE TRIPPING HAZARDS.
PLOPP!!
ECONDLY, SOME OF THEM RE KNOWN CARRIERS F >UGH!< SUNLIGHT.
THIRD--AND WORST OF ALL--THEY INTERFERE WITH ZOMBIE PLANS TO DINE ON EVERYONE'S BRAINS!

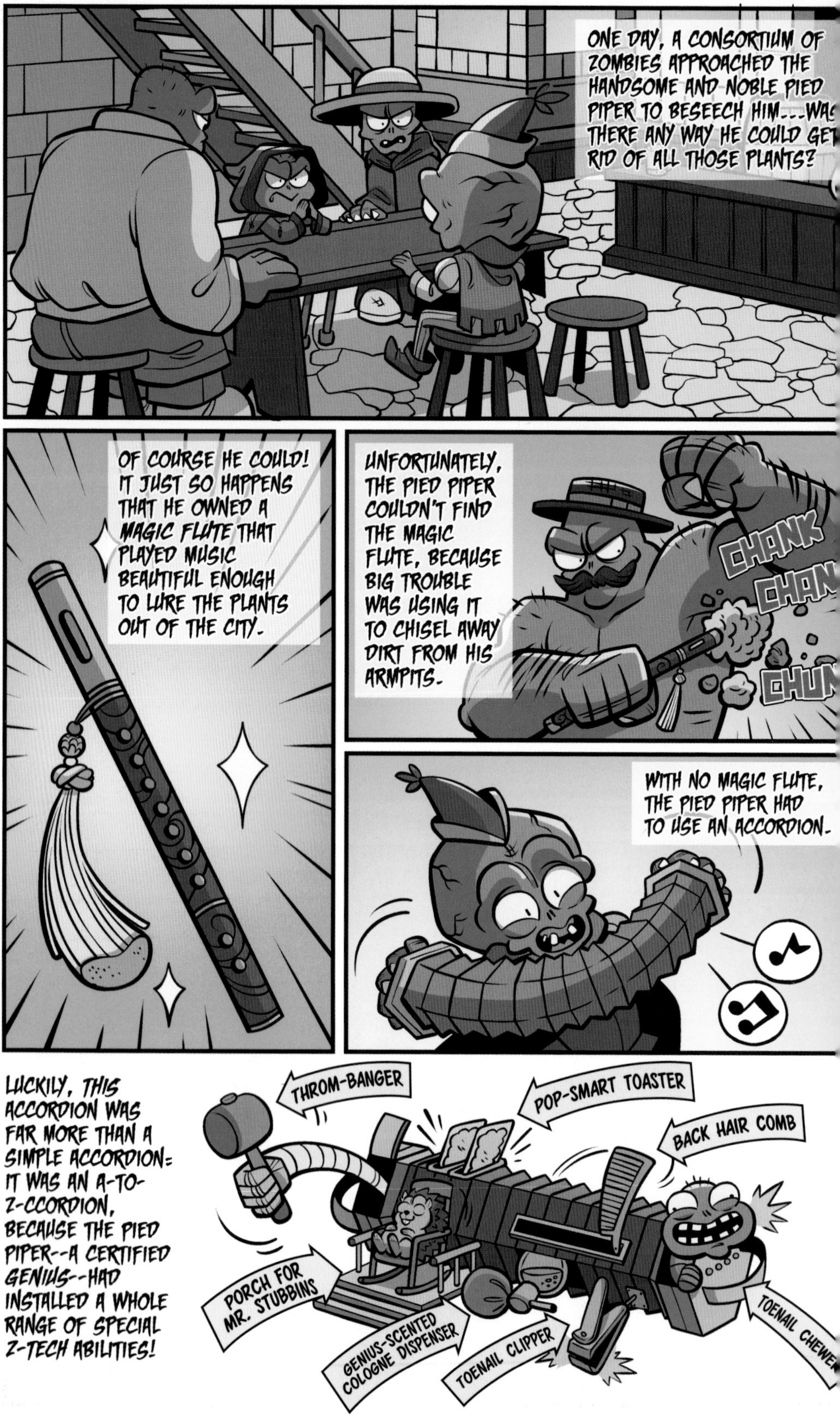
ONE DAY, A CONSORTIUM OF ZOMBIES APPROACHED THE HANDSOME AND NOBLE PIED PIPER TO BESEECH HIM...WA THERE ANY WAY HE COULD GE RID OF ALL THOSE PLANTS?
OF COURSE HE COULD! IT JUST SO HAPPENS THAT HE OWNED A MAGIC FLUTE THAT PLAYED MUSIC BEAUTIFUL ENOUGH TO LURE THE PLANTS OUT OF THE CITY.
UNFORTUNATELY, THE PIED PIPER COULDN'T FIND THE MAGIC FLUTE, BECAUSE BIG TROUBLE WAS USING IT TO CHISEL AWAY DIRT FROM HIS ARMPITS.
CHANK
CHAN
CHUN
WITH NO MAGIC FLUTE, THE PIED PIPER HAD TO USE AN ACCORDION.
LUCKILY, THIS ACCORDION WAS FAR MORE THAN A SIMPLE ACCORDION: IT WAS AN A-TO-Z-CCORDION, BECAUSE THE PIED PIPER--A CERTIFIED GENIUS--HAD INSTALLED A WHOLE RANGE OF SPECIAL Z-TECH ABILITIES!
THROM-BANGER
POP-SMART TOASTER
BACK HAIR COMB
PORCH FOR MR. STUBBINS
GENIUS-SCENTED COLOGNE DISPENSER
TOENAIL CLIPPER
TOENAIL CHEWE

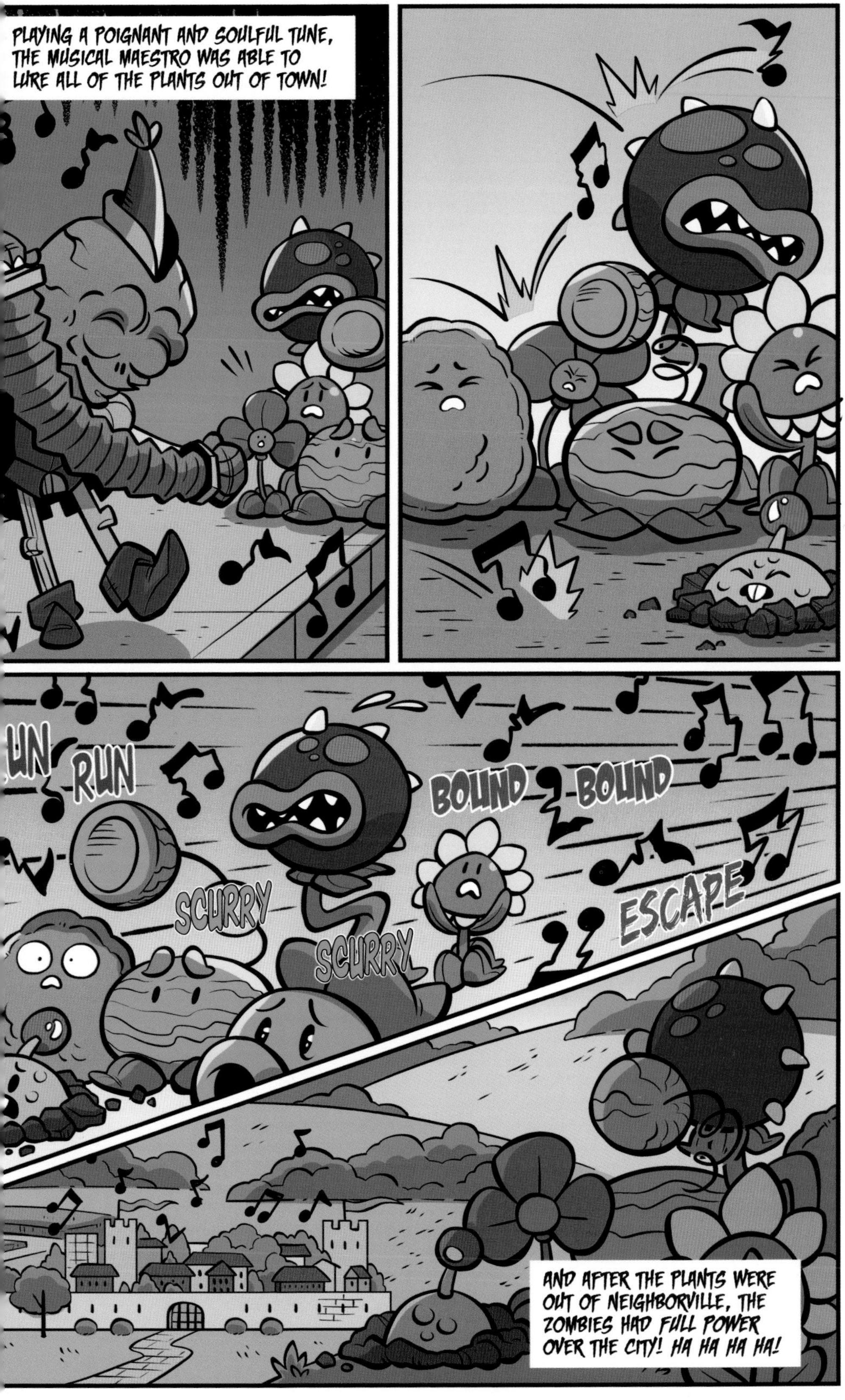
PLAYING A POIGNANT AND SOULFUL TUNE, THE MUSICAL MAESTRO WAS ABLE TO LURE ALL OF THE PLANTS OUT OF TOWN!
UN
RUN
BOUND
BOUND
SCURRY
SCURRY
ESCAPE
AND AFTER THE PLANTS WERE OUT OF NEIGHBORVILLE, THE ZOMBIES HAD FULL POWER OVER THE CITY! HA HA HA HA!

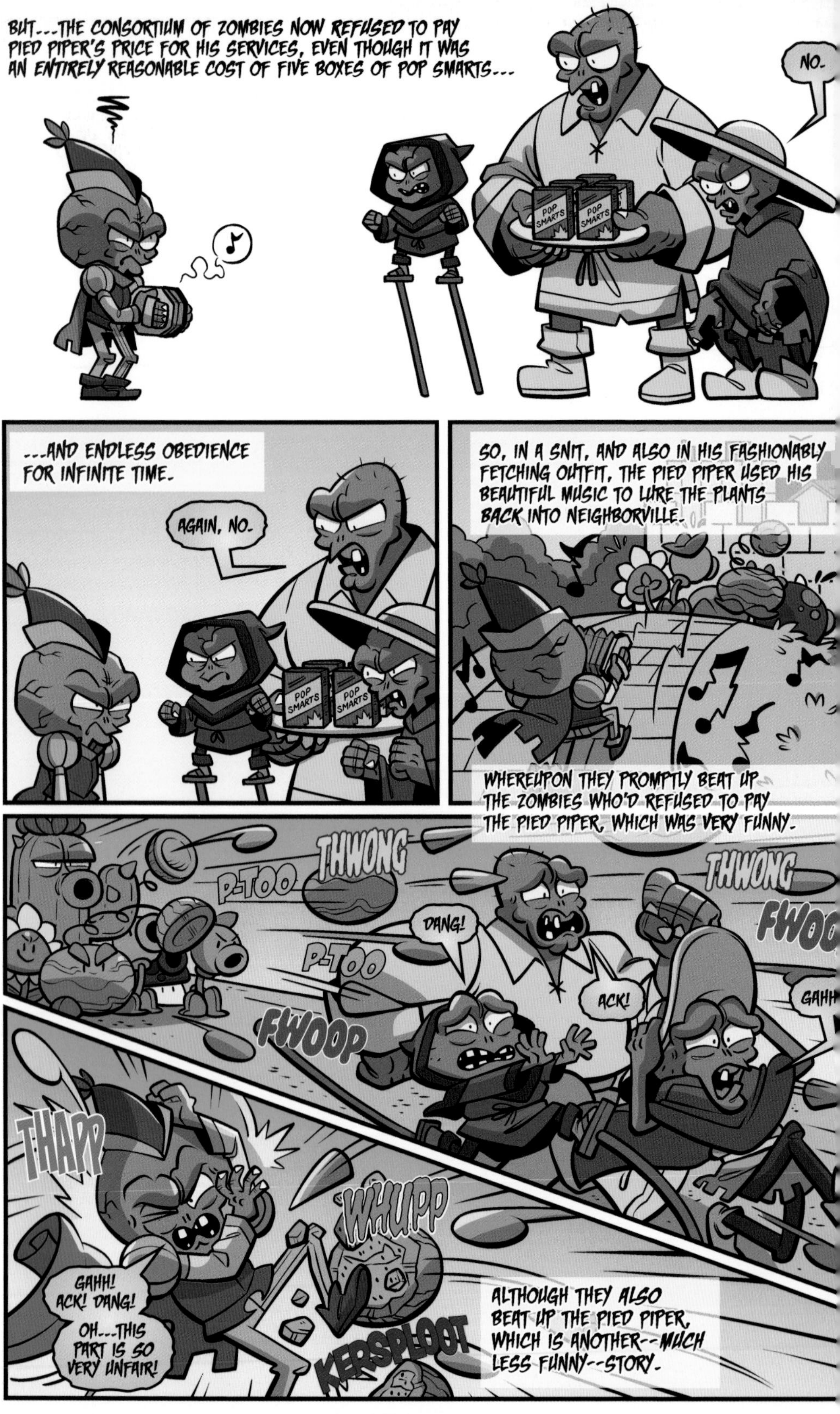
BUT...THE CONSORTIUM OF ZOMBIES NOW REFUSED TO PAY PIED PIPER'S PRICE FOR HIS SERVICES, EVEN THOUGH IT WAS AN ENTIRELY REASONABLE COST OF FIVE BOXES OF POP SMARTS...
POP SMARTS
POP SMARTS
NO.
...AND ENDLESS OBEDIENCE FOR INFINITE TIME.
AGAIN, NO.
POP SMARTS
POP SMARTS
SO, IN A SNIT, AND ALSO IN HIS FASHIONABLY FETCHING OUTFIT, THE PIED PIPER USED HIS BEAUTIFUL MUSIC TO LURE THE PLANTS BACK INTO NEIGHBORVILLE.
WHEREUPON THEY PROMPTLY BEAT UP THE ZOMBIES WHO'D REFUSED TO PAY THE PIED PIPER, WHICH WAS VERY FUNNY.
THWONG
P-TOO
THWONG
DANG!
P-TOO
ACK!
FWOOP
THAPP
WHUPP
GAHH! ACK! DANG!
OH...THIS PART IS SO VERY UNFAIR!
KERSPLOOT
ALTHOUGH THEY ALSO BEAT UP THE PIED PIPER, WHICH IS ANOTHER--MUCH LESS FUNNY--STORY.

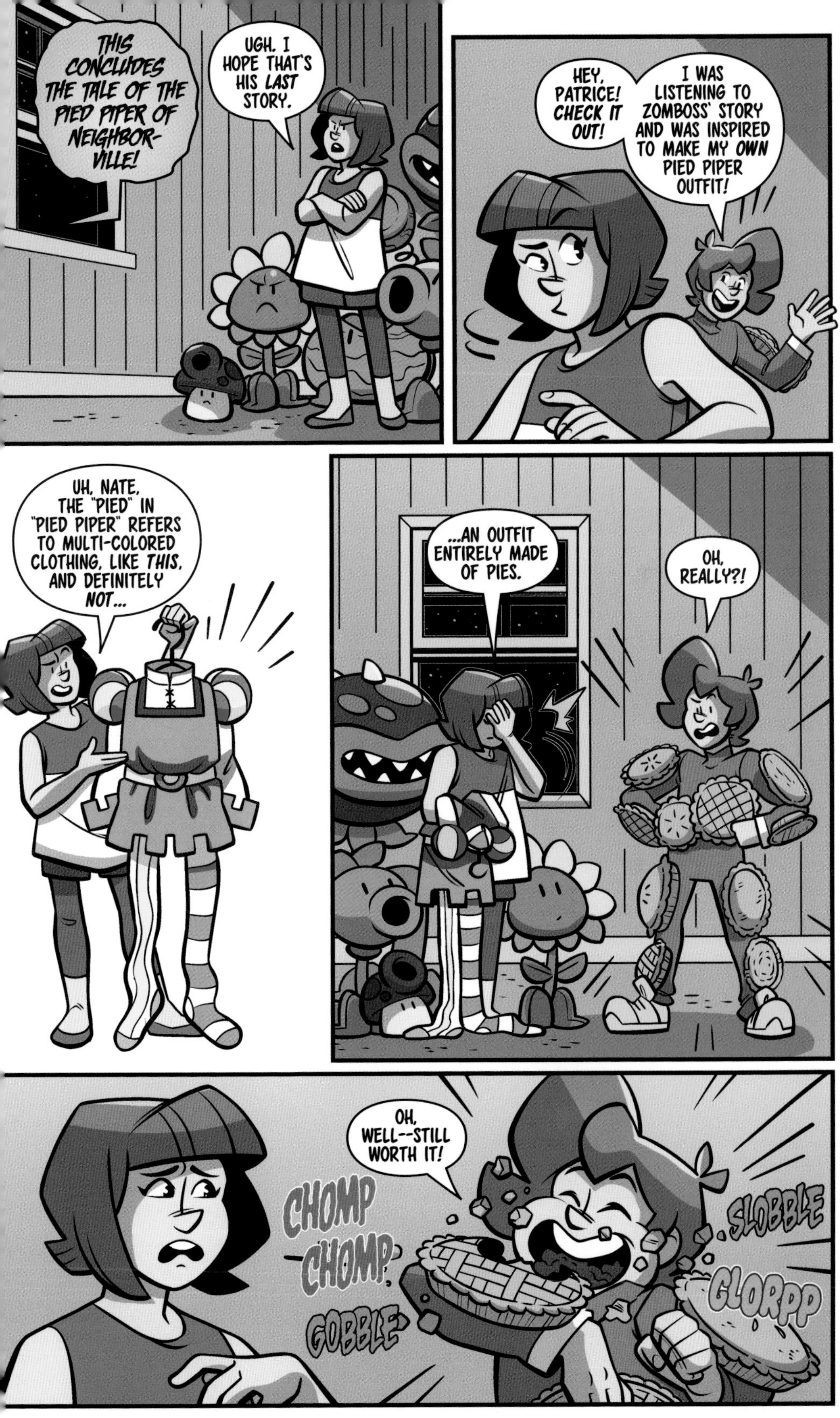
THIS CONCLUDES THE TALE OF THE PIED PIPER OF NEIGHBOR-VILLE!
UGH. I HOPE THAT'S HIS LAST STORY.
HEY, PATRICE! CHECK IT OUT!
I WAS LISTENING TO ZOMBOSS' STORY AND WAS INSPIRED TO MAKE MY OWN PIED PIPER OUTFIT!
UH, NATE, THE "PIED" IN "PIED PIPER" REFERS TO MULTI-COLORED CLOTHING, LIKE THIS, AND DEFINITELY NOT...
...AN OUTFIT ENTIRELY MADE OF PIES.
OH, REALLY?!
OH, WELL--STILL WORTH IT!
CHOMP
CHOMP
GOBBLE
SLOBBLE
GLORPP

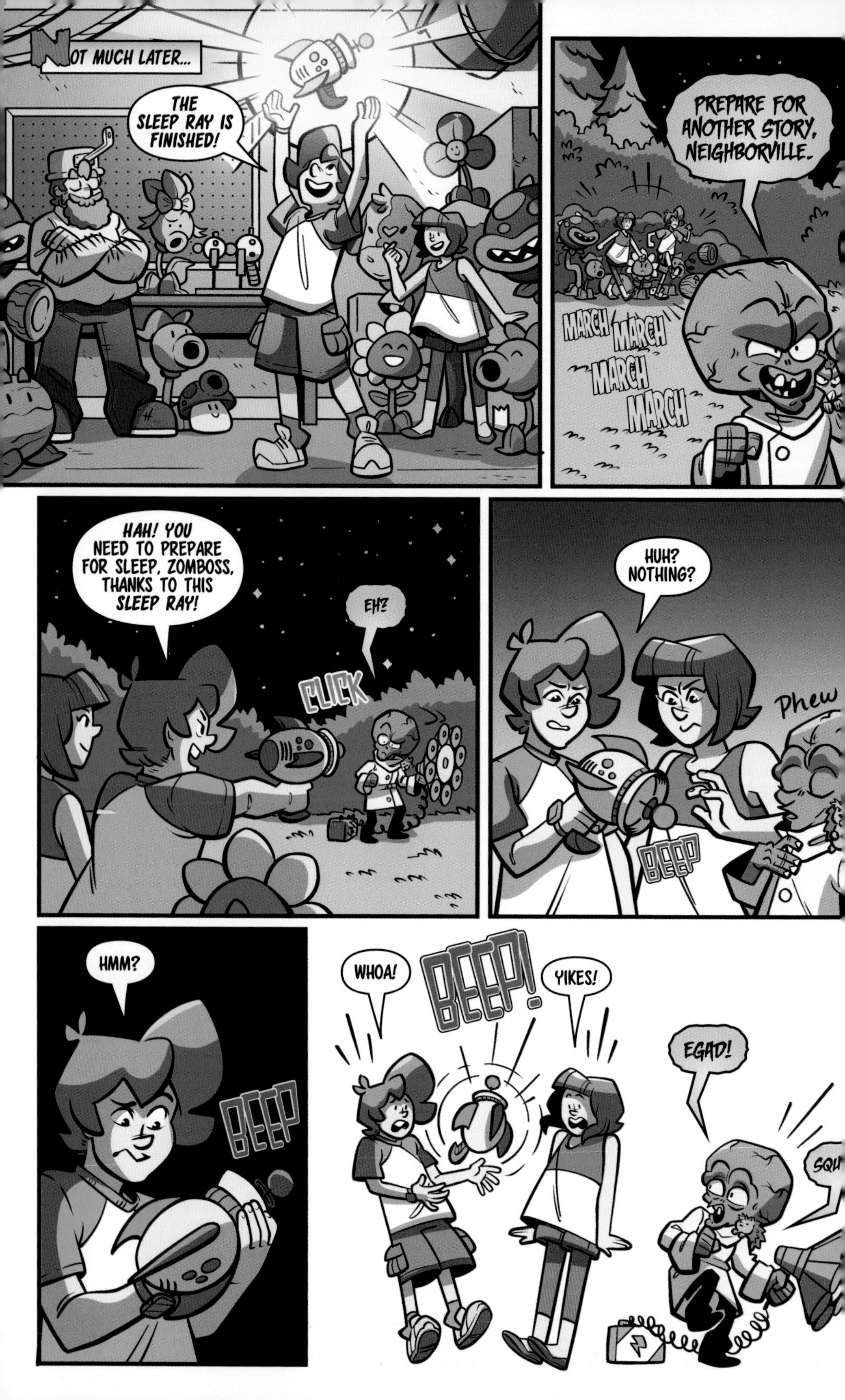
NOT MUCH LATER...
THE SLEEP RAY IS FINISHED!
PREPARE FOR ANOTHER STORY, NEIGHBORVILLE.
MARCH
MARCH
MARCH
MARCH
HAH! YOU NEED TO PREPARE FOR SLEEP, ZOMBOSS, THANKS TO THIS SLEEP RAY!
EH?
CLICK
HUH? NOTHING?
Phew
BEEP
HMM?
BEEP
WHOA!
BEEP!
YIKES!
EGAD!

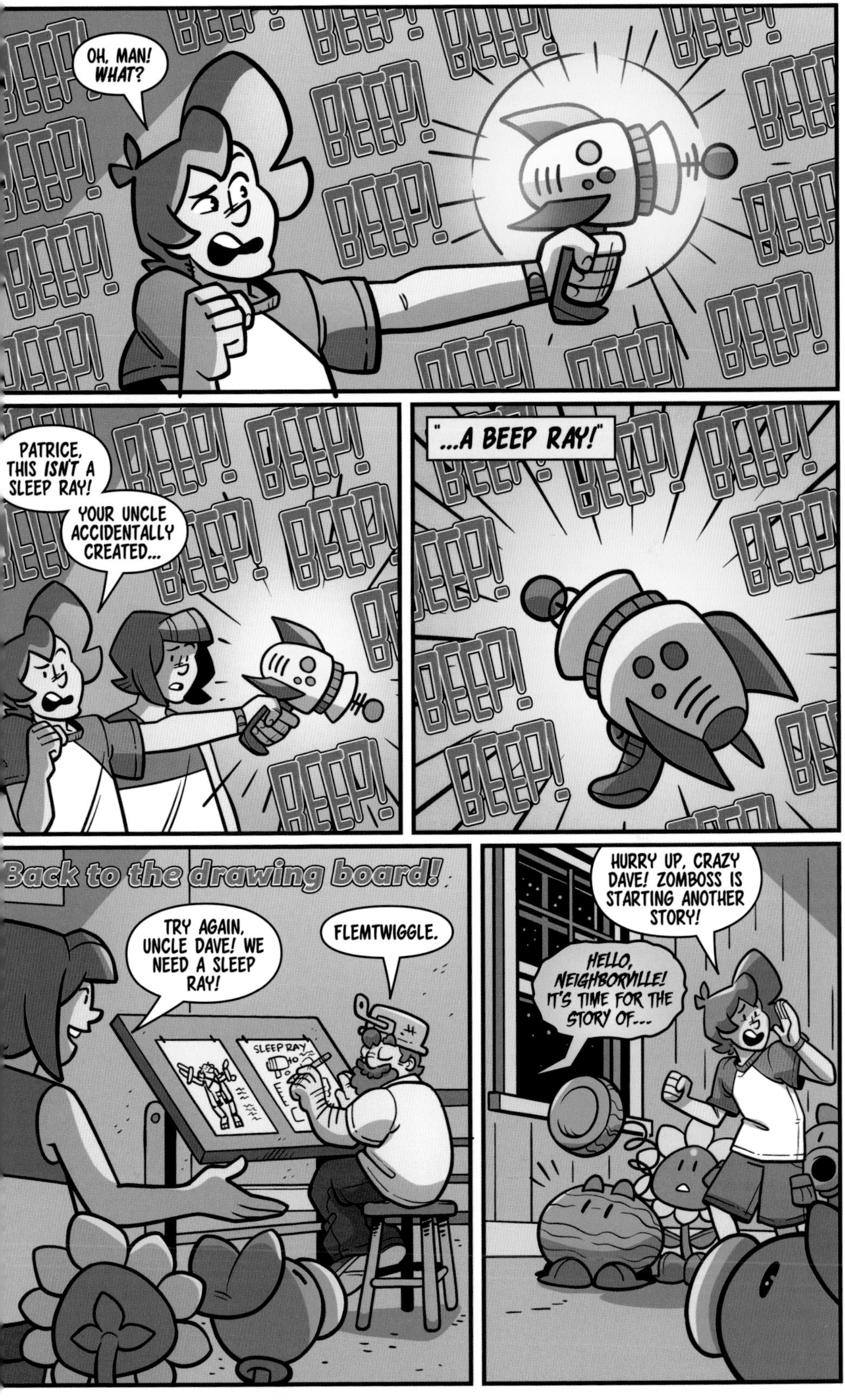
BEEP! BEEP! BEEP!
OH, MAN! WHAT?
PATRICE, THIS ISN'T A SLEEP RAY!
YOUR UNCLE ACCIDENTALLY CREATED...
"...A BEEP RAY!"
Back to the drawing board!
TRY AGAIN, UNCLE DAVE! WE NEED A SLEEP RAY!
FLEMTWIGGLE.
SLEEP RAY
HURRY UP, CRAZY DAVE! ZOMBOSS IS STARTING ANOTHER STORY!
HELLO, NEIGHBORVILLE! IT'S TIME FOR THE STORY OF...

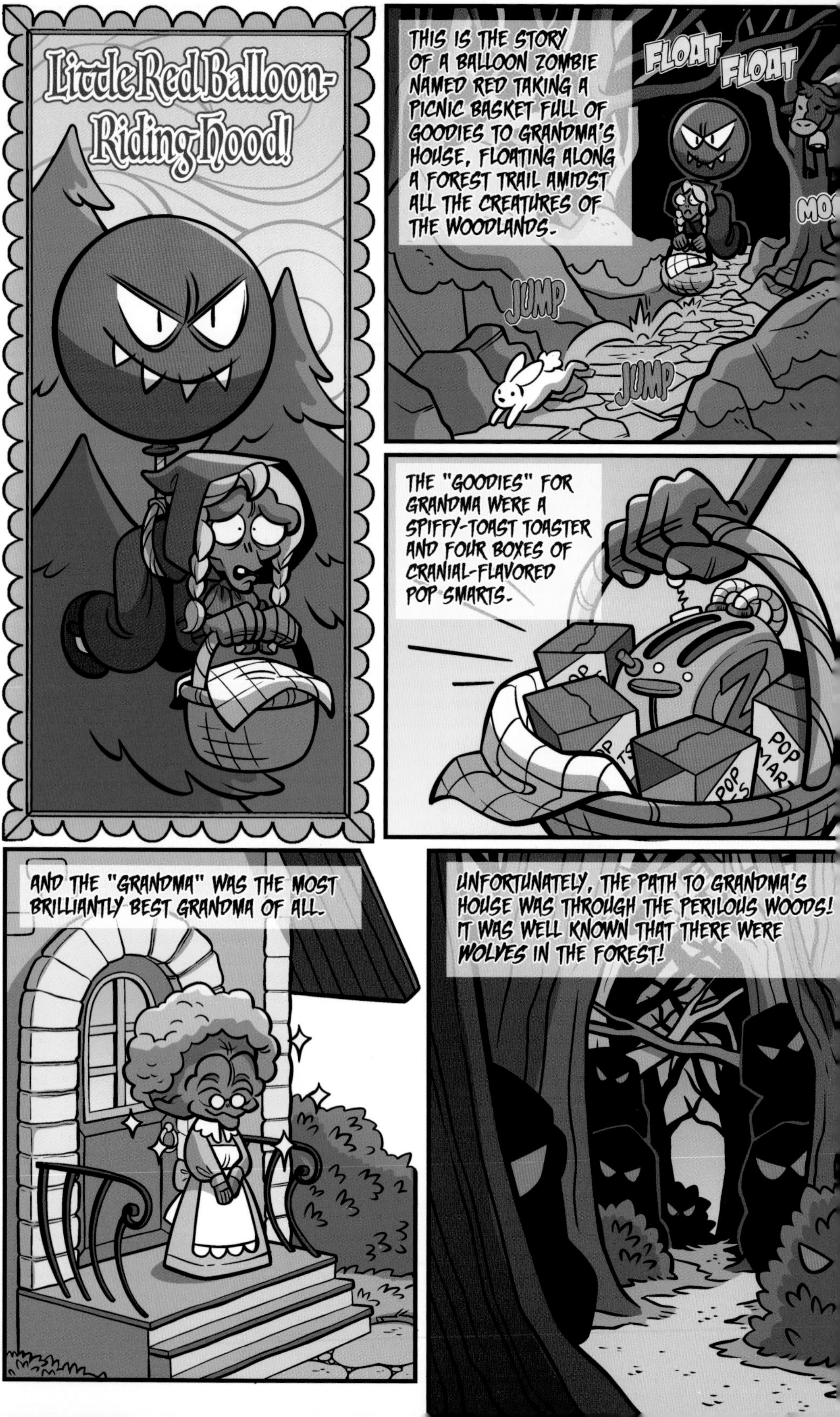
Little Red Balloon-Riding Hood!
THIS IS THE STORY OF A BALLOON ZOMBIE NAMED RED TAKING A PICNIC BASKET FULL OF GOODIES TO GRANDMA'S HOUSE, FLOATING ALONG A FOREST TRAIL AMIDST ALL THE CREATURES OF THE WOODLANDS.
FLOAT
FLOAT
JUMP
JUMP
THE "GOODIES" FOR GRANDMA WERE A SPIFFY-TOAST TOASTER AND FOUR BOXES OF CRANIAL-FLAVORED POP SMARTS.
AND THE "GRANDMA" WAS THE MOST BRILLIANTLY BEST GRANDMA OF ALL.
UNFORTUNATELY, THE PATH TO GRANDMA'S HOUSE WAS THROUGH THE PERILOUS WOODS! IT WAS WELL KNOWN THAT THERE WERE WOLVES IN THE FOREST!

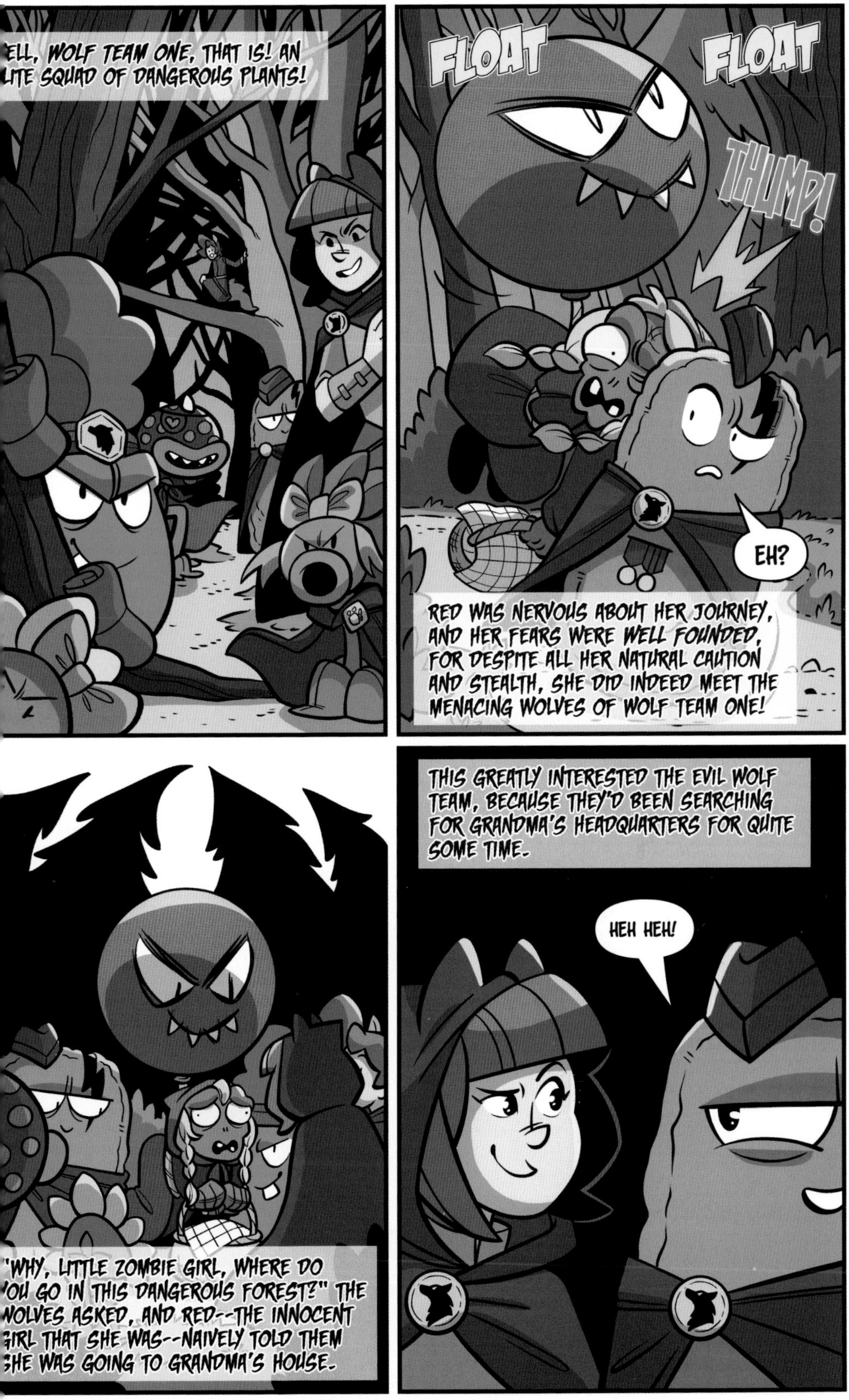
ELL, WOLF TEAM ONE, THAT IS! AN
LITE SQUAD OF DANGEROUS PLANTS!
FLOAT
FLOAT
THUMP!
EH?
RED WAS NERVOUS ABOUT HER JOURNEY, AND HER FEARS WERE WELL FOUNDED, FOR DESPITE ALL HER NATURAL CAUTION AND STEALTH, SHE DID INDEED MEET THE MENACING WOLVES OF WOLF TEAM ONE!
"WHY, LITTLE ZOMBIE GIRL, WHERE DO
OU GO IN THIS DANGEROUS FOREST?" THE
OLVES ASKED, AND RED--THE INNOCENT
IRL THAT SHE WAS--NAIVELY TOLD THEM
HE WAS GOING TO GRANDMA'S HOUSE.
THIS GREATLY INTERESTED THE EVIL WOLF TEAM, BECAUSE THEY'D BEEN SEARCHING FOR GRANDMA'S HEADQUARTERS FOR QUITE SOME TIME.
HEH HEH!

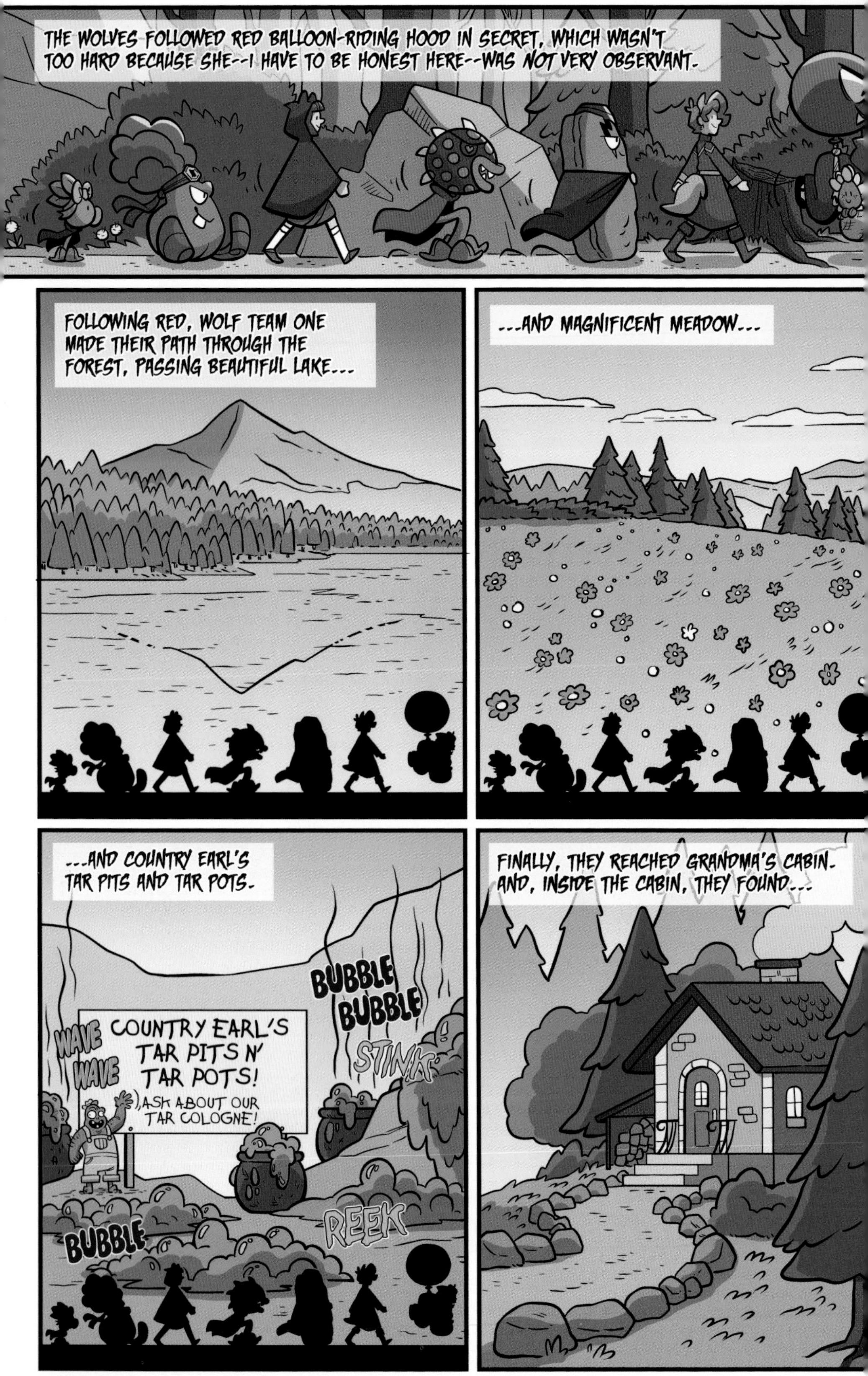
THE WOLVES FOLLOWED RED BALLOON-RIDING HOOD IN SECRET, WHICH WASN'T TOO HARD BECAUSE SHE--I HAVE TO BE HONEST HERE--WAS NOT VERY OBSERVANT.
FOLLOWING RED, WOLF TEAM ONE MADE THEIR PATH THROUGH THE FOREST, PASSING BEAUTIFUL LAKE...
...AND MAGNIFICENT MEADOW...
...AND COUNTRY EARL'S TAR PITS AND TAR POTS.
COUNTRY EARL'S TAR PITS N' TAR POTS!
ASK ABOUT OUR TAR COLOGNE!
WAVE WAVE
BUBBLE BUBBLE
STINK
REEK
BUBBLE
FINALLY, THEY REACHED GRANDMA'S CABIN. AND, INSIDE THE CABIN, THEY FOUND...

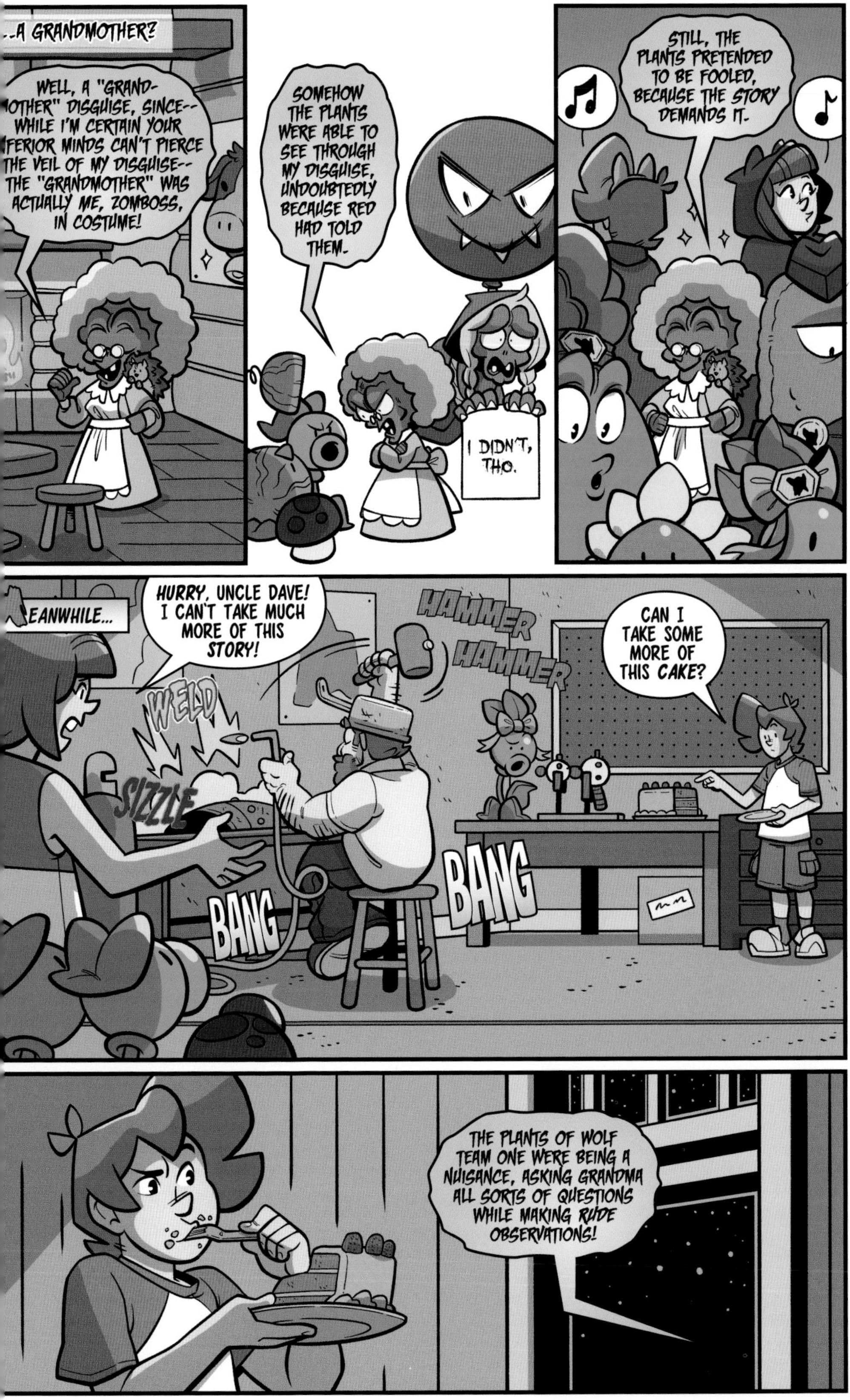
...A GRANDMOTHER?
WELL, A "GRAND-MOTHER" DISGUISE, SINCE--WHILE I'M CERTAIN YOUR INFERIOR MINDS CAN'T PIERCE THE VEIL OF MY DISGUISE--THE "GRANDMOTHER" WAS ACTUALLY ME, ZOMBOSS, IN COSTUME!
SOMEHOW THE PLANTS WERE ABLE TO SEE THROUGH MY DISGUISE, UNDOUBTEDLY BECAUSE RED HAD TOLD THEM.
I DIDN'T, THO.
STILL, THE PLANTS PRETENDED TO BE FOOLED, BECAUSE THE STORY DEMANDS IT.
MEANWHILE...
HURRY, UNCLE DAVE! I CAN'T TAKE MUCH MORE OF THIS STORY!
HAMMER
HAMMER
WELD
SIZZLE
BANG
BANG
CAN I TAKE SOME MORE OF THIS CAKE?
THE PLANTS OF WOLF TEAM ONE WERE BEING A NUISANCE, ASKING GRANDMA ALL SORTS OF QUESTIONS WHILE MAKING RUDE OBSERVATIONS!

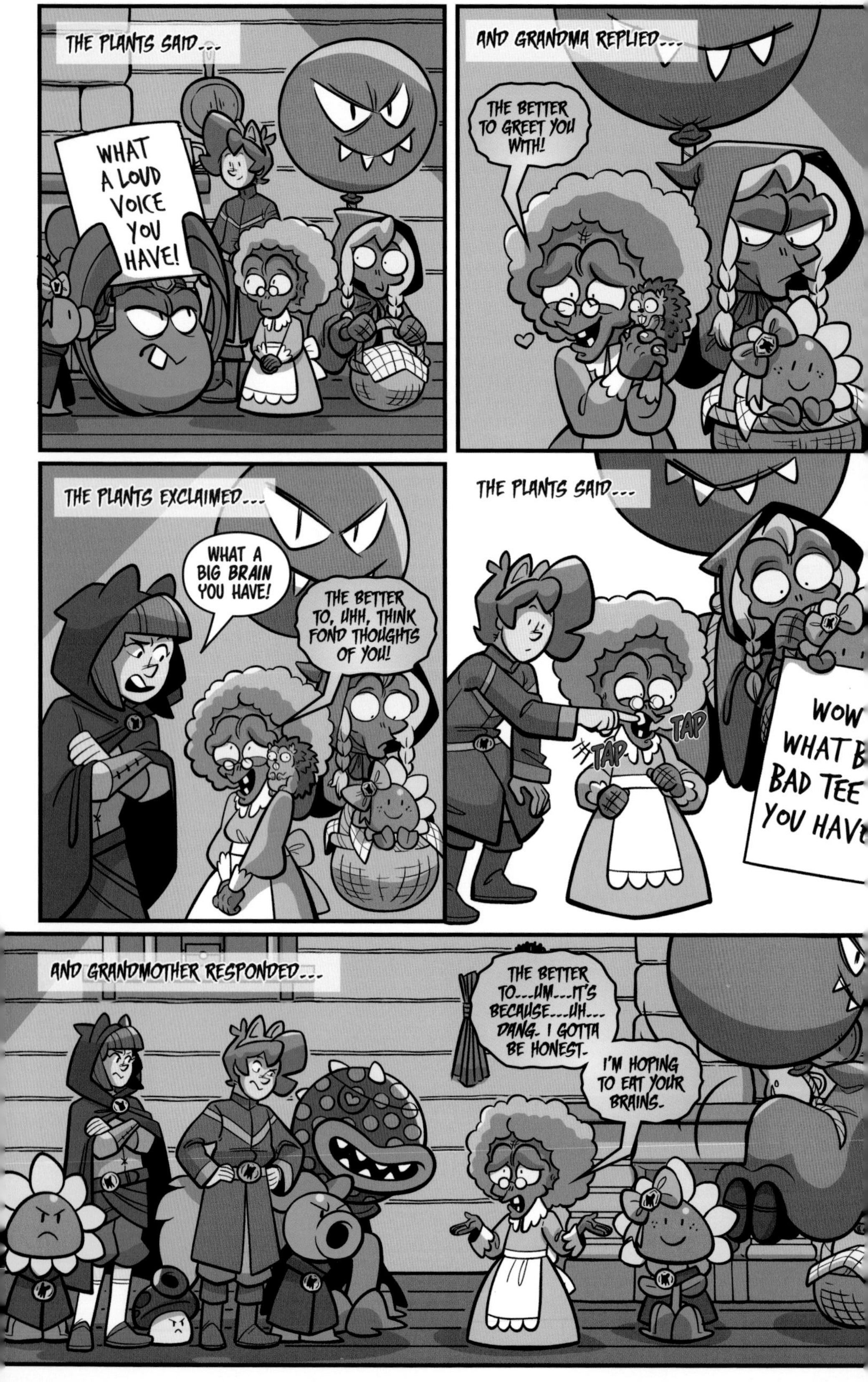

THE PLANTS SAID...
WHAT A LOUD VOICE YOU HAVE!
AND GRANDMA REPLIED...
THE BETTER TO GREET YOU WITH!
THE PLANTS EXCLAIMED...
WHAT A BIG BRAIN YOU HAVE!
THE BETTER TO, UHH, THINK FOND THOUGHTS OF YOU!
THE PLANTS SAID...
TAP
TAP
WOW WHAT B BAD TEE YOU HAV
AND GRANDMOTHER RESPONDED...
THE BETTER TO...UM...IT'S BECAUSE...UH... DANG. I GOTTA BE HONEST.
I'M HOPING TO EAT YOUR BRAINS.

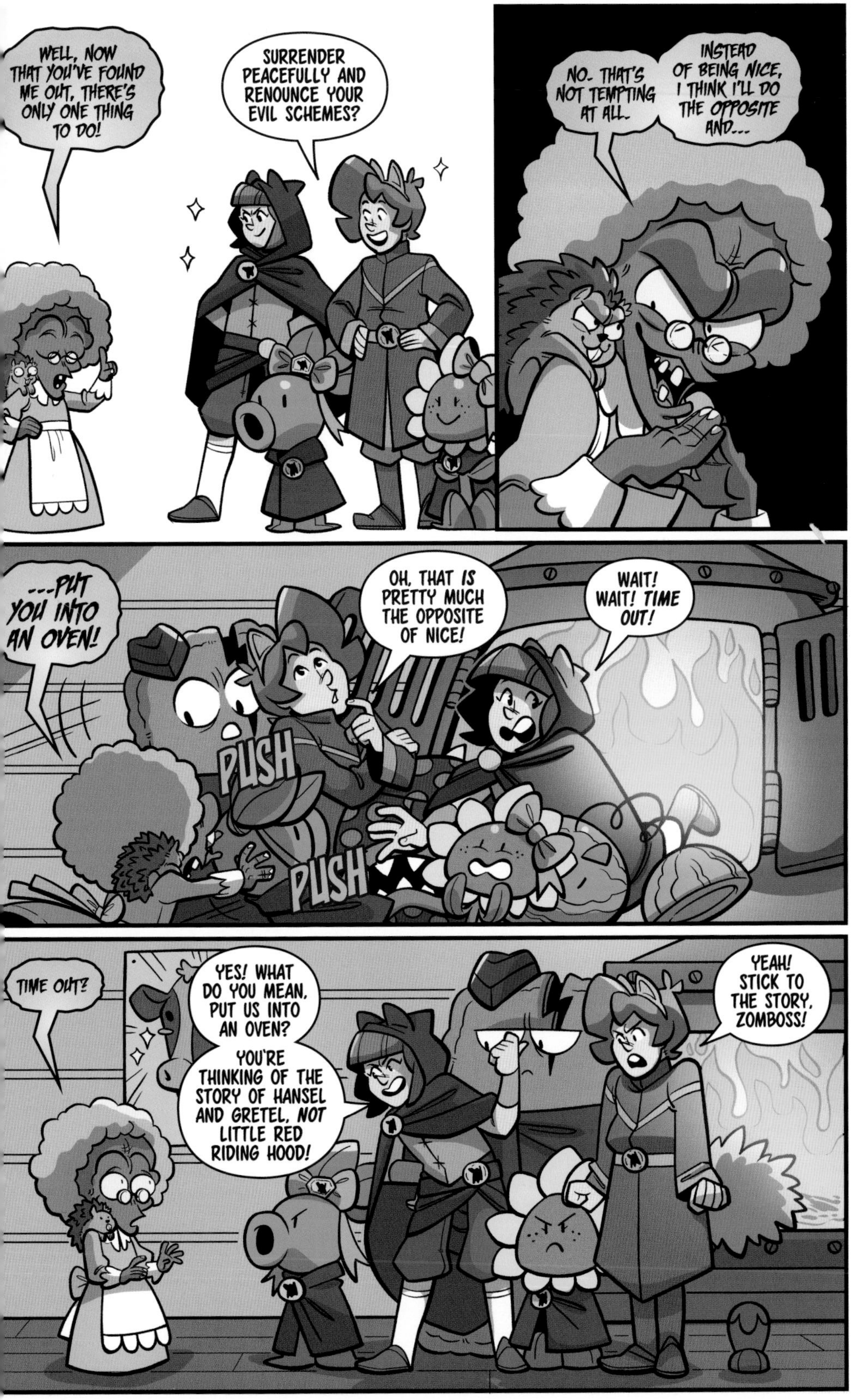
WELL, NOW THAT YOU'VE FOUND ME OUT, THERE'S ONLY ONE THING TO DO!
SURRENDER PEACEFULLY AND RENOUNCE YOUR EVIL SCHEMES?
NO. THAT'S NOT TEMPTING AT ALL.
INSTEAD OF BEING NICE, I THINK I'LL DO THE OPPOSITE AND...
...PUT YOU INTO AN OVEN!
OH, THAT IS PRETTY MUCH THE OPPOSITE OF NICE!
WAIT! WAIT! TIME OUT!
PUSH
PUSH
TIME OUT?
YES! WHAT DO YOU MEAN, PUT US INTO AN OVEN?
YOU'RE THINKING OF THE STORY OF HANSEL AND GRETEL, NOT LITTLE RED RIDING HOOD!
YEAH! STICK TO THE STORY, ZOMBOSS!

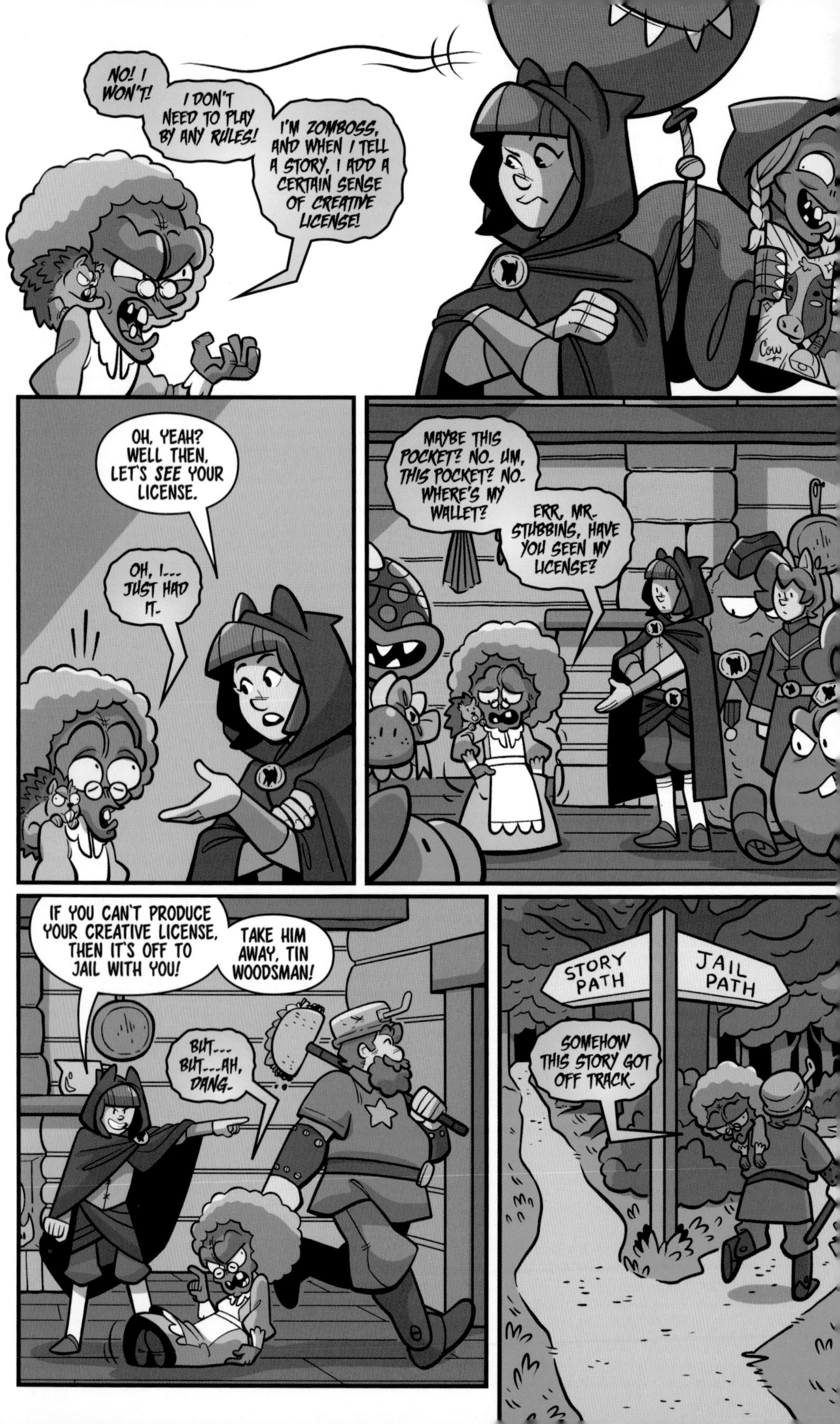

NO! I WON'T!
I DON'T NEED TO PLAY BY ANY RULES!
I'M ZOMBOSS, AND WHEN I TELL A STORY, I ADD A CERTAIN SENSE OF CREATIVE LICENSE!
COW
OH, YEAH? WELL THEN, LET'S SEE YOUR LICENSE.
OH, I... JUST HAD IT.
MAYBE THIS POCKET? NO. UM, THIS POCKET? NO. WHERE'S MY WALLET?
ERR, MR. STUBBINS, HAVE YOU SEEN MY LICENSE?
IF YOU CAN'T PRODUCE YOUR CREATIVE LICENSE, THEN IT'S OFF TO JAIL WITH YOU!
TAKE HIM AWAY, TIN WOODSMAN!
BUT... BUT...AH, DANG.
STORY PATH
JAIL PATH
SOMEHOW THIS STORY GOT OFF TRACK.

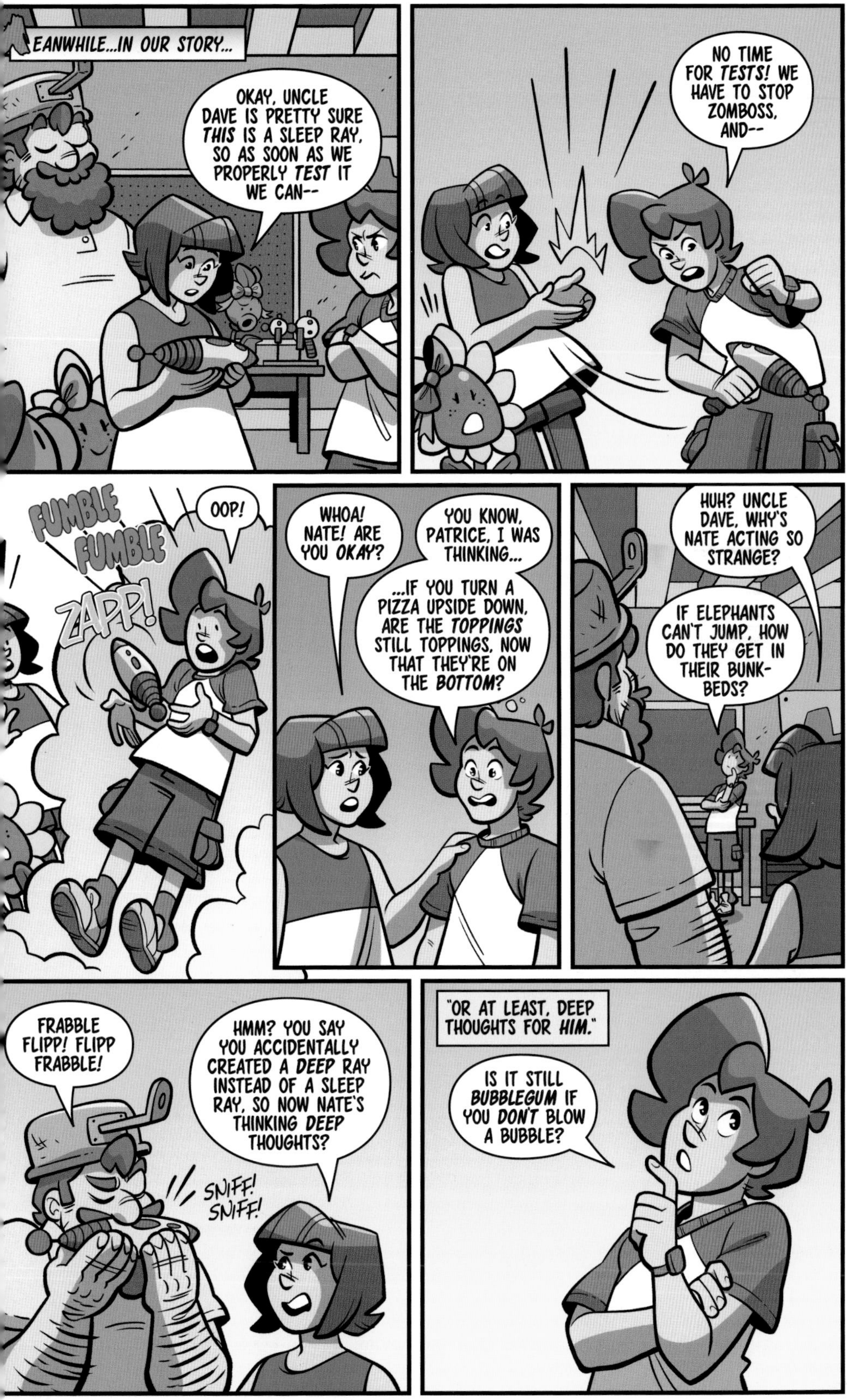

EANWHILE...IN OUR STORY...
OKAY, UNCLE DAVE IS PRETTY SURE *THIS* IS A SLEEP RAY, SO AS SOON AS WE PROPERLY *TEST* IT WE CAN--
NO TIME FOR *TESTS!* WE HAVE TO STOP ZOMBOSS, AND--
FUMBLE FUMBLE
ZAPP!
OOP!
WHOA! NATE! ARE YOU *OKAY*?
YOU KNOW, PATRICE, I WAS THINKING...
...IF YOU TURN A PIZZA UPSIDE DOWN, ARE THE *TOPPINGS* STILL TOPPINGS, NOW THAT THEY'RE ON THE *BOTTOM*?
HUH? UNCLE DAVE, WHY'S NATE ACTING SO STRANGE?
IF ELEPHANTS CAN'T JUMP, HOW DO THEY GET IN THEIR BUNK-BEDS?
FRABBLE FLIPP! FLIPP FRABBLE!
HMM? YOU SAY YOU ACCIDENTALLY CREATED A *DEEP* RAY INSTEAD OF A SLEEP RAY, SO NOW NATE'S THINKING *DEEP* THOUGHTS?
SNIFF! SNIFF!
"OR AT LEAST, DEEP THOUGHTS FOR *HIM*."
IS IT STILL *BUBBLEGUM* IF YOU *DON'T* BLOW A BUBBLE?

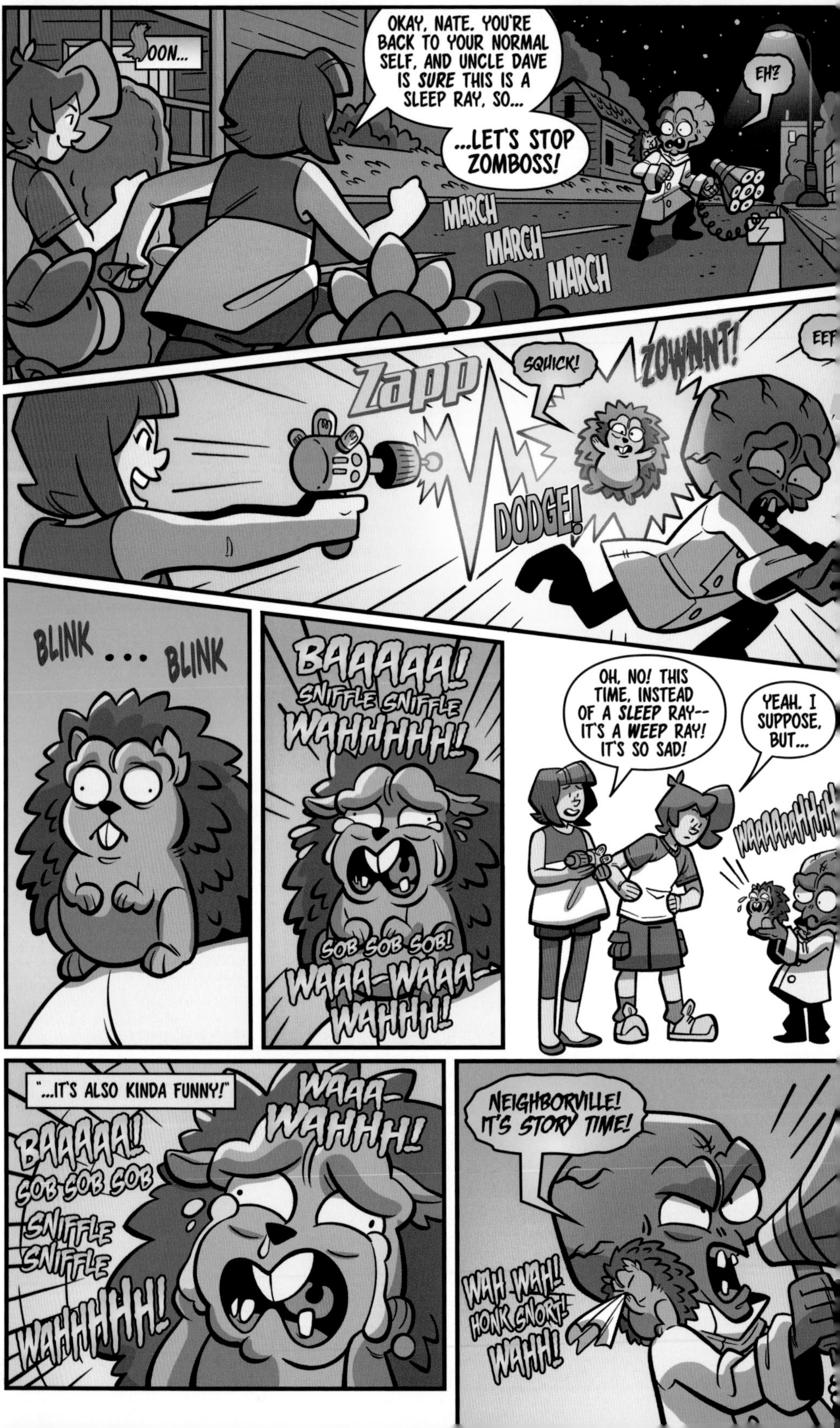
SOON...
OKAY, NATE. YOU'RE BACK TO YOUR NORMAL SELF, AND UNCLE DAVE IS SURE THIS IS A SLEEP RAY, SO...
...LET'S STOP ZOMBOSS!
EH?
MARCH
MARCH
MARCH
ZAPP
SQUICK!
ZOWNNT!
DODGE!
BLINK ... BLINK
BAAAAAA!
SNIFFLE SNIFFLE
WAHHHHHH!
SOB SOB SOB!
WAAA-WAAA-WAHHH!
OH, NO! THIS TIME, INSTEAD OF A SLEEP RAY-- IT'S A WEEP RAY! IT'S SO SAD!
YEAH. I SUPPOSE, BUT...
"...IT'S ALSO KINDA FUNNY!"
WAAA-WAHHH!
BAAAAA!
SOB SOB SOB
SNIFFLE SNIFFLE
WAHHHHH!
NEIGHBORVILLE! IT'S STORY TIME!
WAH WAH!
HONK SNORT
WAHH!

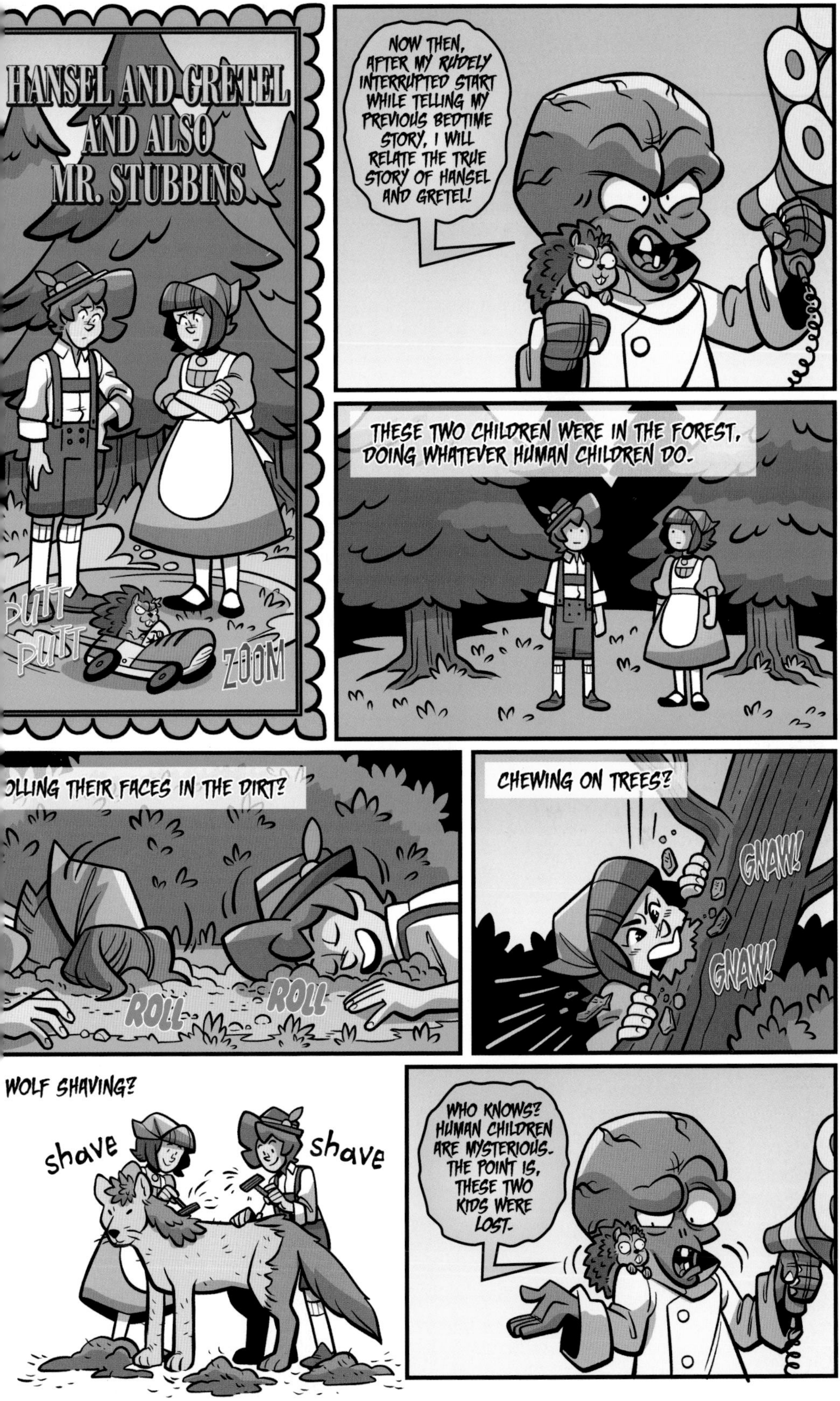
HANSEL AND GRETEL AND ALSO MR. STUBBINS
PUTT PUTT
ZOOM
NOW THEN, AFTER MY RUDELY INTERRUPTED START WHILE TELLING MY PREVIOUS BEDTIME STORY, I WILL RELATE THE TRUE STORY OF HANSEL AND GRETEL!
THESE TWO CHILDREN WERE IN THE FOREST, DOING WHATEVER HUMAN CHILDREN DO.
OLLING THEIR FACES IN THE DIRT?
ROLL
ROLL
CHEWING ON TREES?
GNAW!
GNAW!
WOLF SHAVING?
shave
shave
WHO KNOWS? HUMAN CHILDREN ARE MYSTERIOUS. THE POINT IS, THESE TWO KIDS WERE LOST.

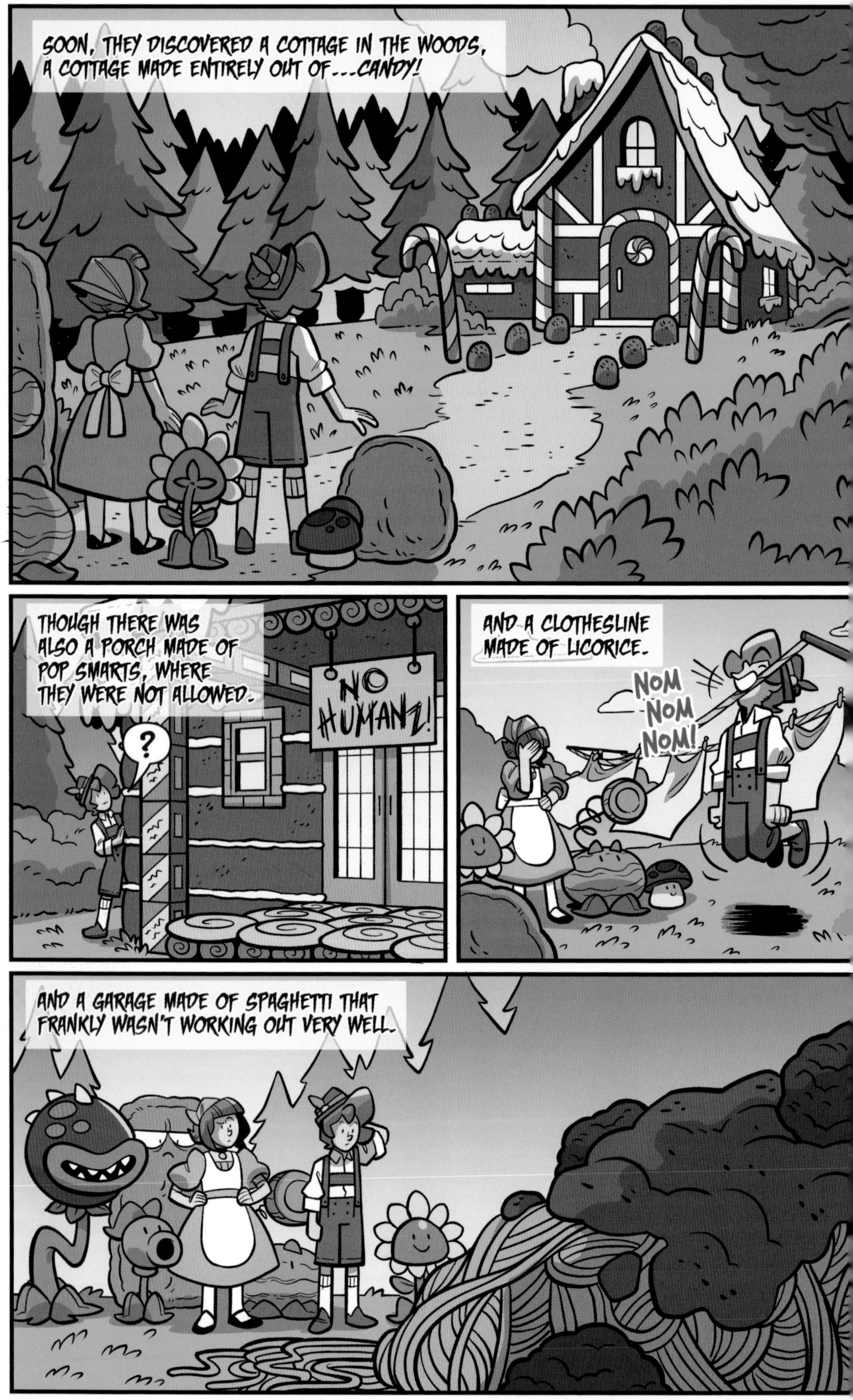
SOON, THEY DISCOVERED A COTTAGE IN THE WOODS, A COTTAGE MADE ENTIRELY OUT OF...CANDY!
THOUGH THERE WAS ALSO A PORCH MADE OF POP SMARTS, WHERE THEY WERE NOT ALLOWED.
NO HUMANZ!
?
AND A CLOTHESLINE MADE OF LICORICE.
NOM NOM NOM!
AND A GARAGE MADE OF SPAGHETTI THAT FRANKLY WASN'T WORKING OUT VERY WELL.

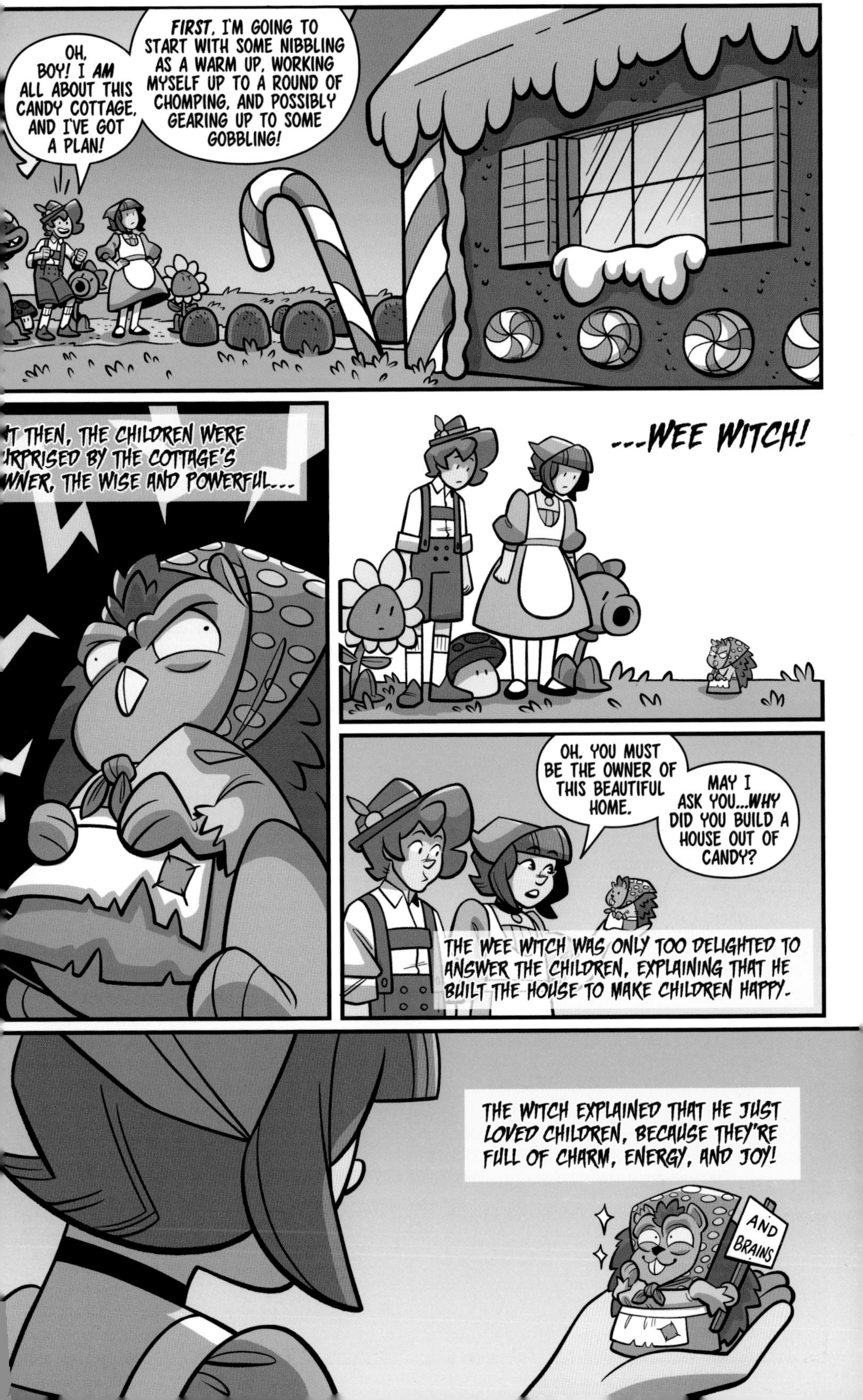
OH, BOY! I AM ALL ABOUT THIS CANDY COTTAGE, AND I'VE GOT A PLAN!
FIRST, I'M GOING TO START WITH SOME NIBBLING AS A WARM UP, WORKING MYSELF UP TO A ROUND OF CHOMPING, AND POSSIBLY GEARING UP TO SOME GOBBLING!
T THEN, THE CHILDREN WERE IRPRISED BY THE COTTAGE'S WNER, THE WISE AND POWERFUL...
---WEE WITCH!
OH. YOU MUST BE THE OWNER OF THIS BEAUTIFUL HOME.
MAY I ASK YOU...WHY DID YOU BUILD A HOUSE OUT OF CANDY?
THE WEE WITCH WAS ONLY TOO DELIGHTED TO ANSWER THE CHILDREN, EXPLAINING THAT HE BUILT THE HOUSE TO MAKE CHILDREN HAPPY.
THE WITCH EXPLAINED THAT HE JUST LOVED CHILDREN, BECAUSE THEY'RE FULL OF CHARM, ENERGY, AND JOY!
AND BRAINS

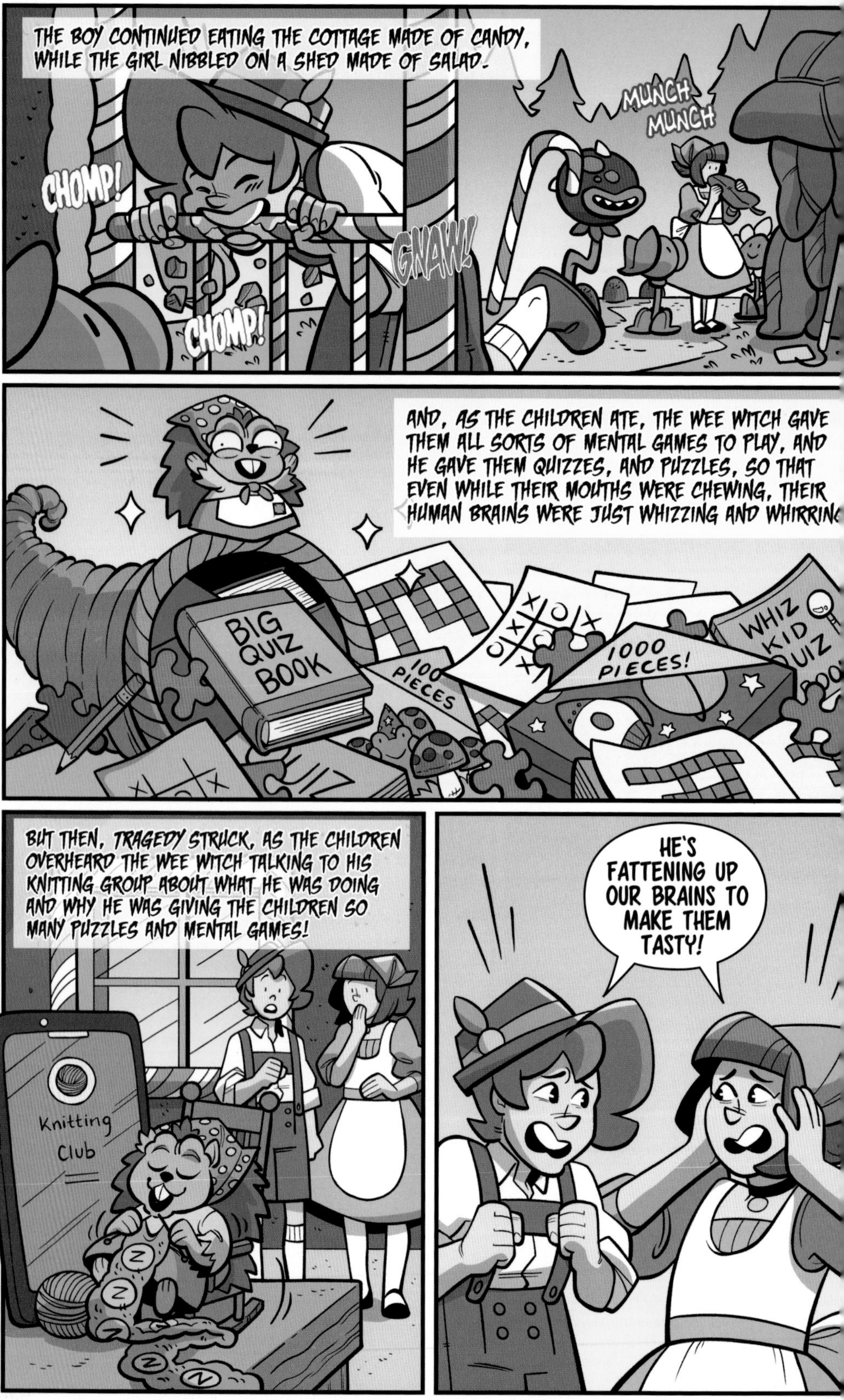
THE BOY CONTINUED EATING THE COTTAGE MADE OF CANDY, WHILE THE GIRL NIBBLED ON A SHED MADE OF SALAD.
CHOMP!
CHOMP!
GNAW!
MUNCH MUNCH
AND, AS THE CHILDREN ATE, THE WEE WITCH GAVE THEM ALL SORTS OF MENTAL GAMES TO PLAY, AND HE GAVE THEM QUIZZES, AND PUZZLES, SO THAT EVEN WHILE THEIR MOUTHS WERE CHEWING, THEIR HUMAN BRAINS WERE JUST WHIZZING AND WHIRRING
BIG QUIZ BOOK
100 PIECES
1000 PIECES!
WHIZ KID QUIZ
BUT THEN, TRAGEDY STRUCK, AS THE CHILDREN OVERHEARD THE WEE WITCH TALKING TO HIS KNITTING GROUP ABOUT WHAT HE WAS DOING AND WHY HE WAS GIVING THE CHILDREN SO MANY PUZZLES AND MENTAL GAMES!
Knitting Club
HE'S FATTENING UP OUR BRAINS TO MAKE THEM TASTY!

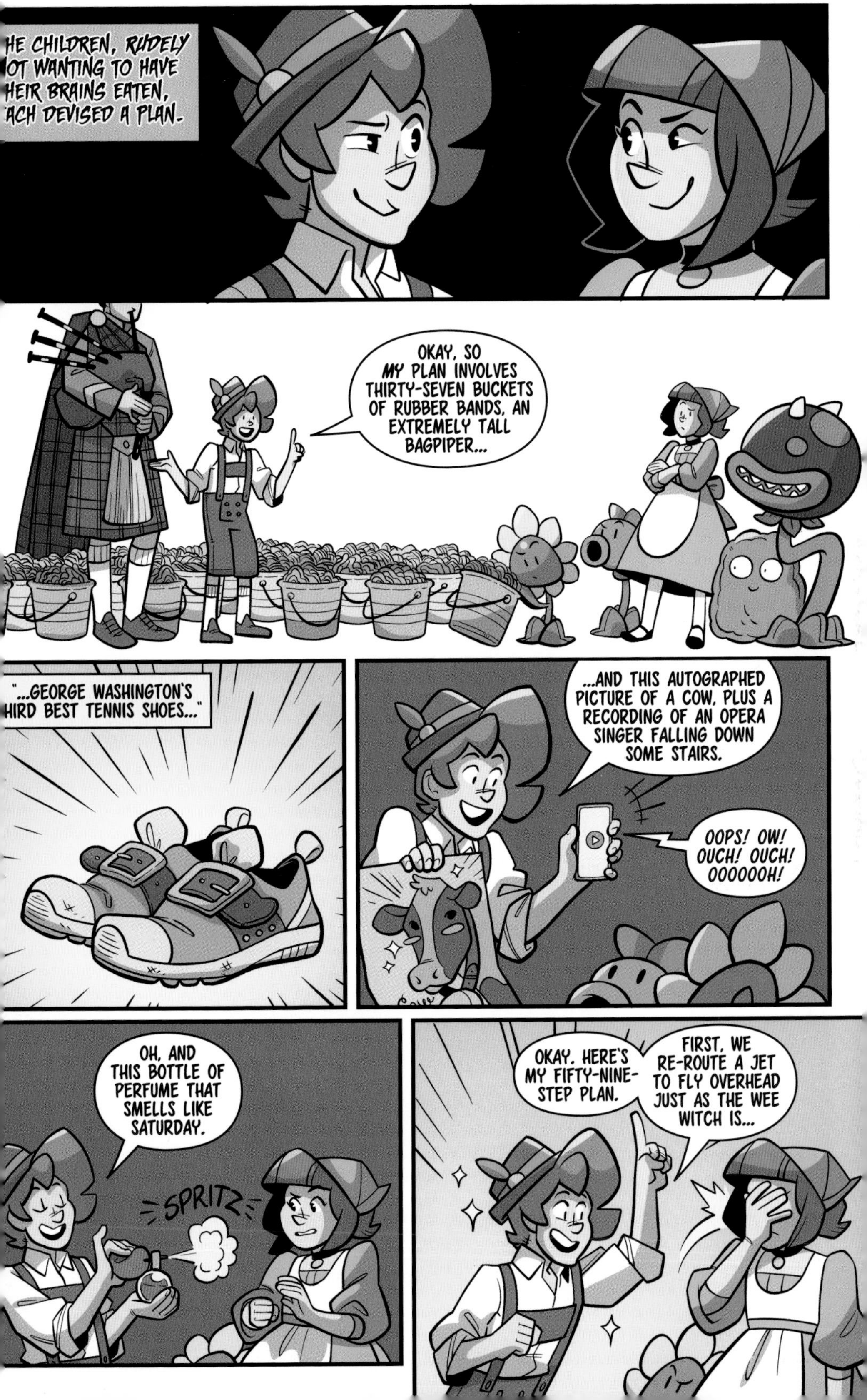
HE CHILDREN, RUDELY
OT WANTING TO HAVE
HEIR BRAINS EATEN,
ACH DEVISED A PLAN.
OKAY, SO MY PLAN INVOLVES THIRTY-SEVEN BUCKETS OF RUBBER BANDS, AN EXTREMELY TALL BAGPIPER...
"...GEORGE WASHINGTON'S HIRD BEST TENNIS SHOES..."
...AND THIS AUTOGRAPHED PICTURE OF A COW, PLUS A RECORDING OF AN OPERA SINGER FALLING DOWN SOME STAIRS.
OOPS! OW! OUCH! OUCH! OOOOOOH!
OH, AND THIS BOTTLE OF PERFUME THAT SMELLS LIKE SATURDAY.
SPRITZ
OKAY. HERE'S MY FIFTY-NINE-STEP PLAN.
FIRST, WE RE-ROUTE A JET TO FLY OVERHEAD JUST AS THE WEE WITCH IS...

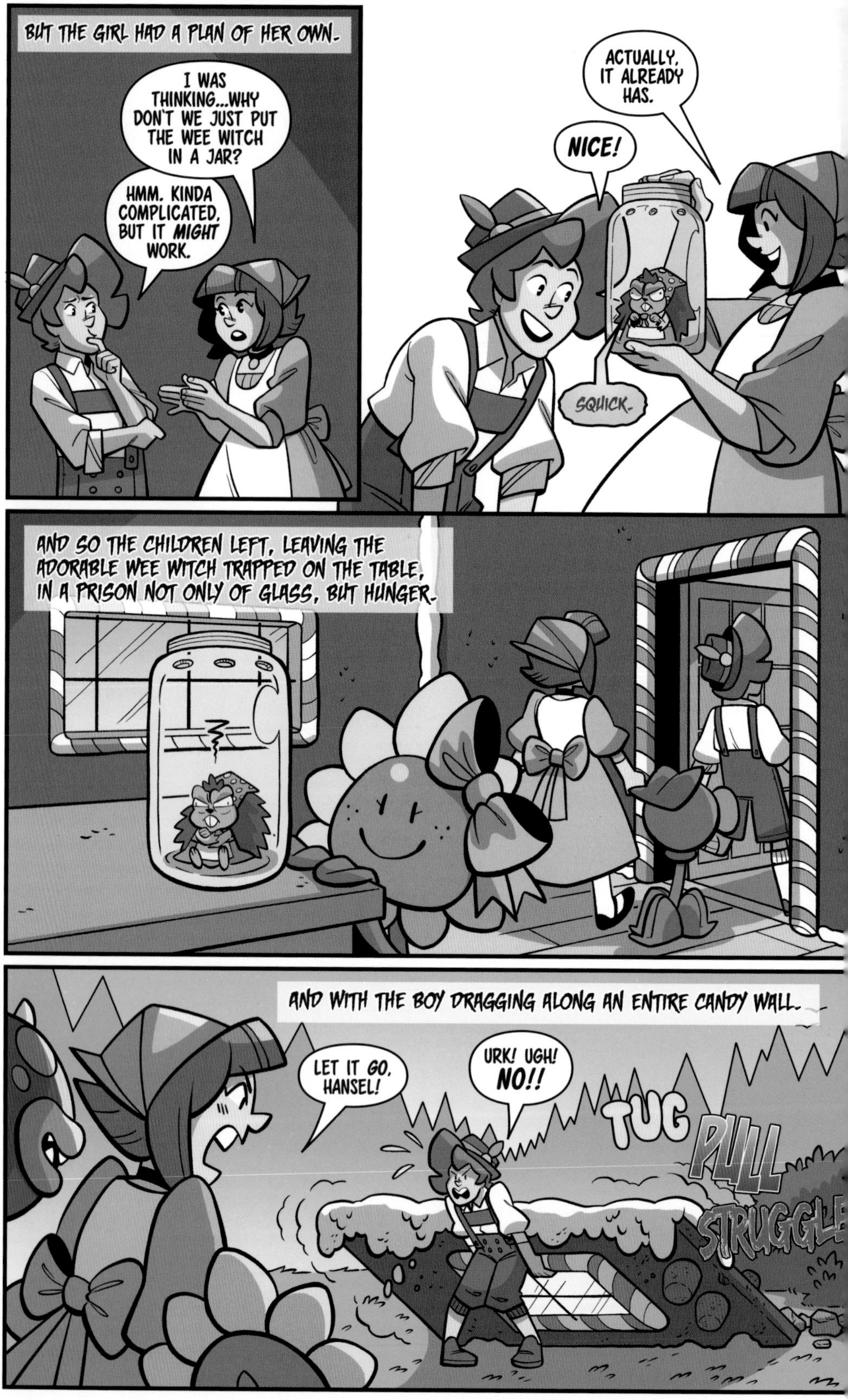
BUT THE GIRL HAD A PLAN OF HER OWN.
I WAS THINKING...WHY DON'T WE JUST PUT THE WEE WITCH IN A JAR?
HMM. KINDA COMPLICATED, BUT IT MIGHT WORK.
ACTUALLY, IT ALREADY HAS.
NICE!
SQUICK.
AND SO THE CHILDREN LEFT, LEAVING THE ADORABLE WEE WITCH TRAPPED ON THE TABLE, IN A PRISON NOT ONLY OF GLASS, BUT HUNGER.
AND WITH THE BOY DRAGGING ALONG AN ENTIRE CANDY WALL.
LET IT GO, HANSEL!
URK! UGH! NO!!
TUG
PULL
STRUGGLE

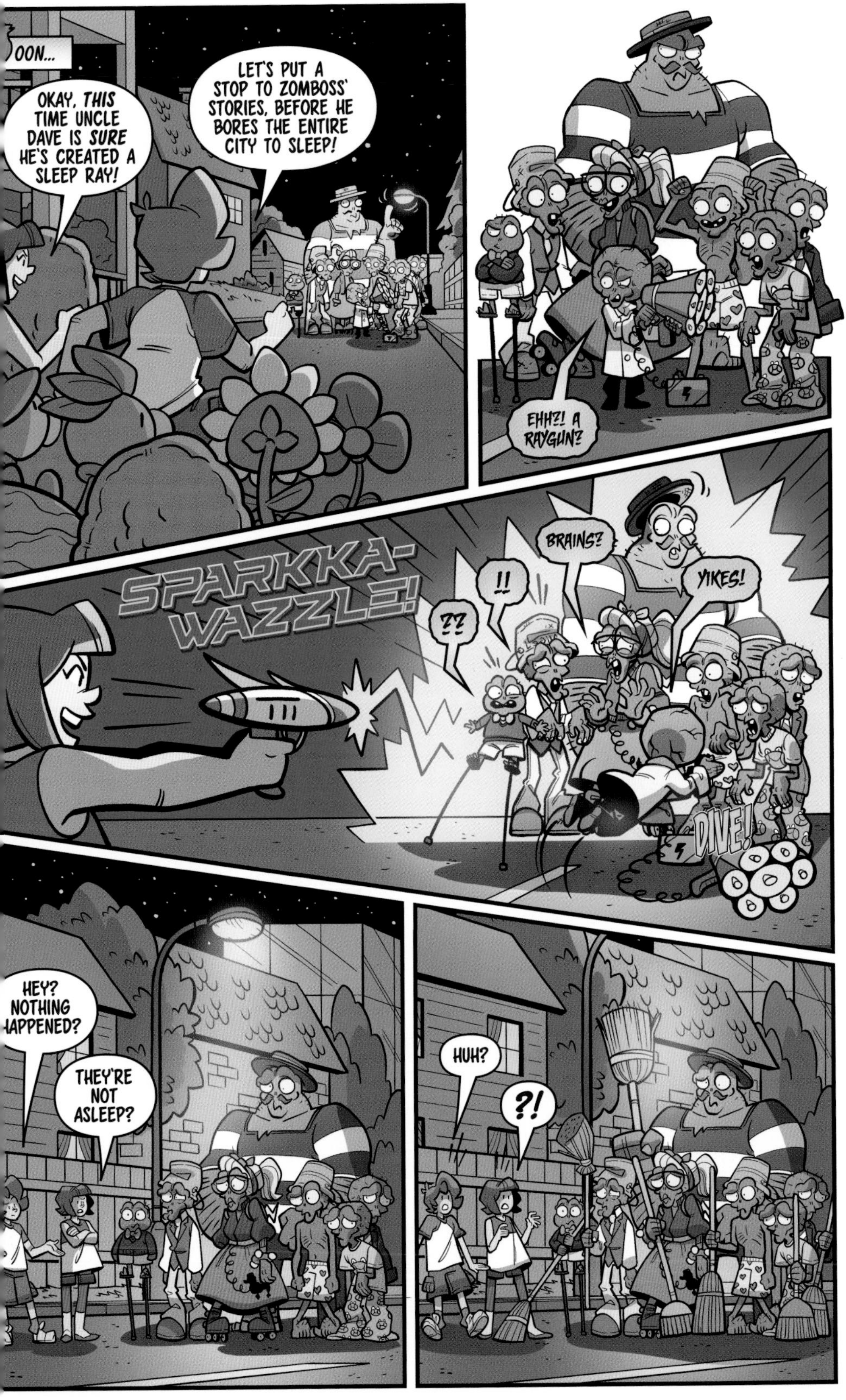

OON...
OKAY, THIS TIME UNCLE DAVE IS SURE HE'S CREATED A SLEEP RAY!
LET'S PUT A STOP TO ZOMBOSS' STORIES, BEFORE HE BORES THE ENTIRE CITY TO SLEEP!
EHH?! A RAYGUN?
SPARKKA-WAZZLE!
??
!!
BRAINS?
YIKES!
DIVE!
HEY? NOTHING HAPPENED?
THEY'RE NOT ASLEEP?
HUH?
?!

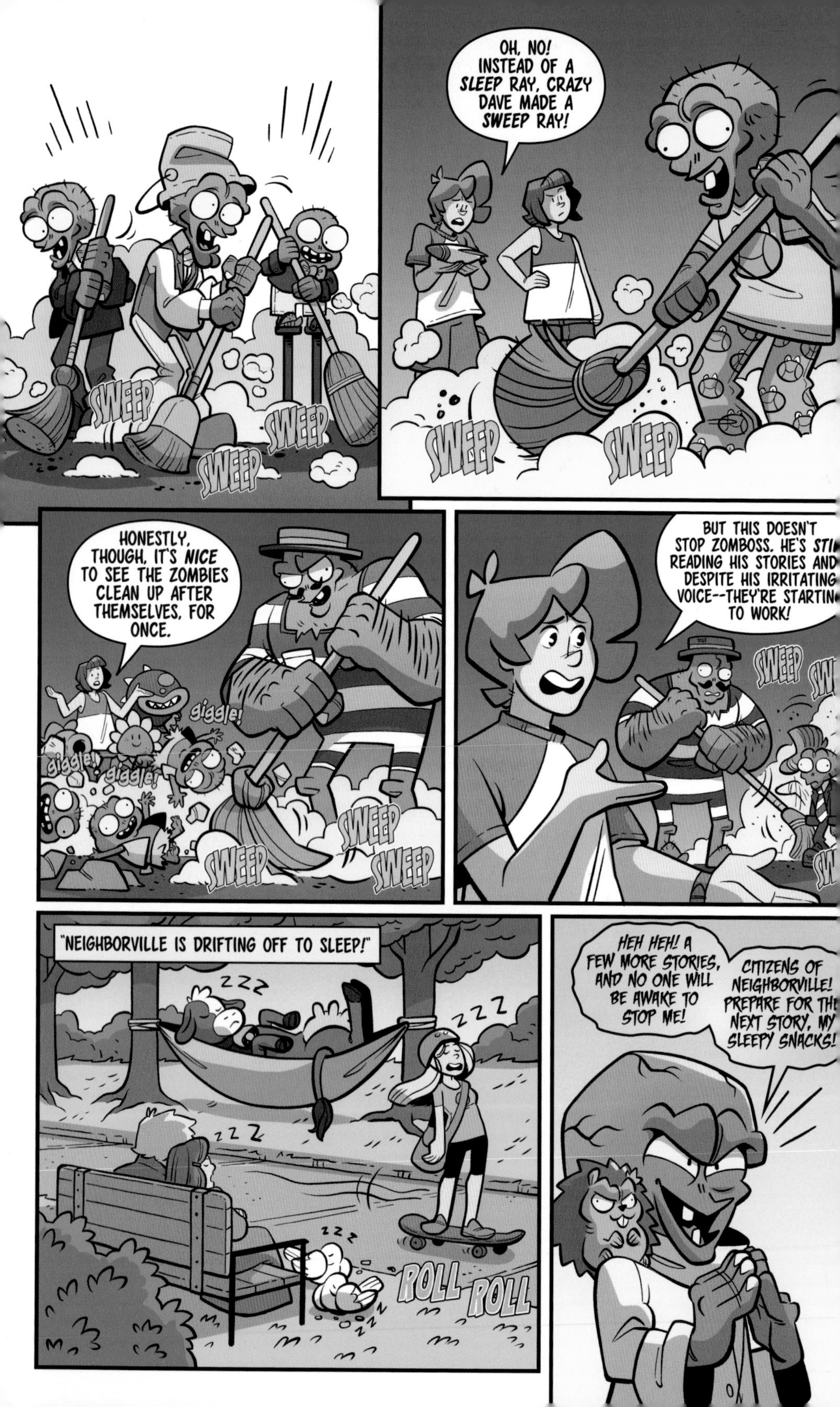
SWEEP
SWEEP
SWEEP
OH, NO! INSTEAD OF A SLEEP RAY, CRAZY DAVE MADE A SWEEP RAY!
SWEEP
SWEEP
HONESTLY, THOUGH, IT'S NICE TO SEE THE ZOMBIES CLEAN UP AFTER THEMSELVES, FOR ONCE.
giggle!
giggle!
giggle!
SWEEP
SWEEP
SWEEP
BUT THIS DOESN'T STOP ZOMBOSS. HE'S STI READING HIS STORIES AND DESPITE HIS IRRITATING VOICE--THEY'RE STARTIN TO WORK!
SWEEP
"NEIGHBORVILLE IS DRIFTING OFF TO SLEEP!"
Z Z Z
Z Z Z
Z Z Z
Z Z Z
ROLL ROLL
HEH HEH! A FEW MORE STORIES, AND NO ONE WILL BE AWAKE TO STOP ME!
CITIZENS OF NEIGHBORVILLE! PREPARE FOR TH NEXT STORY, MY SLEEPY SNACKS!

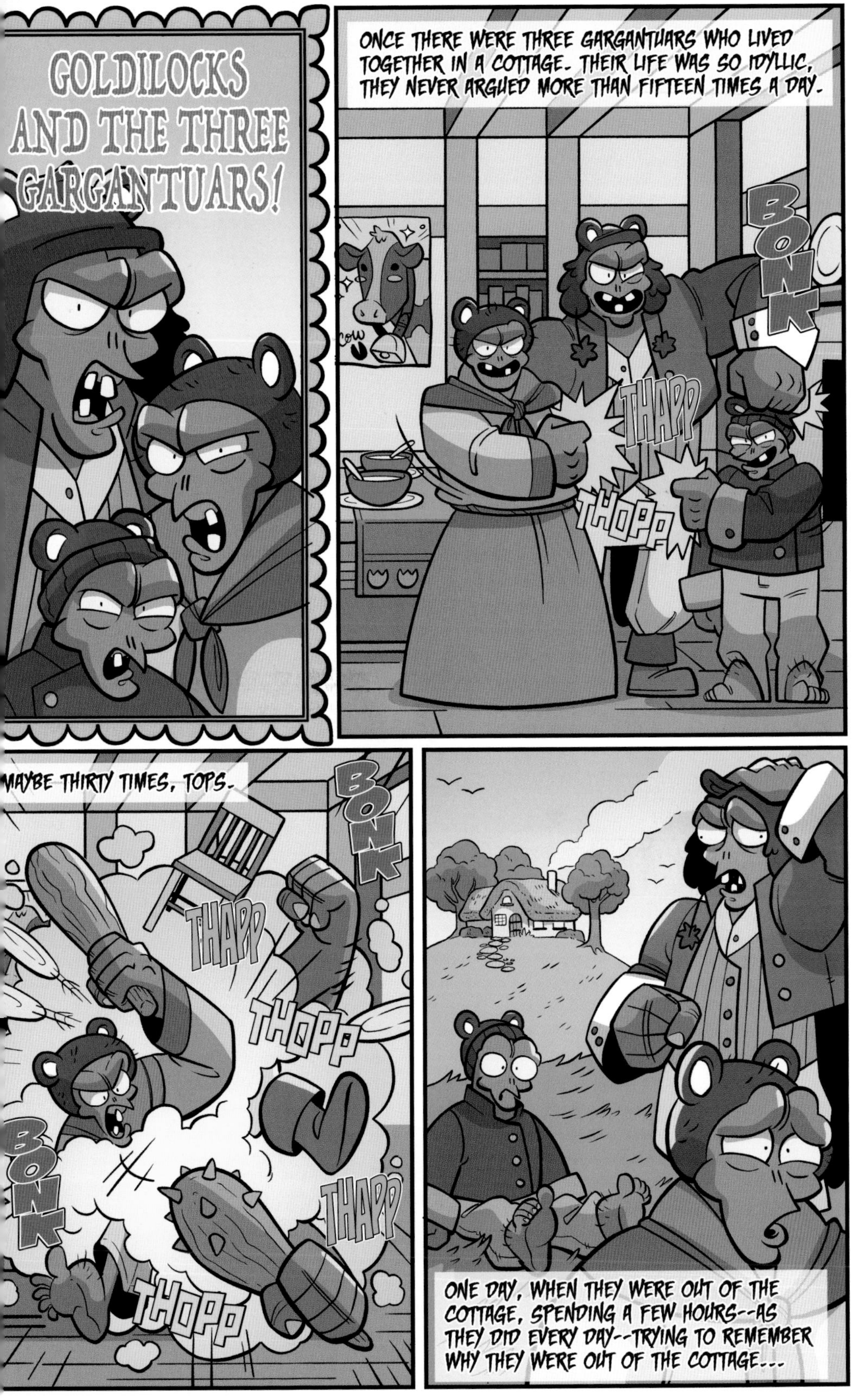
GOLDILOCKS AND THE THREE GARGANTUARS!
ONCE THERE WERE THREE GARGANTUARS WHO LIVED TOGETHER IN A COTTAGE. THEIR LIFE WAS SO IDYLLIC, THEY NEVER ARGUED MORE THAN FIFTEEN TIMES A DAY.
COW
BONK
THAPP
THOPP
MAYBE THIRTY TIMES, TOPS.
BONK
THAPP
THOPP
BONK
THAPP
THOPP
ONE DAY, WHEN THEY WERE OUT OF THE COTTAGE, SPENDING A FEW HOURS--AS THEY DID EVERY DAY--TRYING TO REMEMBER WHY THEY WERE OUT OF THE COTTAGE...

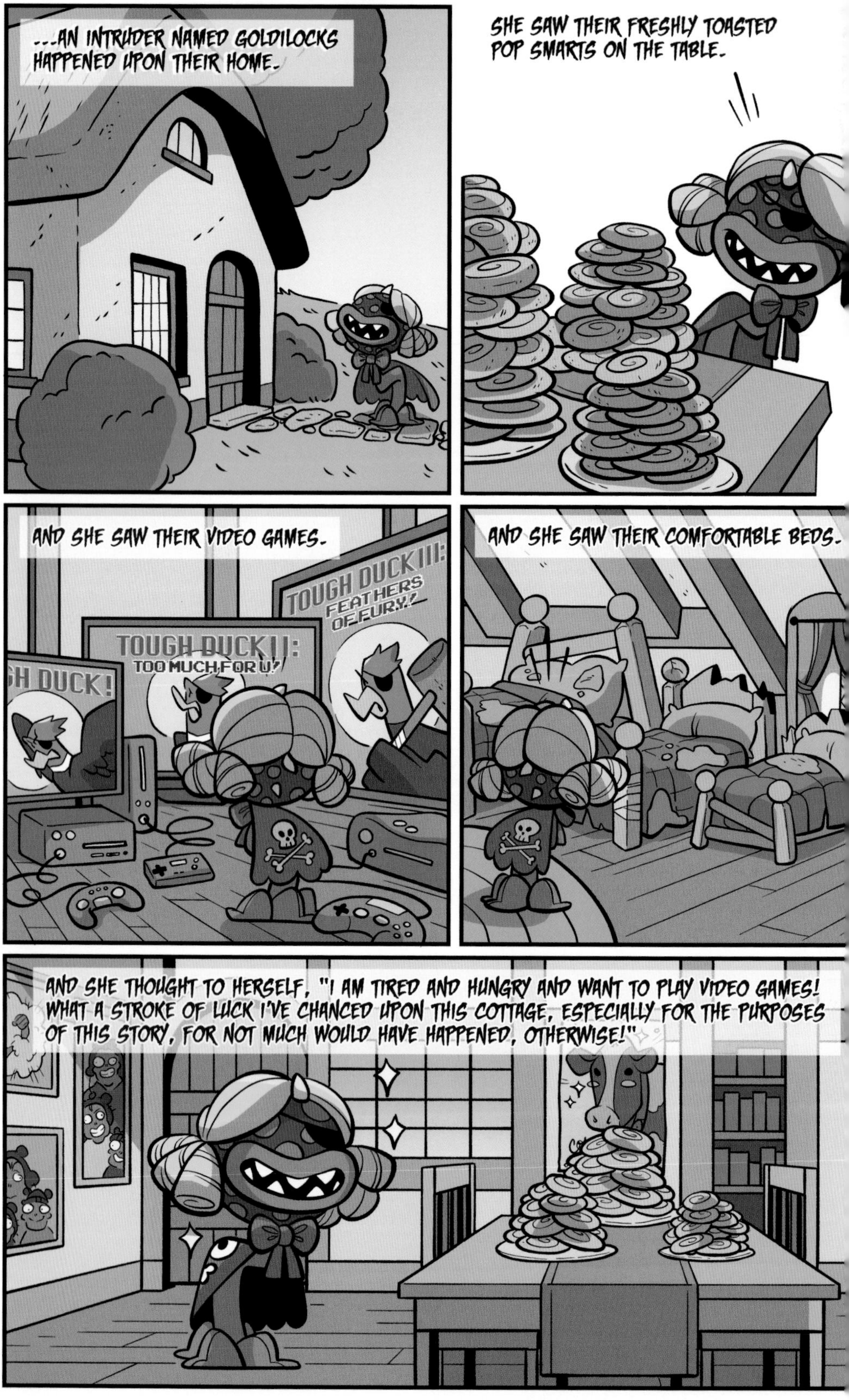
...AN INTRUDER NAMED GOLDILOCKS HAPPENED UPON THEIR HOME.
SHE SAW THEIR FRESHLY TOASTED POP SMARTS ON THE TABLE.
AND SHE SAW THEIR VIDEO GAMES.
TOUGH DUCK III: FEATHERS OF FURY!
TOUGH DUCK II: TOO MUCH FOR U!
H DUCK!
AND SHE SAW THEIR COMFORTABLE BEDS.
AND SHE THOUGHT TO HERSELF, "I AM TIRED AND HUNGRY AND WANT TO PLAY VIDEO GAMES! WHAT A STROKE OF LUCK I'VE CHANCED UPON THIS COTTAGE, ESPECIALLY FOR THE PURPOSES OF THIS STORY, FOR NOT MUCH WOULD HAVE HAPPENED, OTHERWISE!"

SOON, THE THREE GARGANTUARS CAME HOME, AND THEY IMMEDIATELY NOTICED SOMEONE HAD BEEN IN THEIR COTTAGE.

GRR-

GARR?

GUHH.

THEY LOOKED AT THEIR PLATES OF POP SMARTS, AND THE PAPA GARGANTUAR SAID, "SOMEONE HAS BEEN EATING MY POP SMARTS!"

TAP

TAP

THEN THE MAMA GARGANTUAR SAID, "SOMEONE HAS BEEN EATING MY POP SMARTS, TOO!"

AND THEN THE BABY GARGANTUAR SAID, "SOMEBODY HAS BEEN EATING MY POP SMARTS, TOO, AND THEY STILL ARE!"

YEAH. IT'S ME.

SORRY TO BUTT INTO THE STORY, BUT THESE POP SMARTS ARE SO DELICIOUS!

GOBBLE GOBBLE CHOMP

SLOBBER

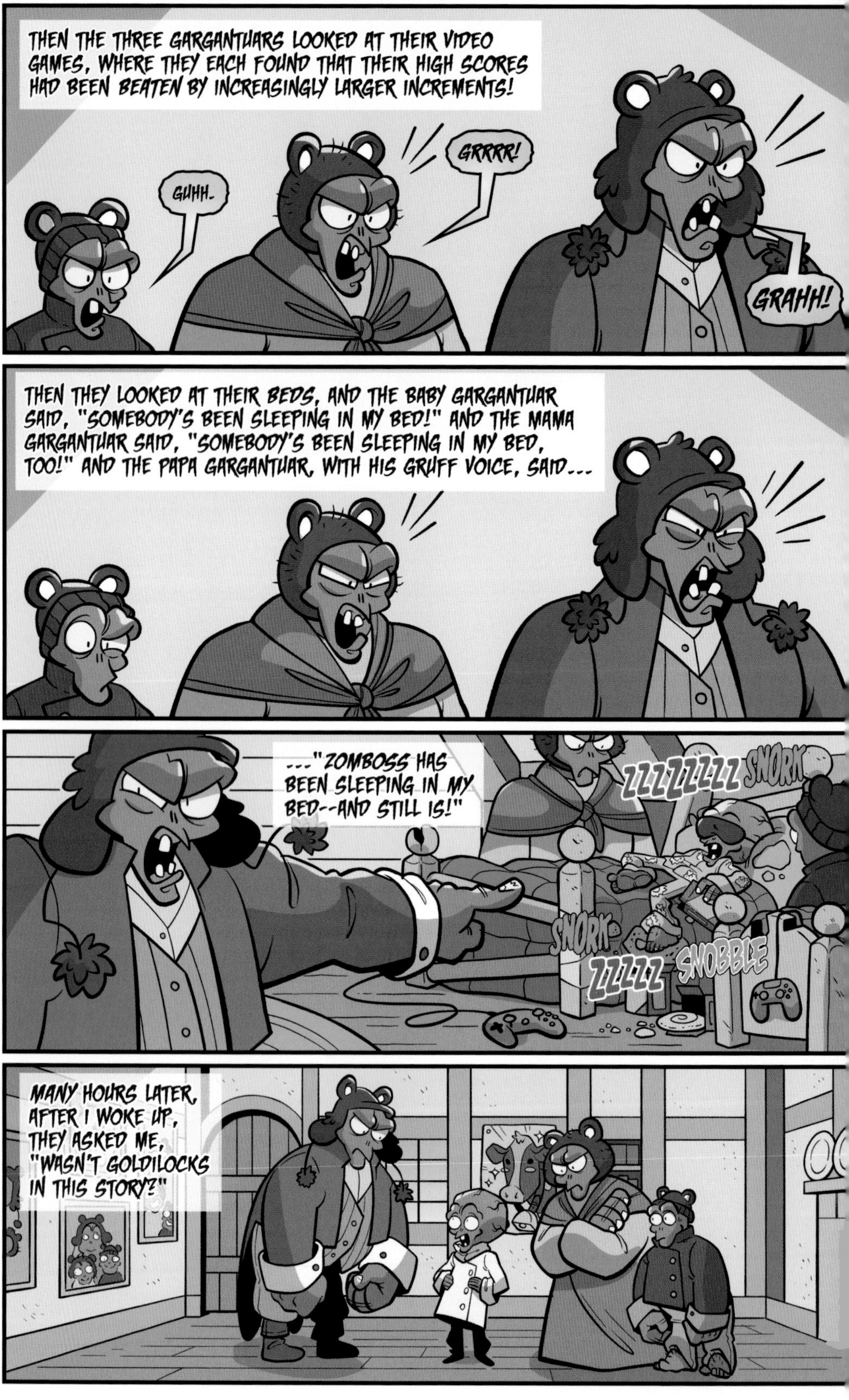
THEN THE THREE GARGANTUARS LOOKED AT THEIR VIDEO GAMES, WHERE THEY EACH FOUND THAT THEIR HIGH SCORES HAD BEEN BEATEN BY INCREASINGLY LARGER INCREMENTS!
GUHH.
GRRRR!
GRAHH!
THEN THEY LOOKED AT THEIR BEDS, AND THE BABY GARGANTUAR SAID, "SOMEBODY'S BEEN SLEEPING IN MY BED!" AND THE MAMA GARGANTUAR SAID, "SOMEBODY'S BEEN SLEEPING IN MY BED, TOO!" AND THE PAPA GARGANTUAR, WITH HIS GRUFF VOICE, SAID...
..."ZOMBOSS HAS BEEN SLEEPING IN MY BED--AND STILL IS!"
ZZZZZZZZZ SNORK
SNORK
ZZZZZ
SNOBBLE
MANY HOURS LATER, AFTER I WOKE UP, THEY ASKED ME, "WASN'T GOLDILOCKS IN THIS STORY?"

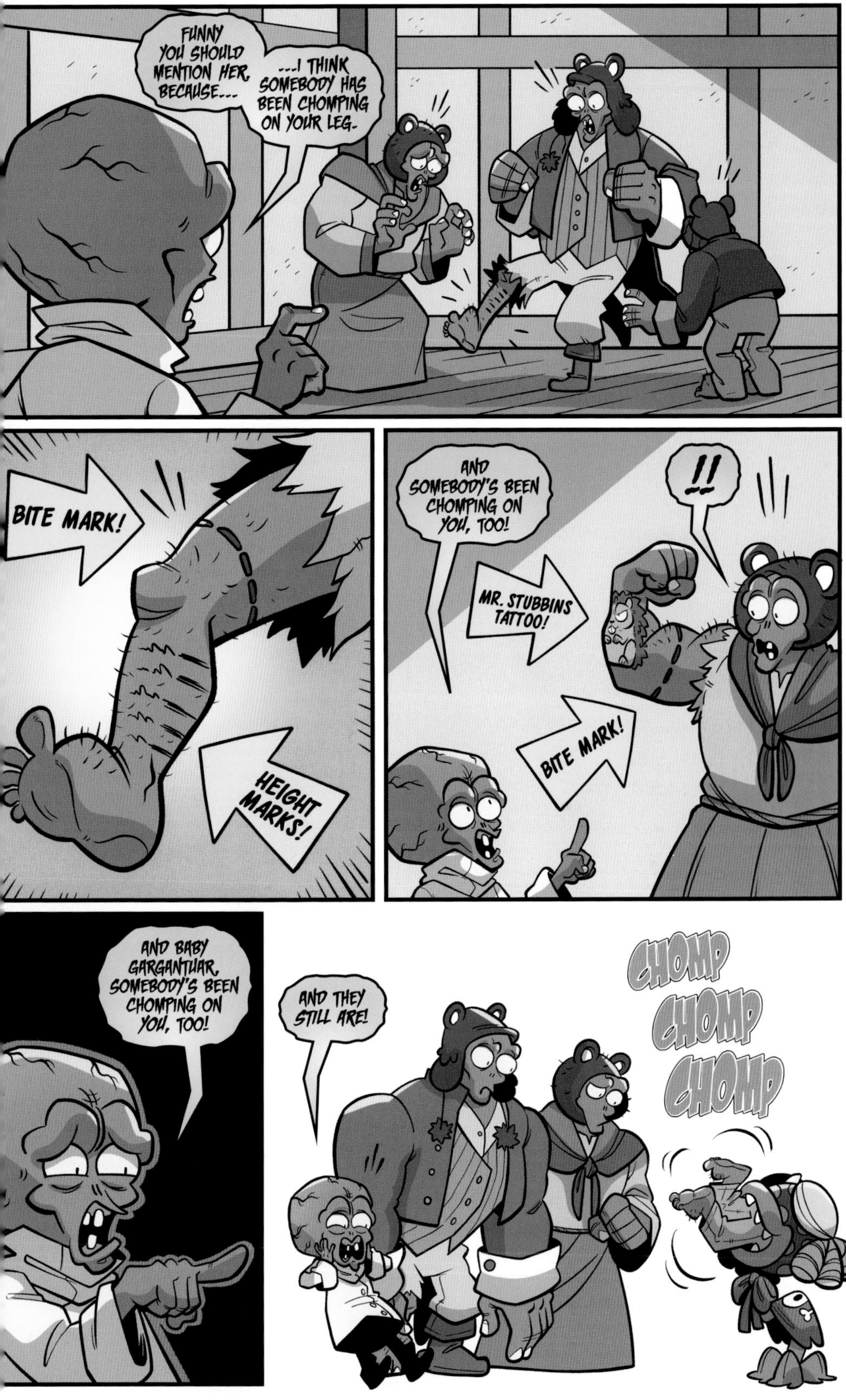
FUNNY YOU SHOULD MENTION HER, BECAUSE...
...I THINK SOMEBODY HAS BEEN CHOMPING ON YOUR LEG.
BITE MARK!
HEIGHT MARKS!
AND SOMEBODY'S BEEN CHOMPING ON YOU, TOO!
!!
MR. STUBBINS TATTOO!
BITE MARK!
AND BABY GARGANTUAR, SOMEBODY'S BEEN CHOMPING ON YOU, TOO!
AND THEY STILL ARE!
CHOMP
CHOMP
CHOMP

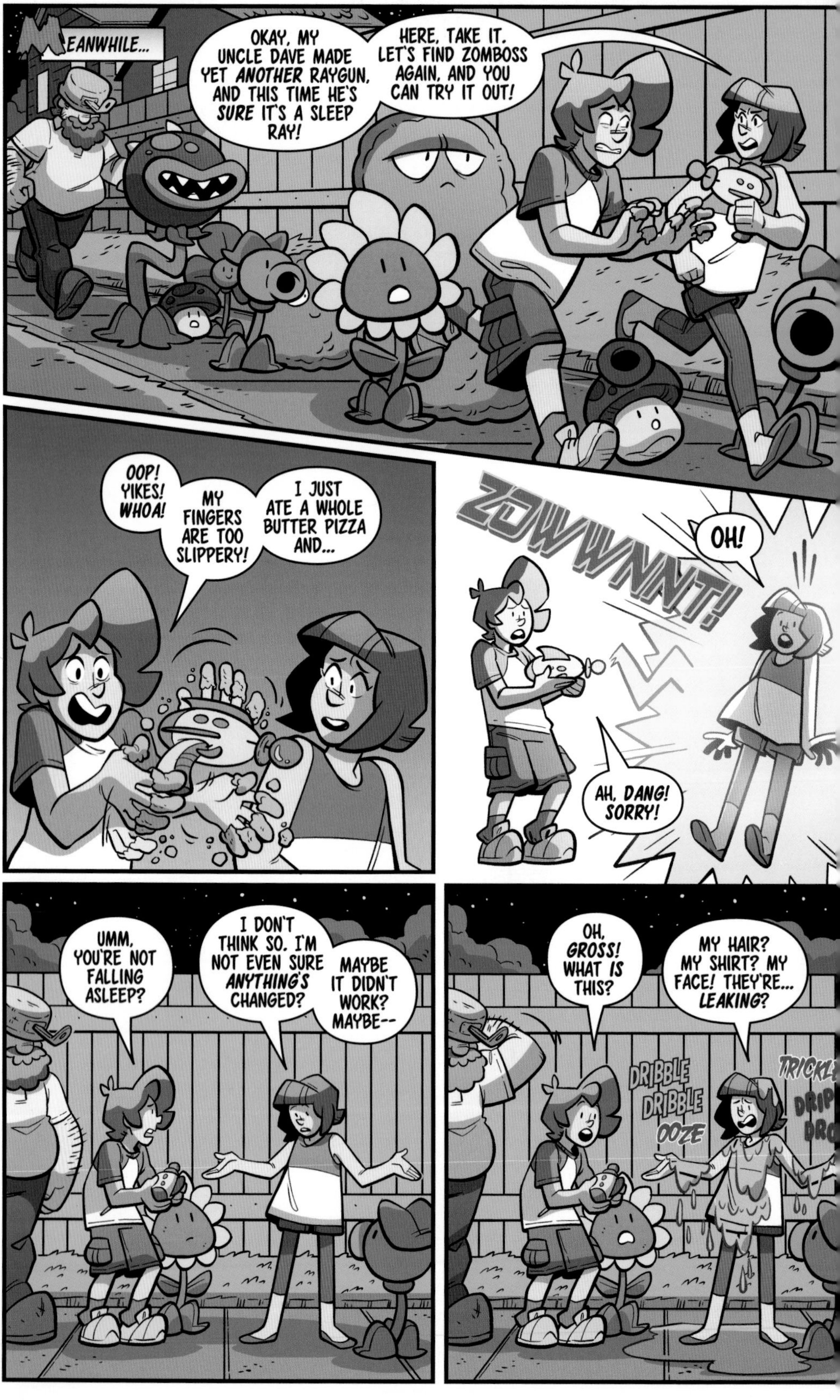
MEANWHILE...
OKAY, MY UNCLE DAVE MADE YET ANOTHER RAYGUN, AND THIS TIME HE'S SURE IT'S A SLEEP RAY!
HERE, TAKE IT. LET'S FIND ZOMBOSS AGAIN, AND YOU CAN TRY IT OUT!
OOP! YIKES! WHOA!
MY FINGERS ARE TOO SLIPPERY!
I JUST ATE A WHOLE BUTTER PIZZA AND...
ZDWWNNT!
OH!
AH, DANG! SORRY!
UMM, YOU'RE NOT FALLING ASLEEP?
I DON'T THINK SO. I'M NOT EVEN SURE ANYTHING'S CHANGED?
MAYBE IT DIDN'T WORK? MAYBE--
OH, GROSS! WHAT IS THIS?
MY HAIR? MY SHIRT? MY FACE! THEY'RE... LEAKING?
DRIBBLE
DRIBBLE
OOZE

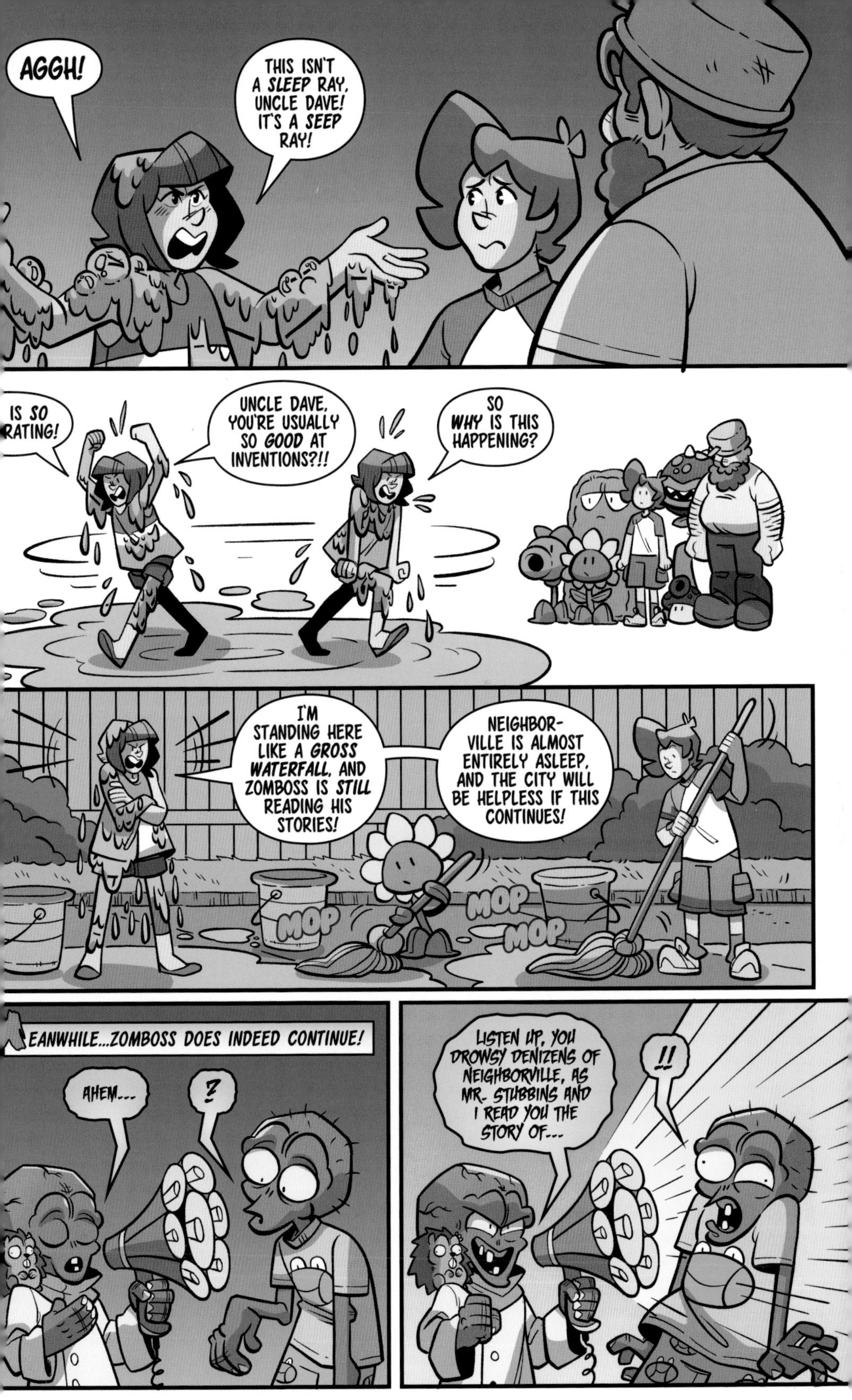

AGGH!
THIS ISN'T A *SLEEP RAY*, UNCLE DAVE! IT'S A *SEEP* RAY!
IS *SO* RATING!
UNCLE DAVE, YOU'RE USUALLY SO *GOOD* AT INVENTIONS?!!
SO *WHY* IS THIS HAPPENING?
I'M STANDING HERE LIKE A *GROSS WATERFALL*, AND ZOMBOSS IS *STILL* READING HIS STORIES!
NEIGHBOR-VILLE IS ALMOST ENTIRELY ASLEEP, AND THE CITY WILL BE HELPLESS IF THIS CONTINUES!
MOP
MOP
MOP
EANWHILE...ZOMBOSS DOES INDEED CONTINUE!
AHEM...
?
LISTEN UP, YOU DROWSY DENIZENS OF NEIGHBORVILLE, AS MR. STUBBINS AND I READ YOU THE STORY OF...
!!

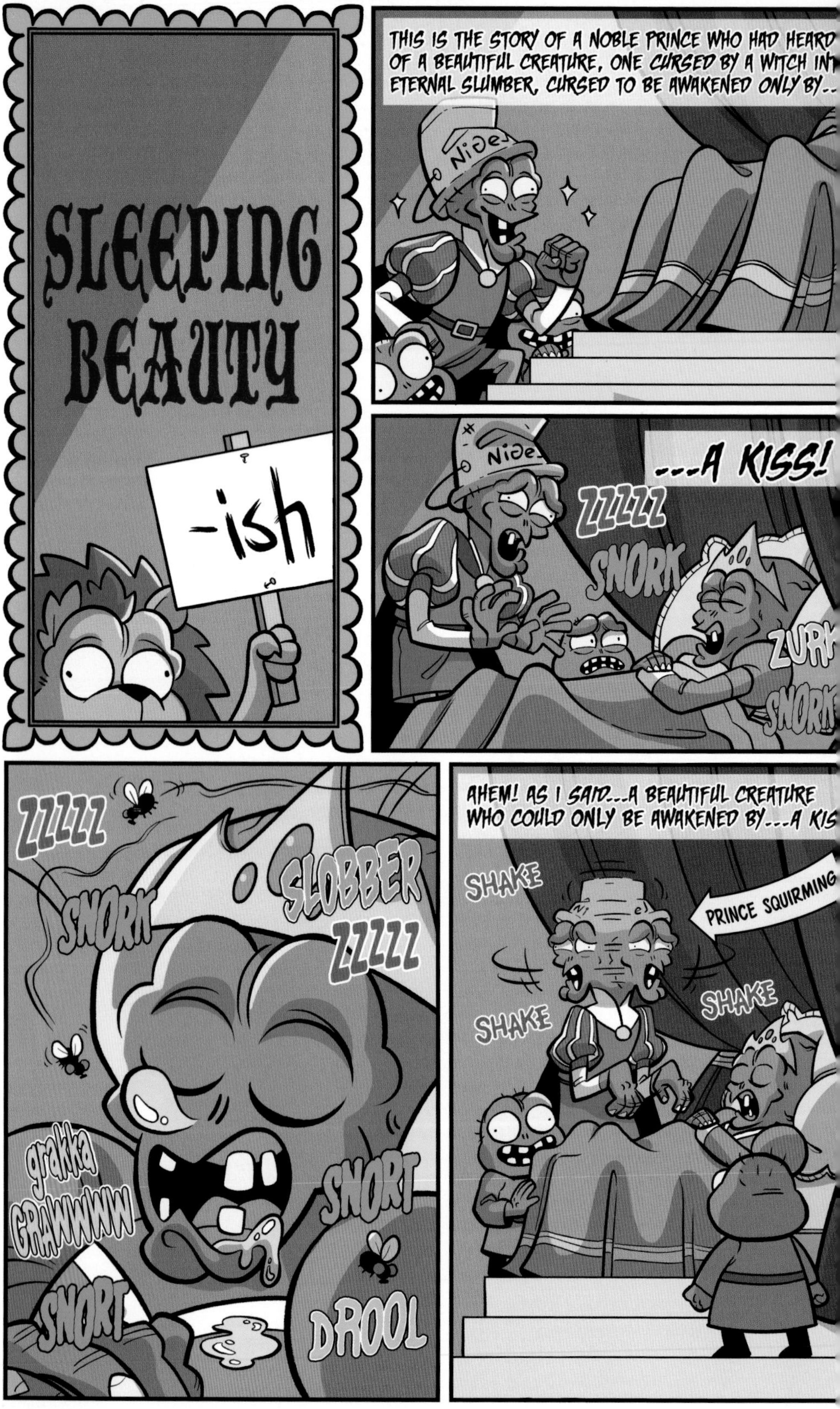
SLEEPING BEAUTY
-ish
THIS IS THE STORY OF A NOBLE PRINCE WHO HAD HEARD OF A BEAUTIFUL CREATURE, ONE CURSED BY A WITCH INTO ETERNAL SLUMBER, CURSED TO BE AWAKENED ONLY BY...
...A KISS!
ZZZZZ
SNORK
ZURK
SNORK
ZZZZZ
SNORK
SLOBBER
ZZZZZ
grakka
GRAWWWW
SNORT
SNORT
DROOL
AHEM! AS I SAID...A BEAUTIFUL CREATURE WHO COULD ONLY BE AWAKENED BY...A KISS
SHAKE
PRINCE SQUIRMING
SHAKE
SHAKE

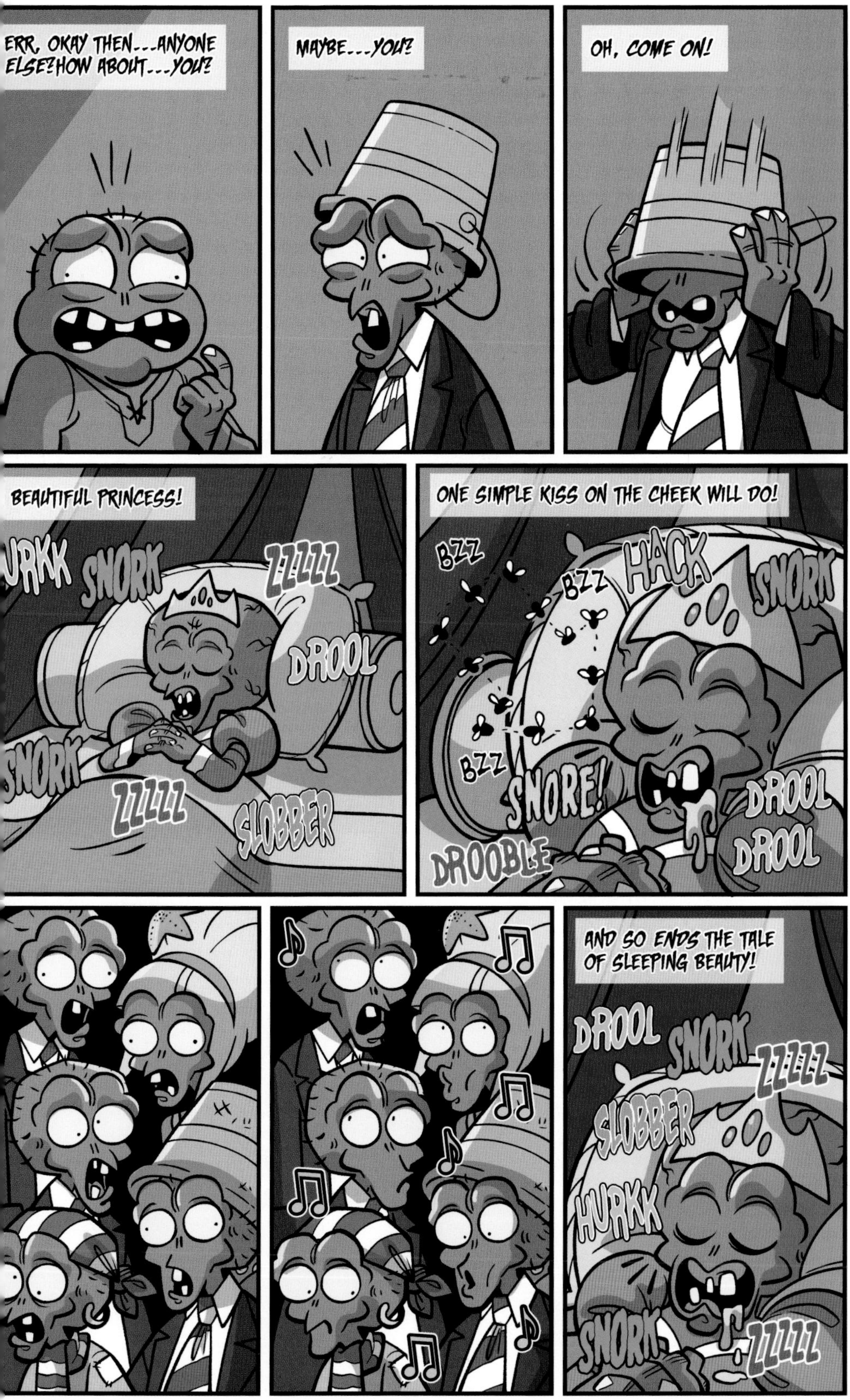
ERR, OKAY THEN...ANYONE ELSE? HOW ABOUT...YOU?
MAYBE...YOU?
OH, COME ON!
BEAUTIFUL PRINCESS!
URKK
SNORK
ZZZZZ
DROOL
SNORK
ZZZZZ
SLOBBER
ONE SIMPLE KISS ON THE CHEEK WILL DO!
BZZ
BZZ
HACK
SNORK
BZZ
SNORE!
DROOL
DROOL
DROOBLE
AND SO ENDS THE TALE OF SLEEPING BEAUTY!
DROOL
SNORK
ZZZZZ
SLOBBER
HURKK
SNORK
ZZZZZ

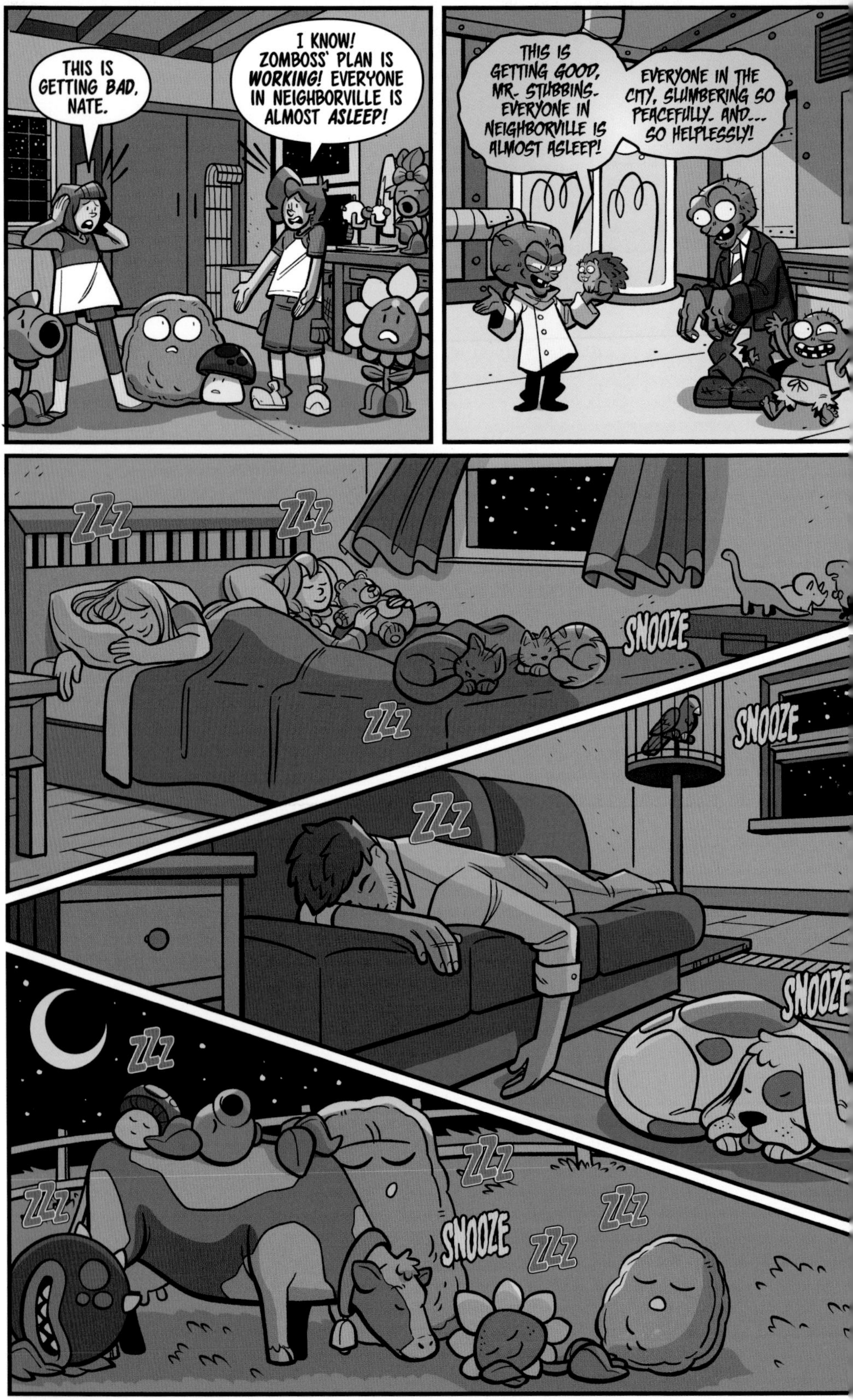
THIS IS GETTING BAD, NATE.
I KNOW! ZOMBOSS' PLAN IS WORKING! EVERYONE IN NEIGHBORVILLE IS ALMOST ASLEEP!
THIS IS GETTING GOOD, MR. STUBBINS. EVERYONE IN NEIGHBORVILLE IS ALMOST ASLEEP!
EVERYONE IN THE CITY, SLUMBERING SO PEACEFULLY. AND... SO HELPLESSLY!
ZZZ
ZZZ
SNOOZE
ZZZ
SNOOZE
ZZZ
SNOOZE
ZZZ
ZZZ
ZZZ
SNOOZE
ZZZ
ZZZ

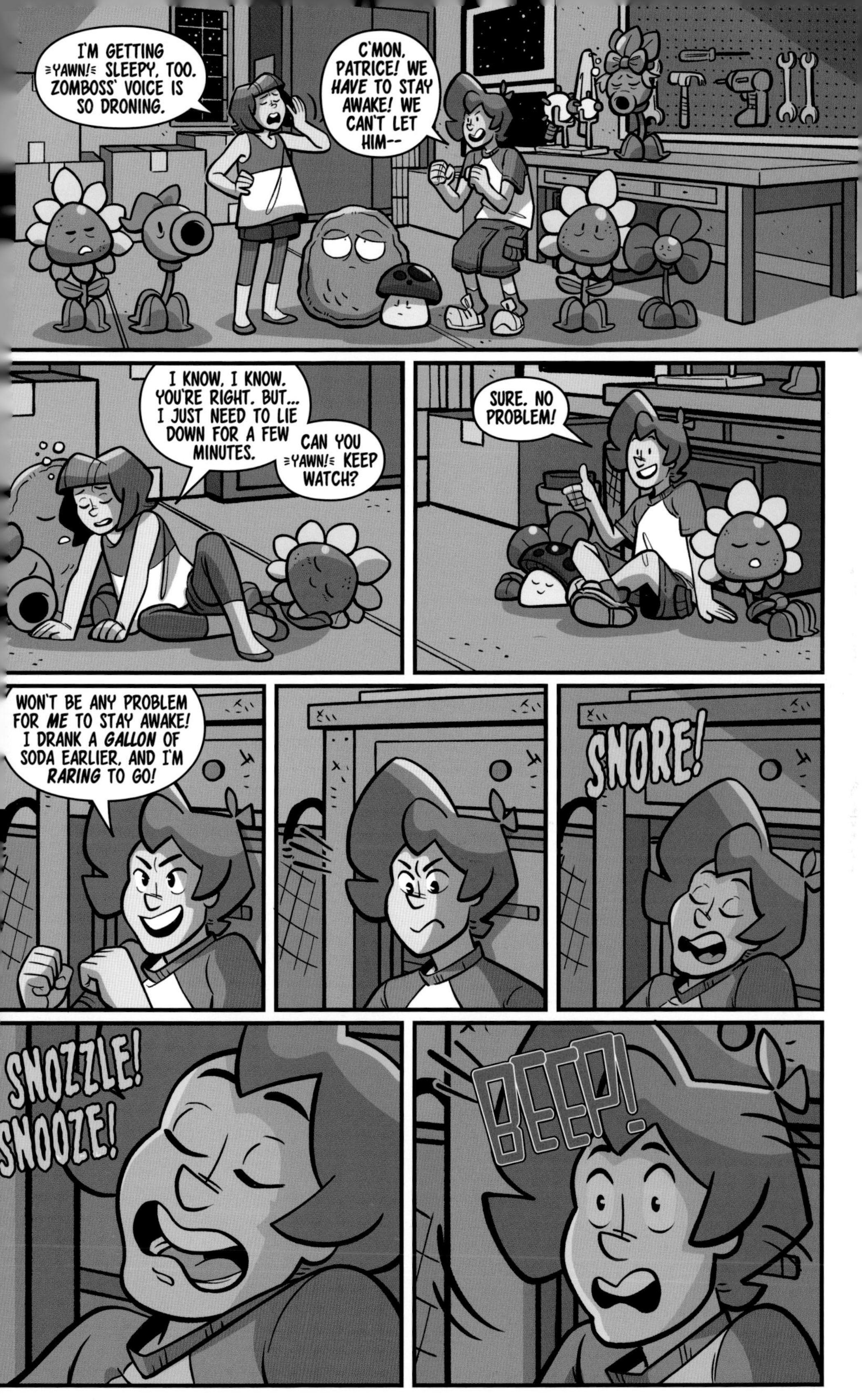
I'M GETTING ≡YAWN!≡ SLEEPY, TOO. ZOMBOSS' VOICE IS SO DRONING.
C'MON, PATRICE! WE HAVE TO STAY AWAKE! WE CAN'T LET HIM--
I KNOW, I KNOW. YOU'RE RIGHT. BUT... I JUST NEED TO LIE DOWN FOR A FEW MINUTES.
CAN YOU ≡YAWN!≡ KEEP WATCH?
SURE. NO PROBLEM!
WON'T BE ANY PROBLEM FOR ME TO STAY AWAKE! I DRANK A GALLON OF SODA EARLIER, AND I'M RARING TO GO!
SNORE!
SNOZZLE!
SNOOZE!
BEEP!

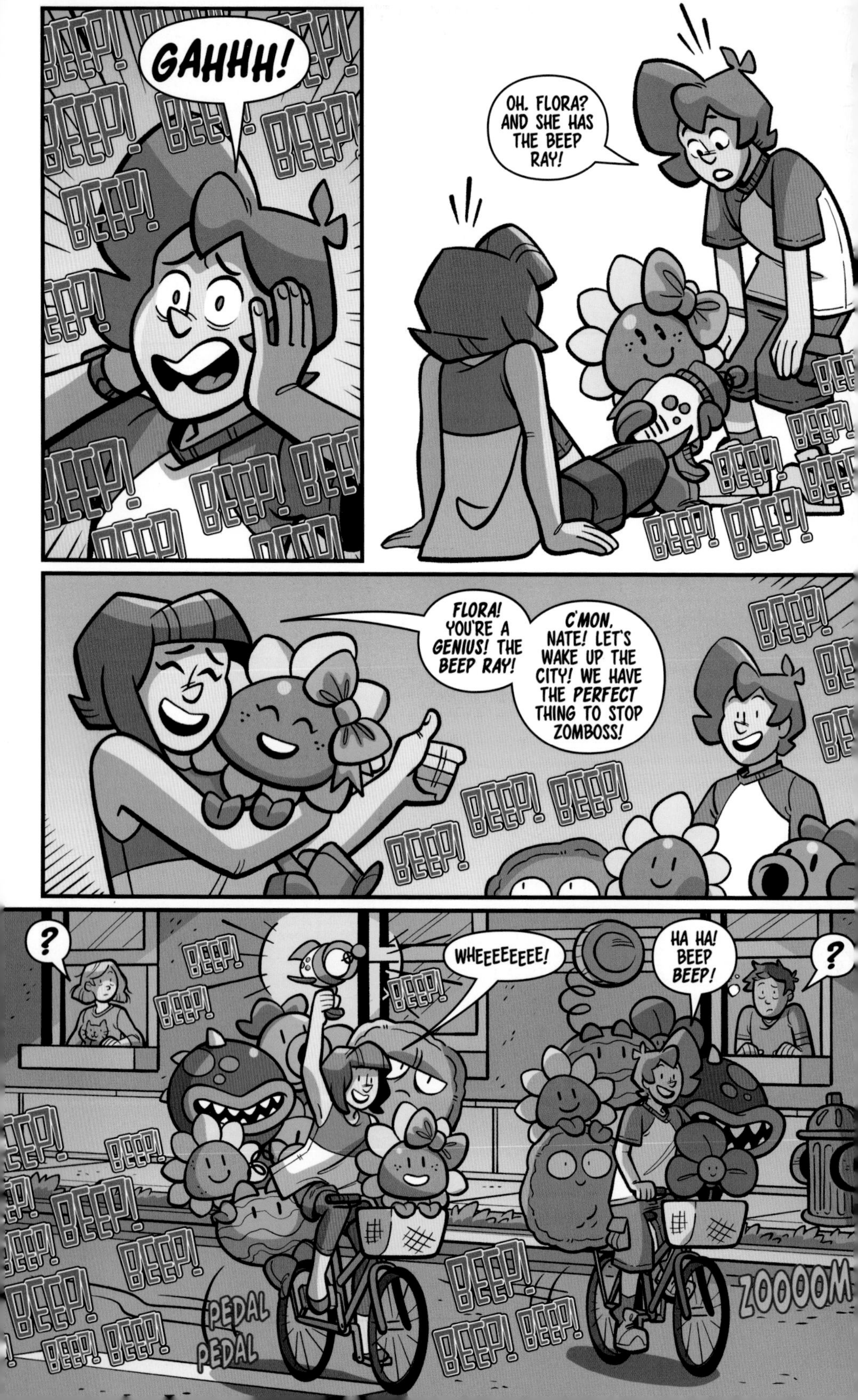
GAHHH!
BEEP! BEEP! BEEP! BEEP! BEEP!
OH, FLORA? AND SHE HAS THE BEEP RAY!
BEEP! BEEP! BEEP! BEEP!
FLORA! YOU'RE A GENIUS! THE BEEP RAY!
C'MON, NATE! LET'S WAKE UP THE CITY! WE HAVE THE PERFECT THING TO STOP ZOMBOSS!
BEEP! BEEP! BEEP!
?
WHEEEEEEEE!
HA HA! BEEP BEEP!
?
BEEP! BEEP! BEEP!
PEDAL PEDAL
ZOOOOM

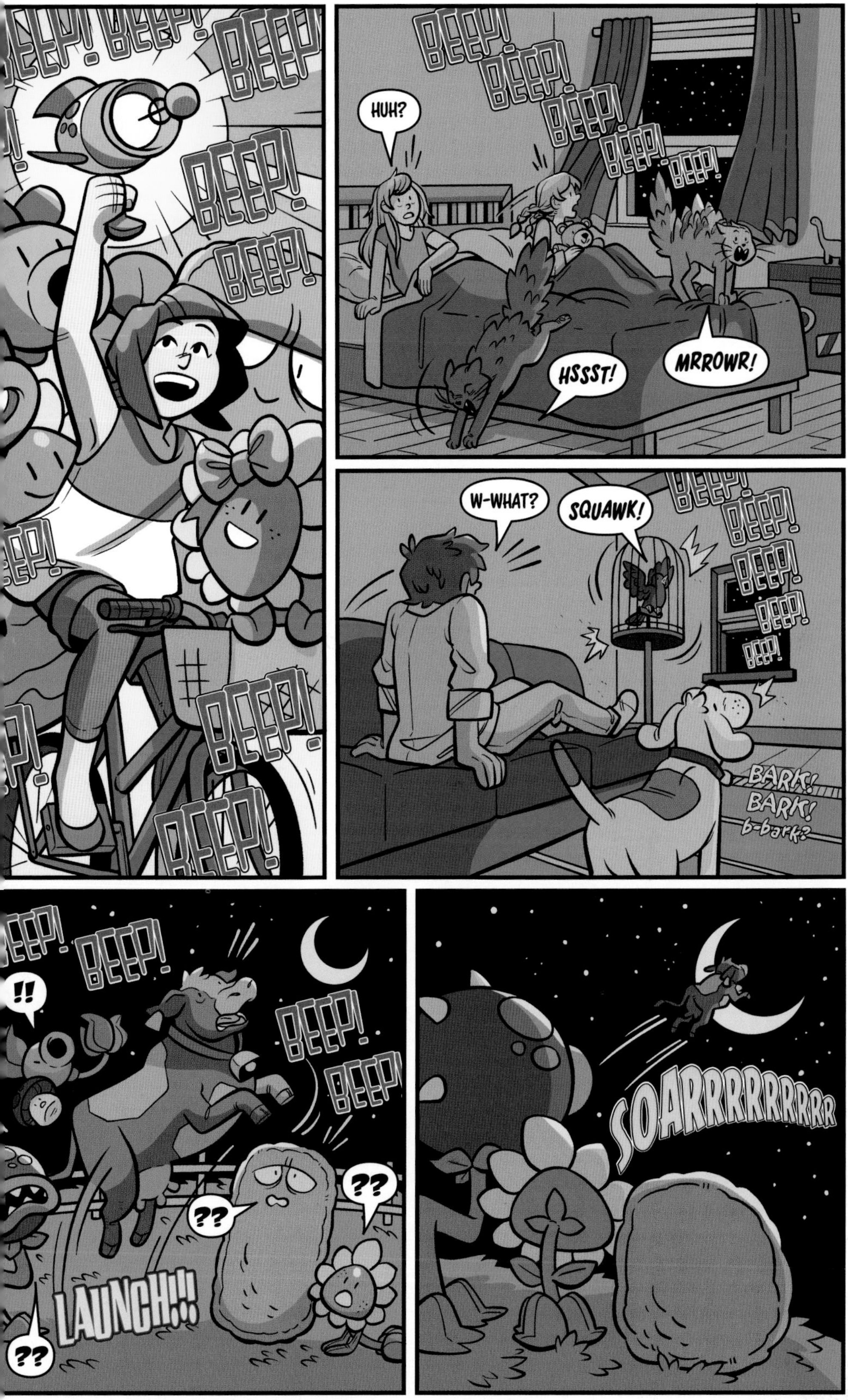
BEEP! BEEP!
BEEP!
BEEP!
BEEP!
BEEP!
BEEP!
BEEP!
BEEP!
HUH?
BEEP!
BEEP!
BEEP!
BEEP!
BEEP!
HSSST!
MRROWR!
W-WHAT?
SQUAWK!
BEEP!
BEEP!
BEEP!
BEEP!
BEEP!
BARK!
BARK!
b-bark?
BEEP!
BEEP!
!!
BEEP!
BEEP!
??
??
LAUNCH!!!
??
SOARRRRRRRRR

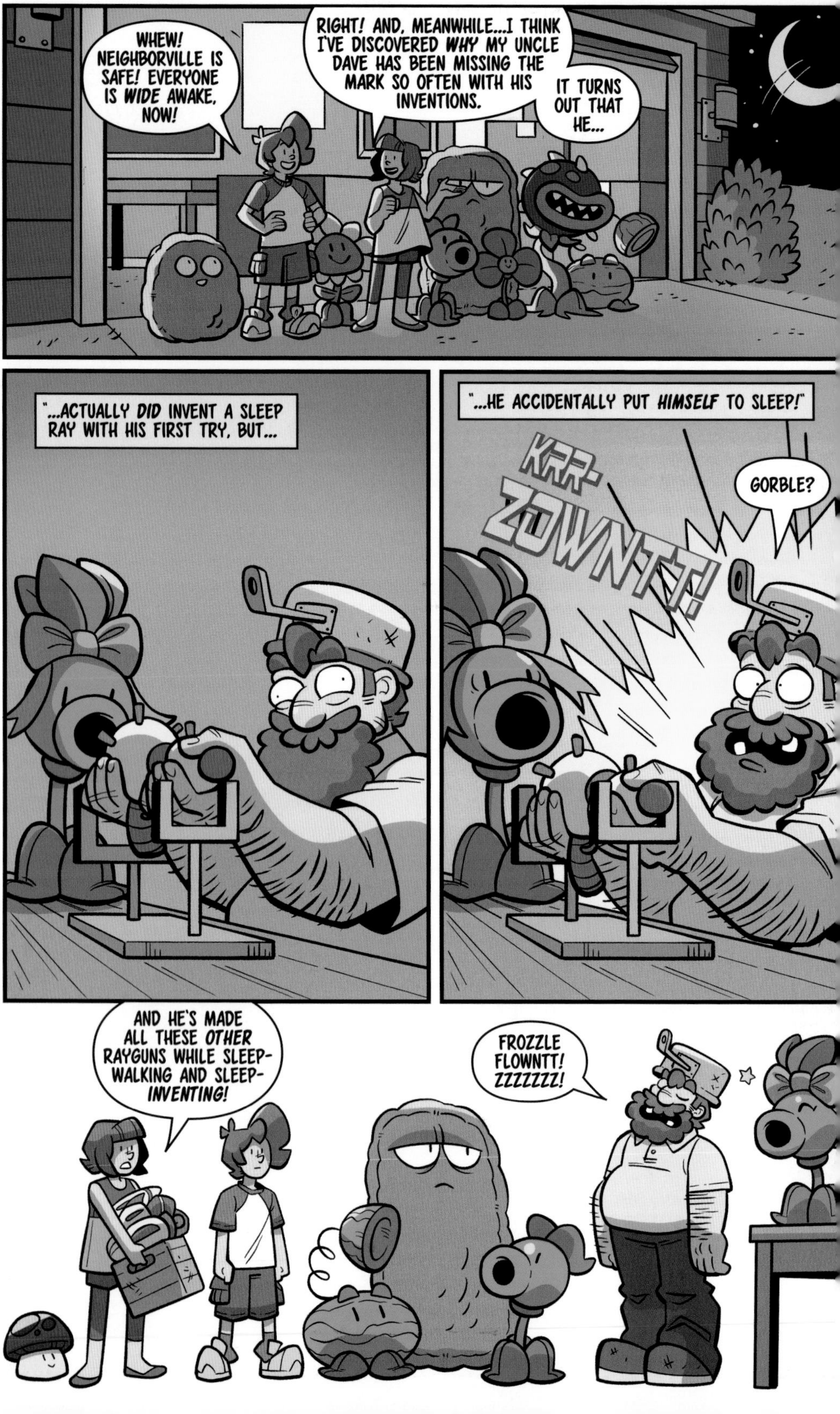
WHEW! NEIGHBORVILLE IS SAFE! EVERYONE IS WIDE AWAKE, NOW!
RIGHT! AND, MEANWHILE...I THINK I'VE DISCOVERED WHY MY UNCLE DAVE HAS BEEN MISSING THE MARK SO OFTEN WITH HIS INVENTIONS.
IT TURNS OUT THAT HE...
"...ACTUALLY DID INVENT A SLEEP RAY WITH HIS FIRST TRY, BUT...
"...HE ACCIDENTALLY PUT HIMSELF TO SLEEP!"
KRR-ZOWNTT!
GORBLE?
AND HE'S MADE ALL THESE OTHER RAYGUNS WHILE SLEEP-WALKING AND SLEEP-INVENTING!
FROZZLE FLOWNTT! ZZZZZZZ!

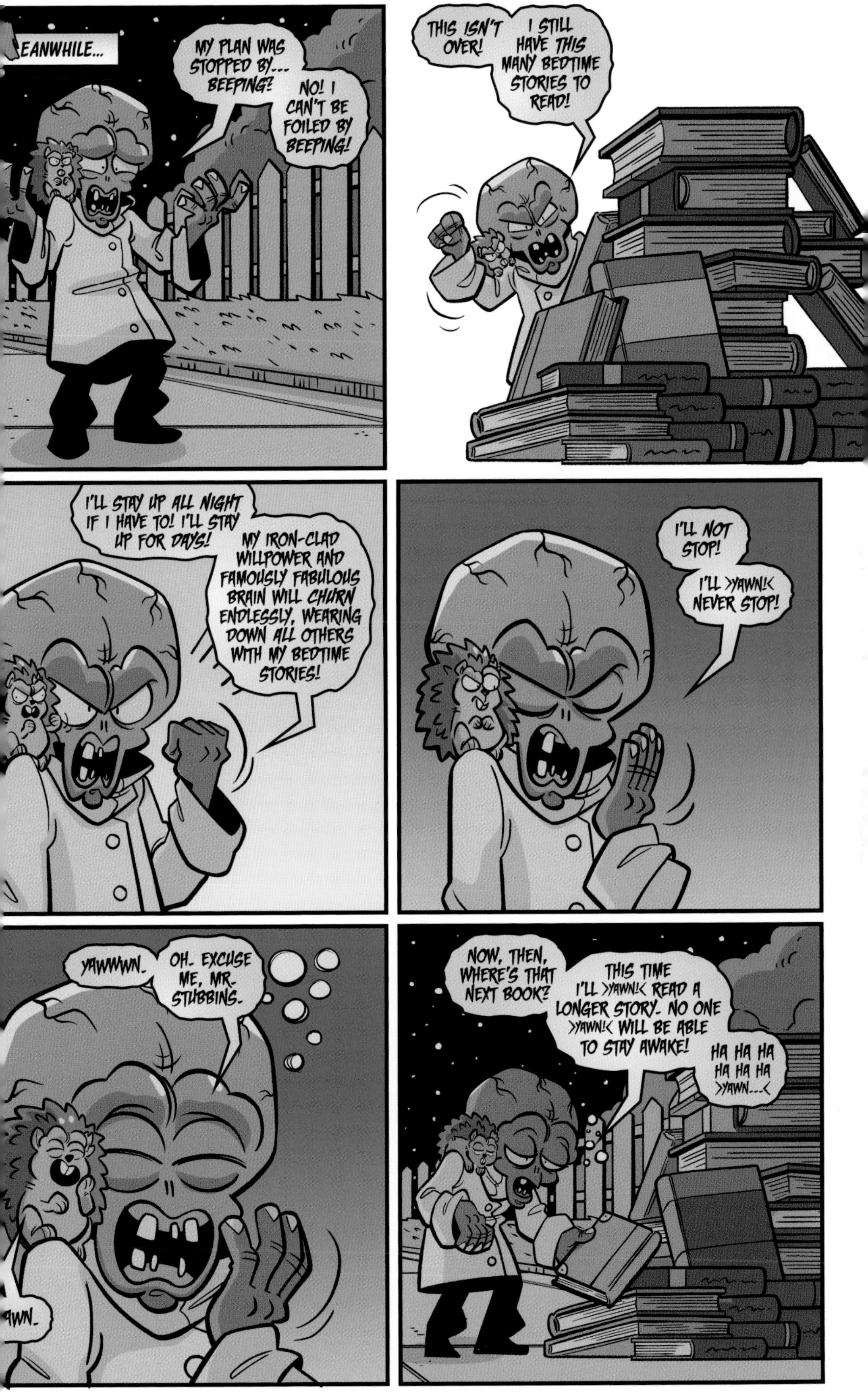
EANWHILE...
MY PLAN WAS STOPPED BY... BEEPING?
NO! I CAN'T BE FOILED BY BEEPING!
THIS ISN'T OVER!
I STILL HAVE THIS MANY BEDTIME STORIES TO READ!
I'LL STAY UP ALL NIGHT IF I HAVE TO! I'LL STAY UP FOR DAYS!
MY IRON-CLAD WILLPOWER AND FAMOUSLY FABULOUS BRAIN WILL CHURN ENDLESSLY, WEARING DOWN ALL OTHERS WITH MY BEDTIME STORIES!
I'LL NOT STOP!
I'LL >YAWN!< NEVER STOP!
YAWWWN.
OH. EXCUSE ME, MR. STUBBINS.
AWN.
NOW, THEN, WHERE'S THAT NEXT BOOK?
THIS TIME I'LL >YAWN!< READ A LONGER STORY. NO ONE >YAWN!< WILL BE ABLE TO STAY AWAKE!
HA HA HA HA HA HA >YAWN...<

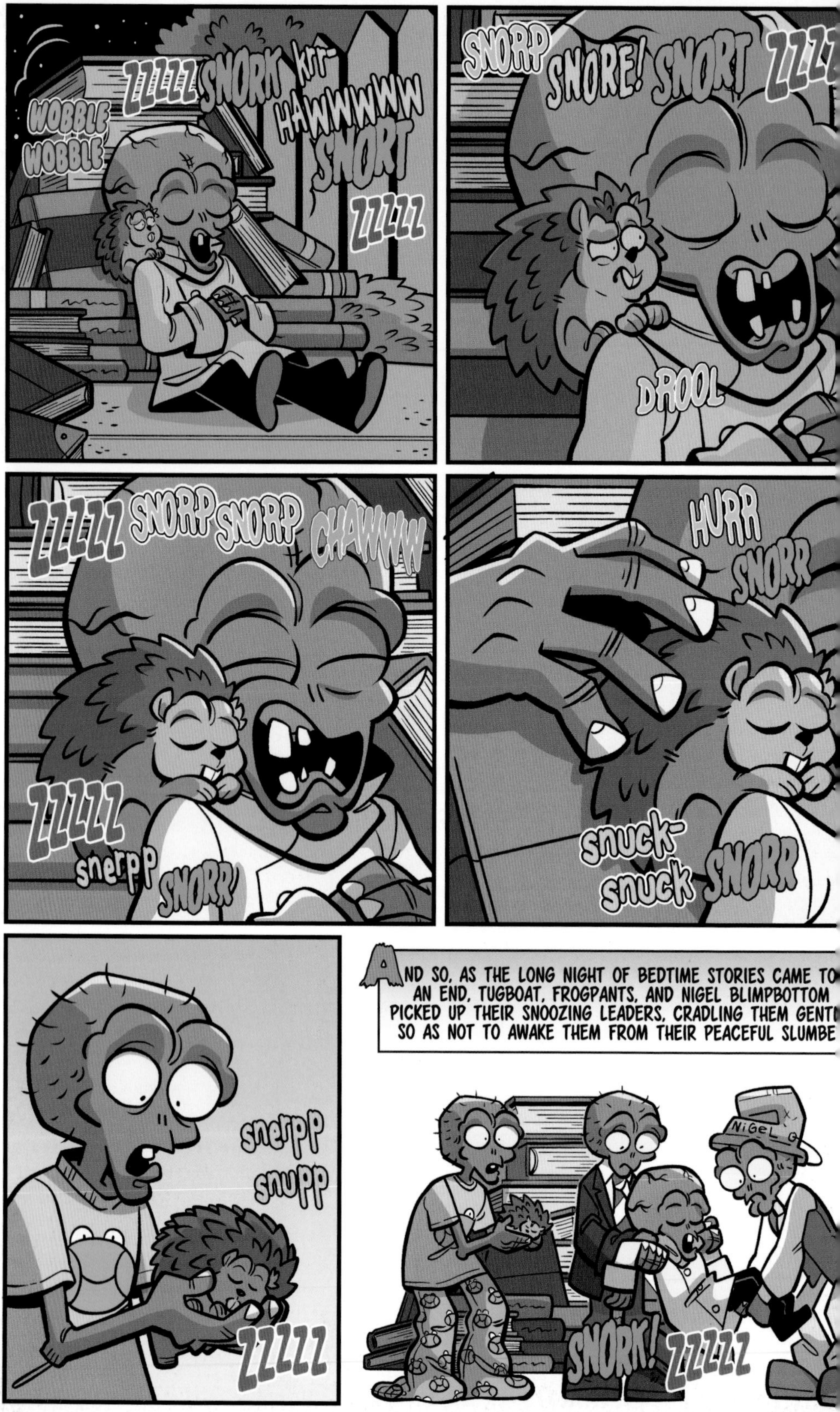
WOBBLE WOBBLE
ZZZZZ SNORK krr-HAWWWWWW SNORT
ZZZZZ
SNORP
SNORE! SNORT ZZZZ
DROOL
ZZZZZ SNORP SNORP
CHAWWW
ZZZZZ
snerpp
SNORR
HURR SNORR
snuck-snuck
SNORR
snerpp snupp
ZZZZZ
AND SO, AS THE LONG NIGHT OF BEDTIME STORIES CAME TO AN END, TUGBOAT, FROGPANTS, AND NIGEL BLIMPBOTTOM PICKED UP THEIR SNOOZING LEADERS, CRADLING THEM GENTL SO AS NOT TO AWAKE THEM FROM THEIR PEACEFUL SLUMBE
NiGeL
SNORK! ZZZZZ

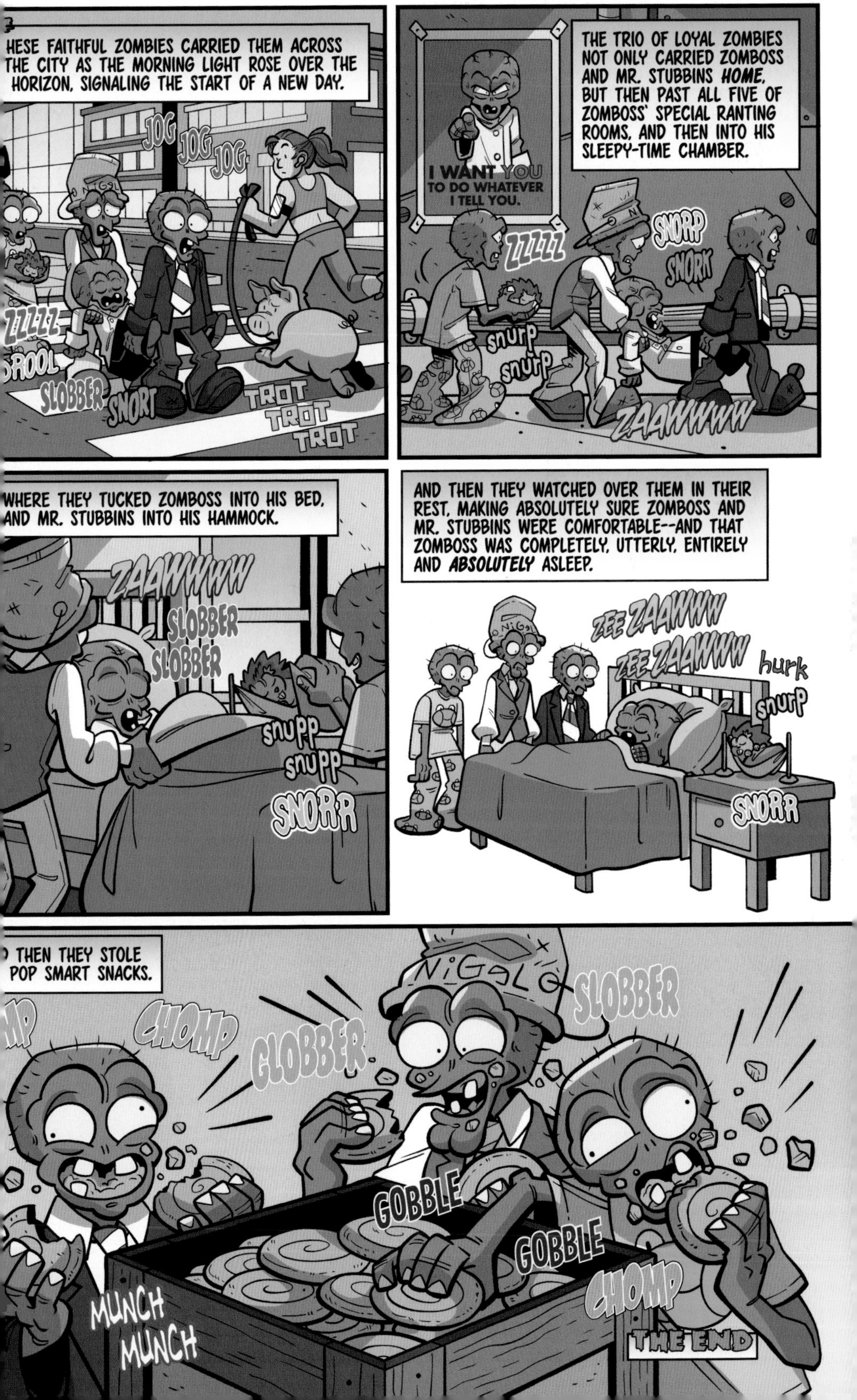
HESE FAITHFUL ZOMBIES CARRIED THEM ACROSS THE CITY AS THE MORNING LIGHT ROSE OVER THE HORIZON, SIGNALING THE START OF A NEW DAY.
JOG JOG JOG
ZZZZZ
DROOL
SLOBBER
SNORT
TROT TROT TROT
THE TRIO OF LOYAL ZOMBIES NOT ONLY CARRIED ZOMBOSS AND MR. STUBBINS HOME, BUT THEN PAST ALL FIVE OF ZOMBOSS' SPECIAL RANTING ROOMS, AND THEN INTO HIS SLEEPY-TIME CHAMBER.
I WANT YOU TO DO WHATEVER I TELL YOU.
ZZZZZ
SNORP
SNORK
snurp
snurp
ZAAWWWW
WHERE THEY TUCKED ZOMBOSS INTO HIS BED, AND MR. STUBBINS INTO HIS HAMMOCK.
ZAAWWWW
SLOBBER
SLOBBER
snupp
snupp
SNORR
AND THEN THEY WATCHED OVER THEM IN THEIR REST, MAKING ABSOLUTELY SURE ZOMBOSS AND MR. STUBBINS WERE COMFORTABLE--AND THAT ZOMBOSS WAS COMPLETELY, UTTERLY, ENTIRELY AND ABSOLUTELY ASLEEP.
ZEE ZAAWWW
ZEE ZAAWWW
hurk
snurp
SNORR
THEN THEY STOLE POP SMART SNACKS.
CHOMP
GLOBBER
SLOBBER
GOBBLE
GOBBLE
CHOMP
MUNCH MUNCH
THE END

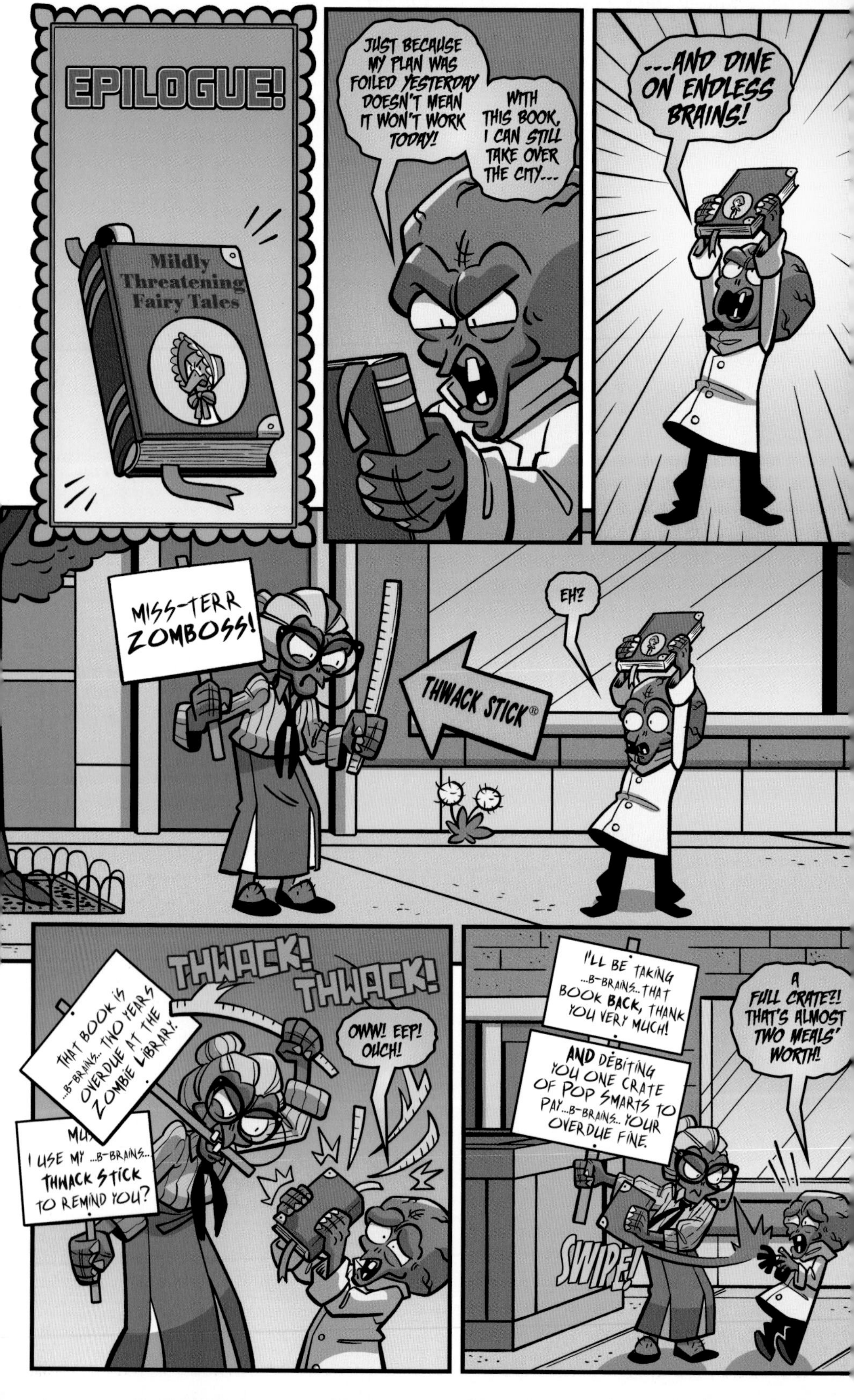
EPILOGUE!
Mildly Threatening Fairy Tales
JUST BECAUSE MY PLAN WAS FOILED YESTERDAY DOESN'T MEAN IT WON'T WORK TODAY!
WITH THIS BOOK, I CAN STILL TAKE OVER THE CITY...
...AND DINE ON ENDLESS BRAINS!
MISS-TERR ZOMBOSS!
THWACK STICK®
EH?
THWACK! THWACK!
THAT BOOK IS ...B-BRAINS... TWO YEARS OVERDUE AT THE ZOMBIE LIBRARY!
MU
I USE MY ...B-BRAINS... THWACK STICK TO REMIND YOU?
OWW! EEP! OUCH!
I'LL BE TAKING ...B-BRAINS... THAT BOOK BACK, THANK YOU VERY MUCH!
AND DEBITING YOU ONE CRATE OF POP SMARTS TO PAY...B-BRAINS... YOUR OVERDUE FINE.
SWIPE!
A FULL CRATE?! THAT'S ALMOST TWO MEALS' WORTH!

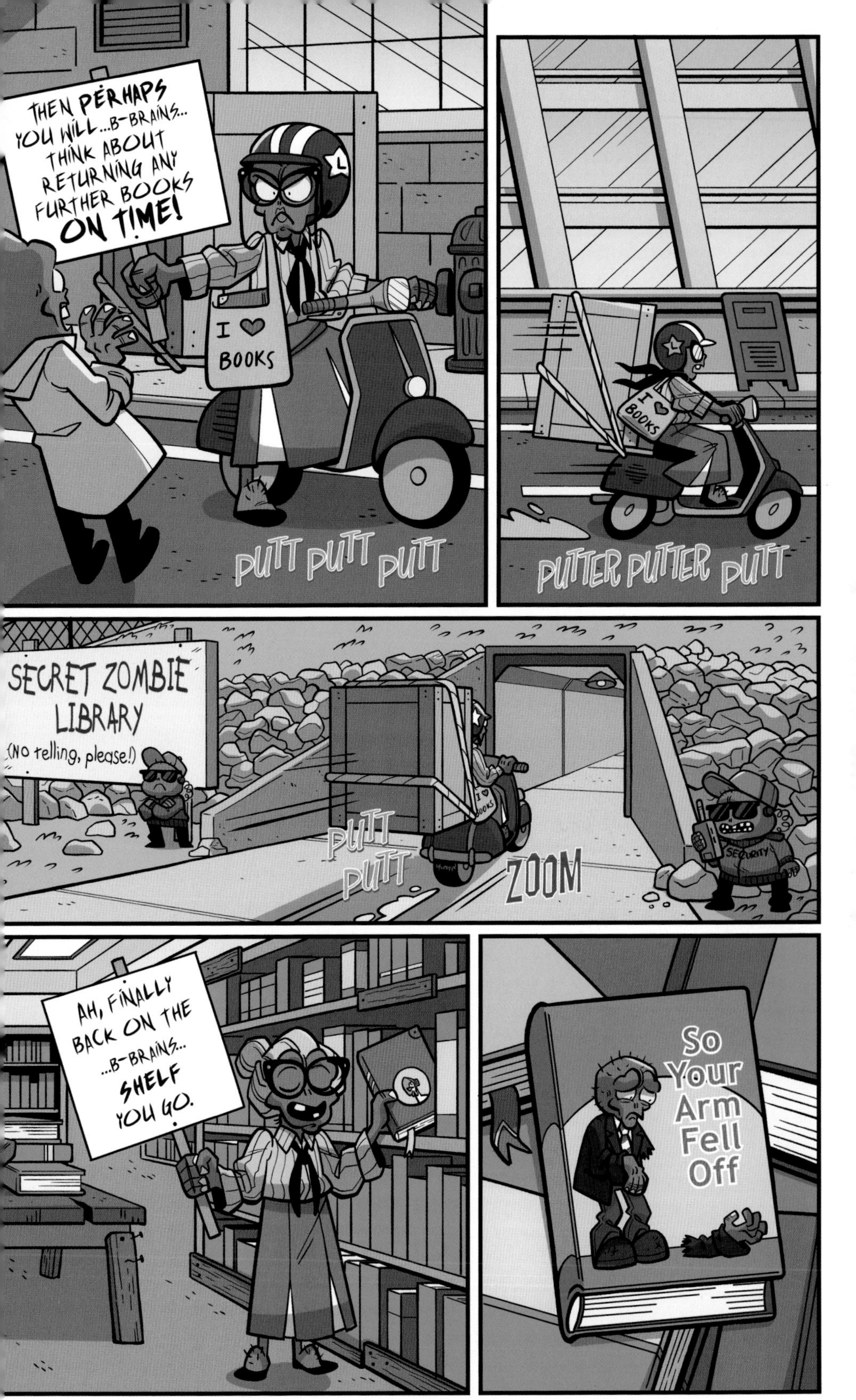

THEN PERHAPS YOU WILL...B-BRAINS... THINK ABOUT RETURNING ANY FURTHER BOOKS ON TIME!
I ♥ BOOKS
PUTT PUTT PUTT
PUTTER PUTTER PUTT
SECRET ZOMBIE LIBRARY
(No telling, please!)
PUTT PUTT
ZOOM
SECURITY
AH, FINALLY BACK ON THE ...B-BRAINS... SHELF YOU GO.
So Your Arm Fell Off

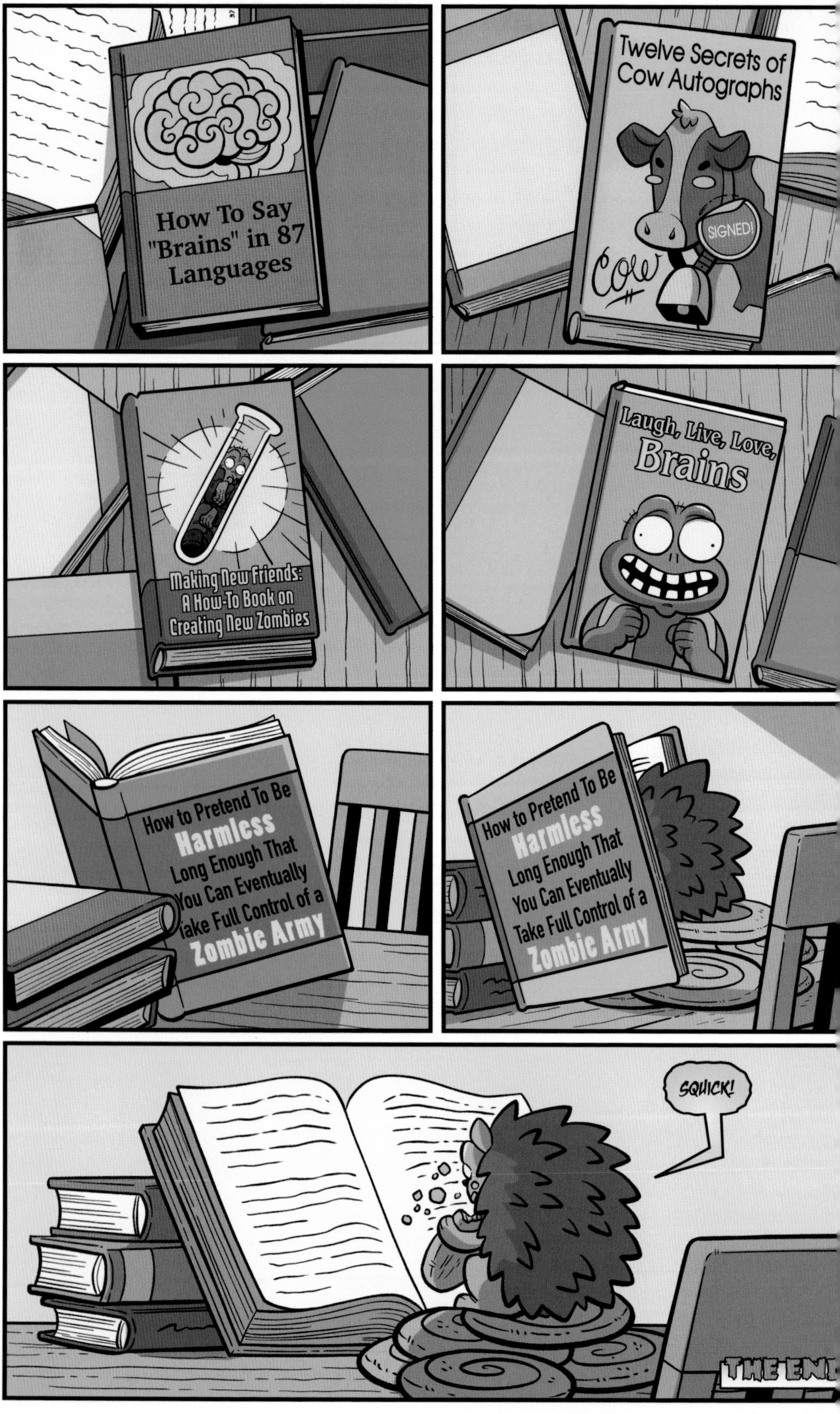

How To Say "Brains" in 87 Languages
Twelve Secrets of Cow Autographs
SIGNED!
COW
Making New Friends: A How-To Book on Creating New Zombies
Laugh, Live, Love, Brains
How to Pretend To Be Harmless Long Enough That You Can Eventually Take Full Control of a Zombie Army
How to Pretend To Be Harmless Long Enough That You Can Eventually Take Full Control of a Zombie Army
SQUICK!
THE EN

FROM CHRISTIANNE GILLENARDO-GOUDREAU'S *PLANTS VS. ZOMBIES* SKETCHBOOK! INITIAL COVER ROUGHS AND INSPIRATIONAL IMAGES FOR THE *PLANTS VS. ZOMBIES: FAULTY FABLES* COVER.

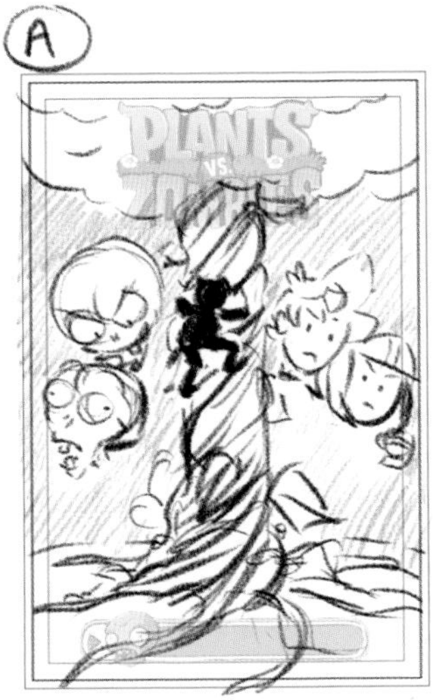
A
PLANTS VS. ZOMBIES

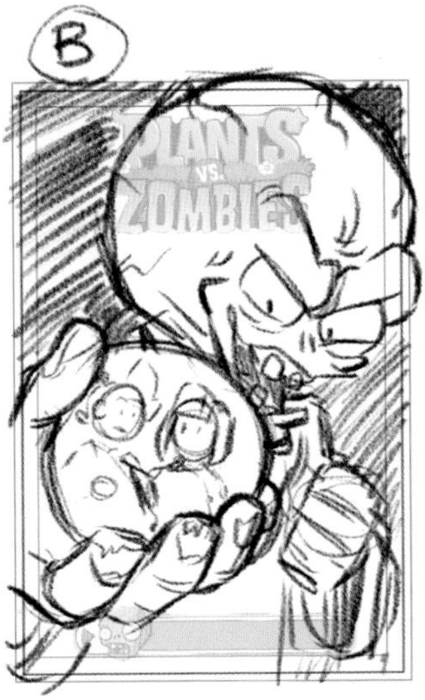
B
PLANTS VS. ZOMBIES

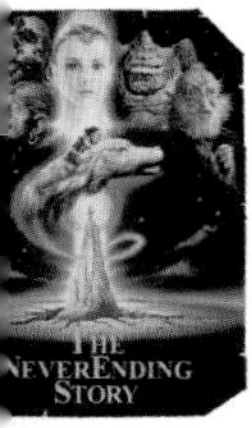
THE NEVERENDING STORY

ovie poster ref

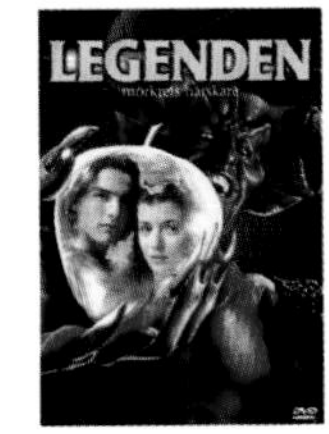
LEGENDEN

movie poster ref

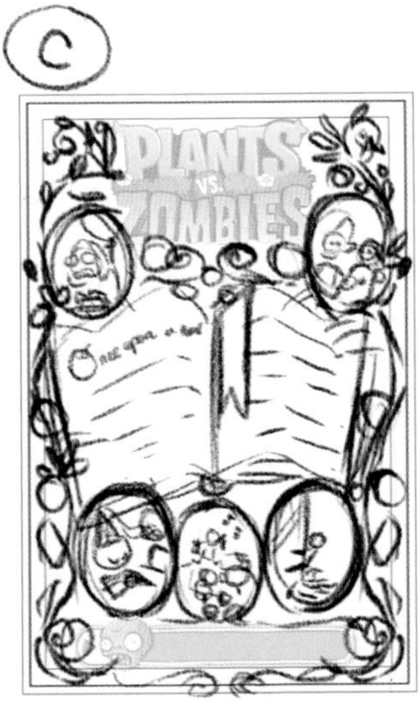
C
PLANTS VS. ZOMBIES

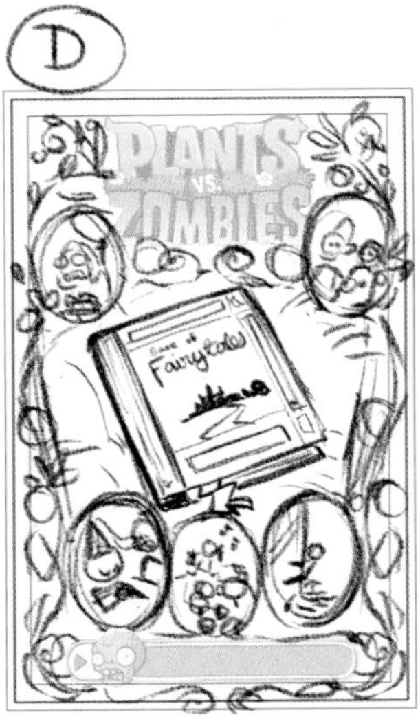
D
PLANTS VS. ZOMBIES
Fairytales

- based off old-school classic fairytale book covers

- vignettes will feature snapshots of the stories (red riding hood, handel + gretel, sleeping beauty, pied piper, jack + bean)

PLANTS VS. ZOMBIES: FAULTY FABLES
COVER PENCILS BY CHRISTIANNE GILLENARDO-GOUDREAU

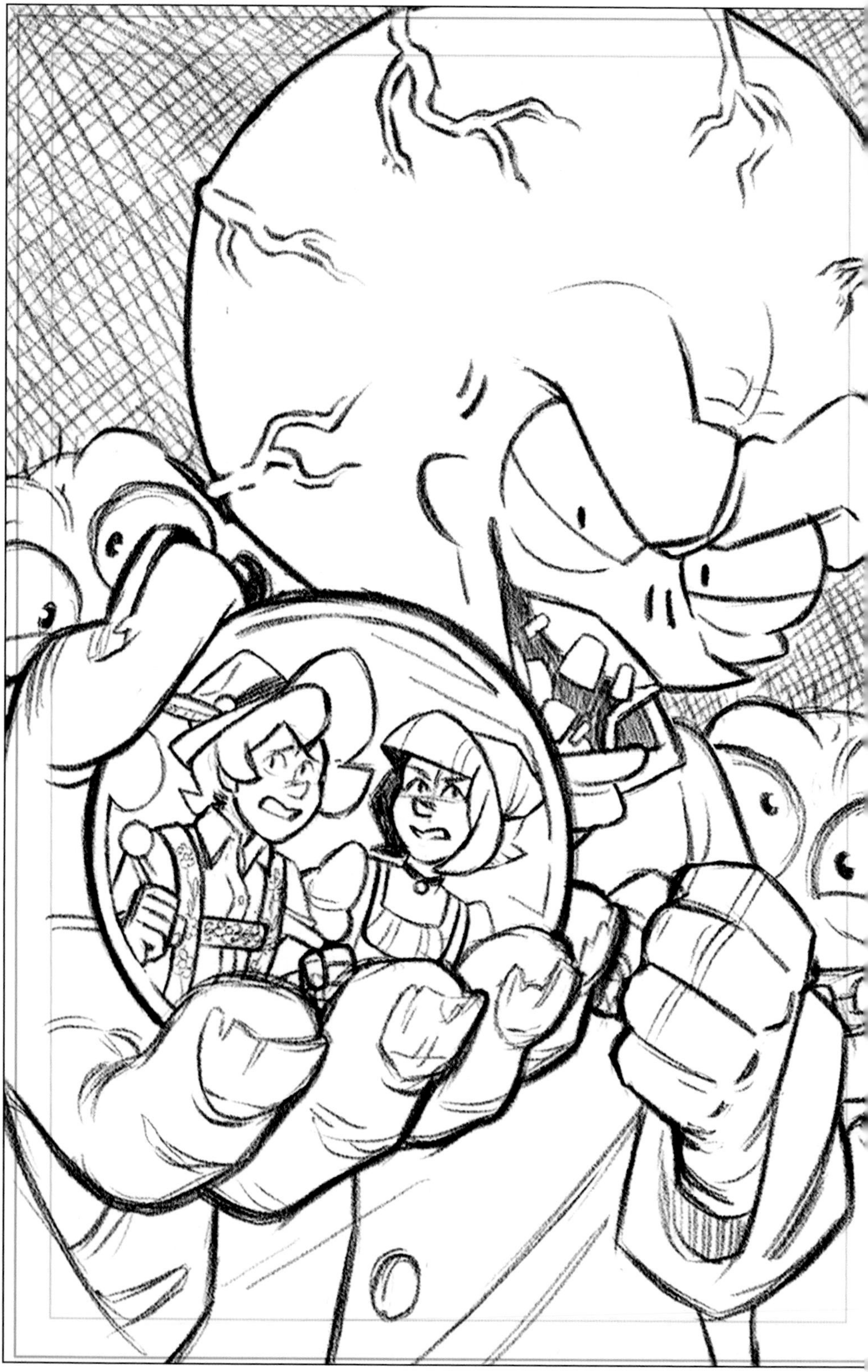

PLANTS VS. ZOMBIES: FAULTY FABLES
COVER INKS BY CHRISTIANNE GILLENARDO-GOUDREAU

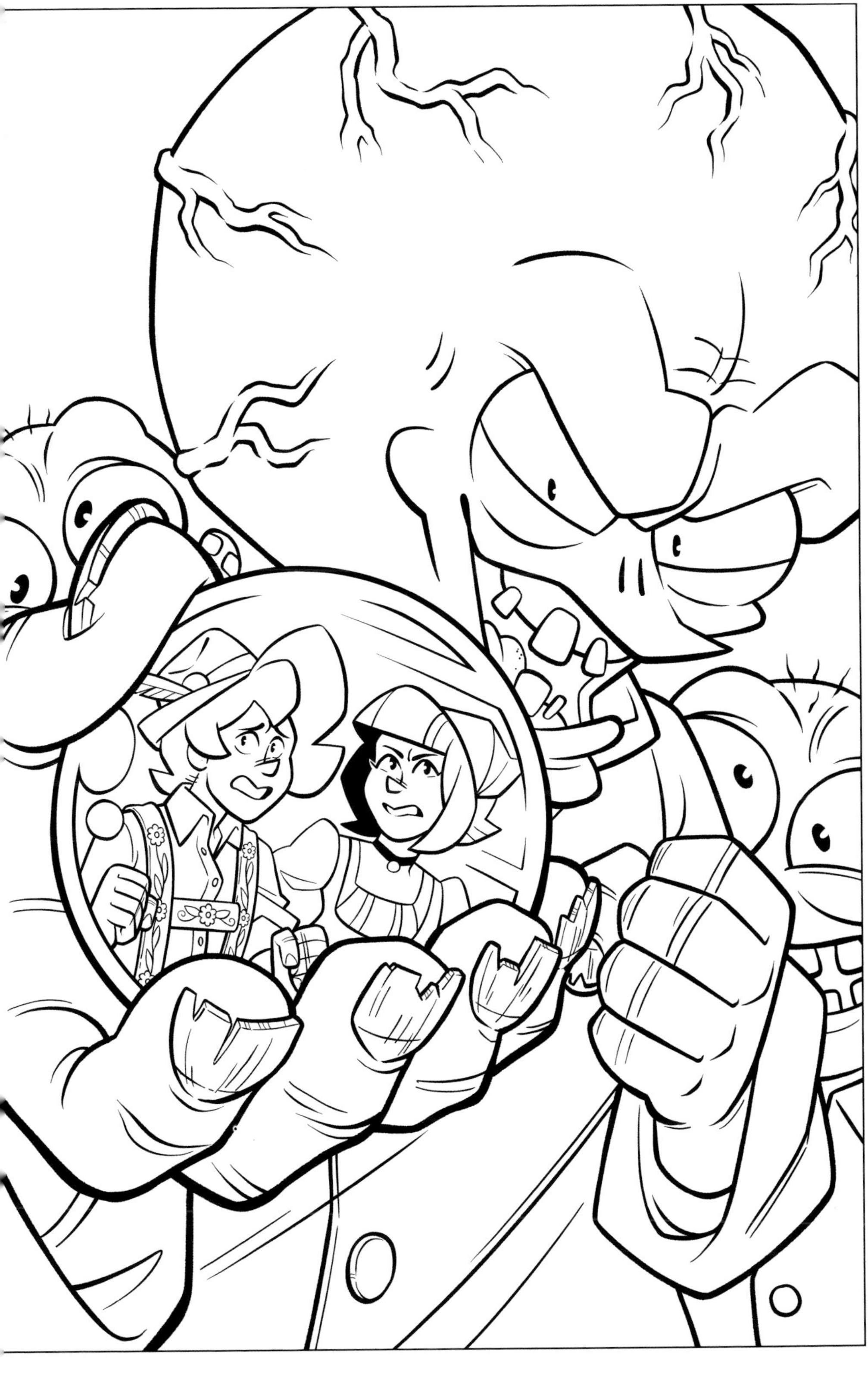

FAULTY FABLES LINE ART GALLERY! ALL PAGES BY ARTIST CHRISTIANNE GILLENARDO-GOUDREAU.

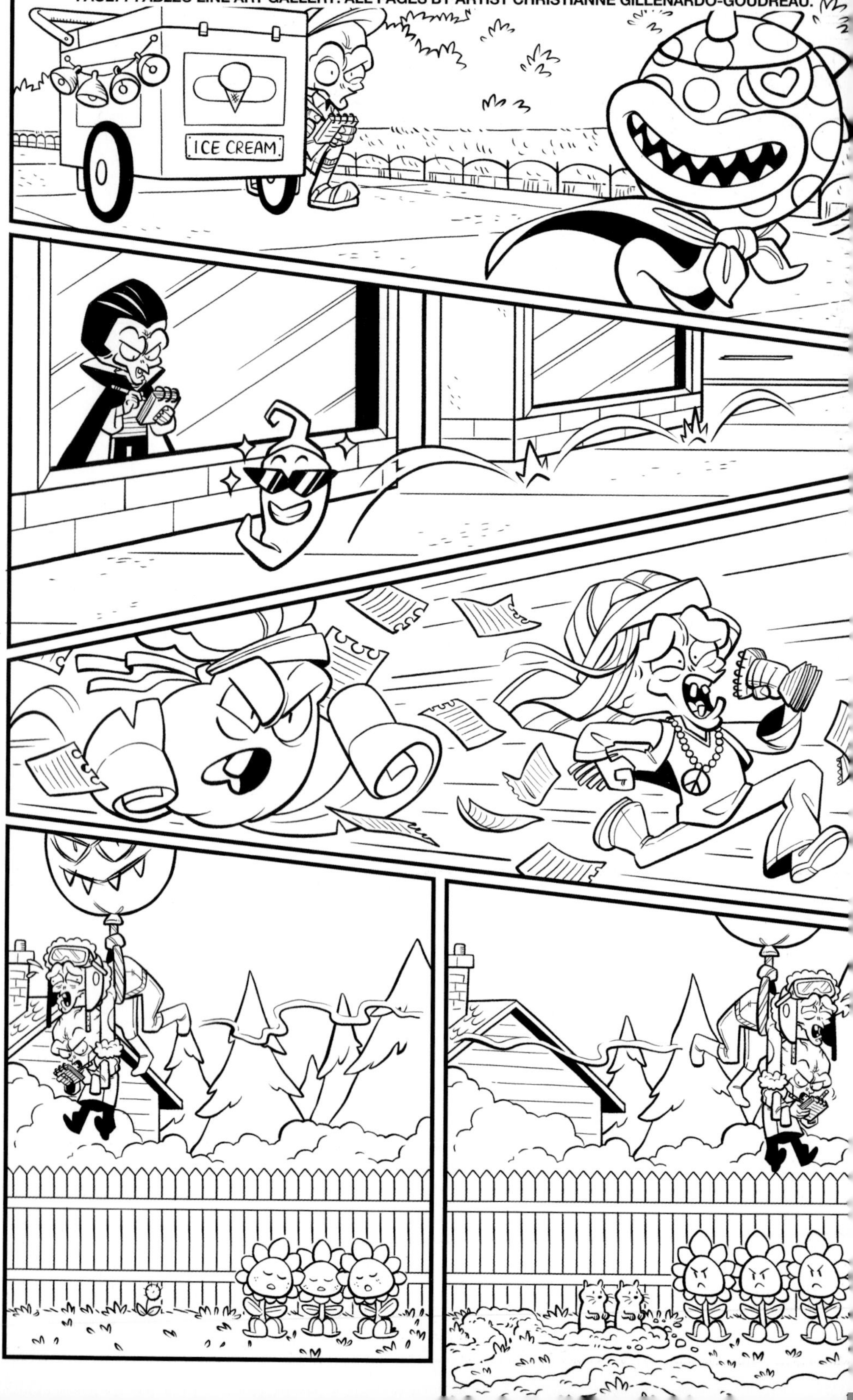
ICE CREAM

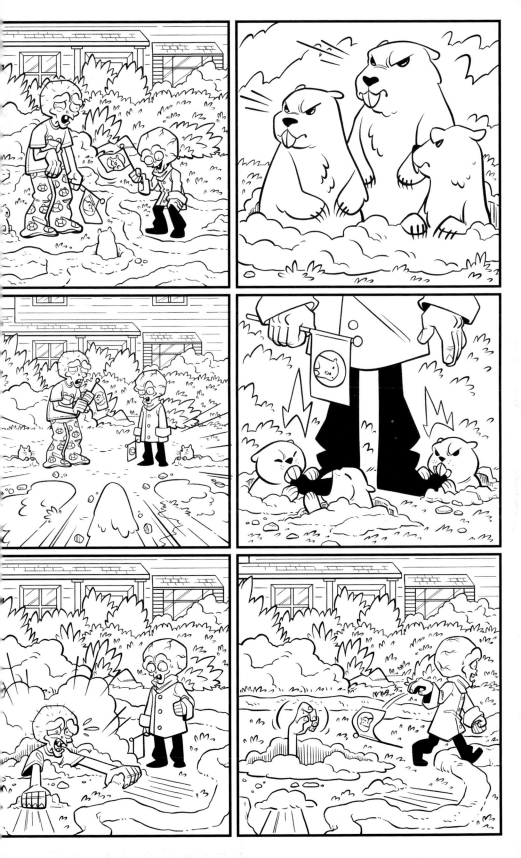

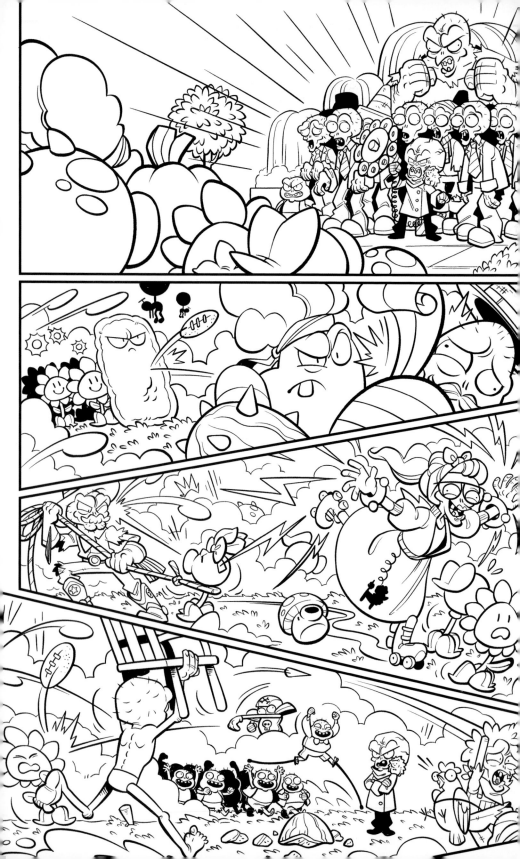

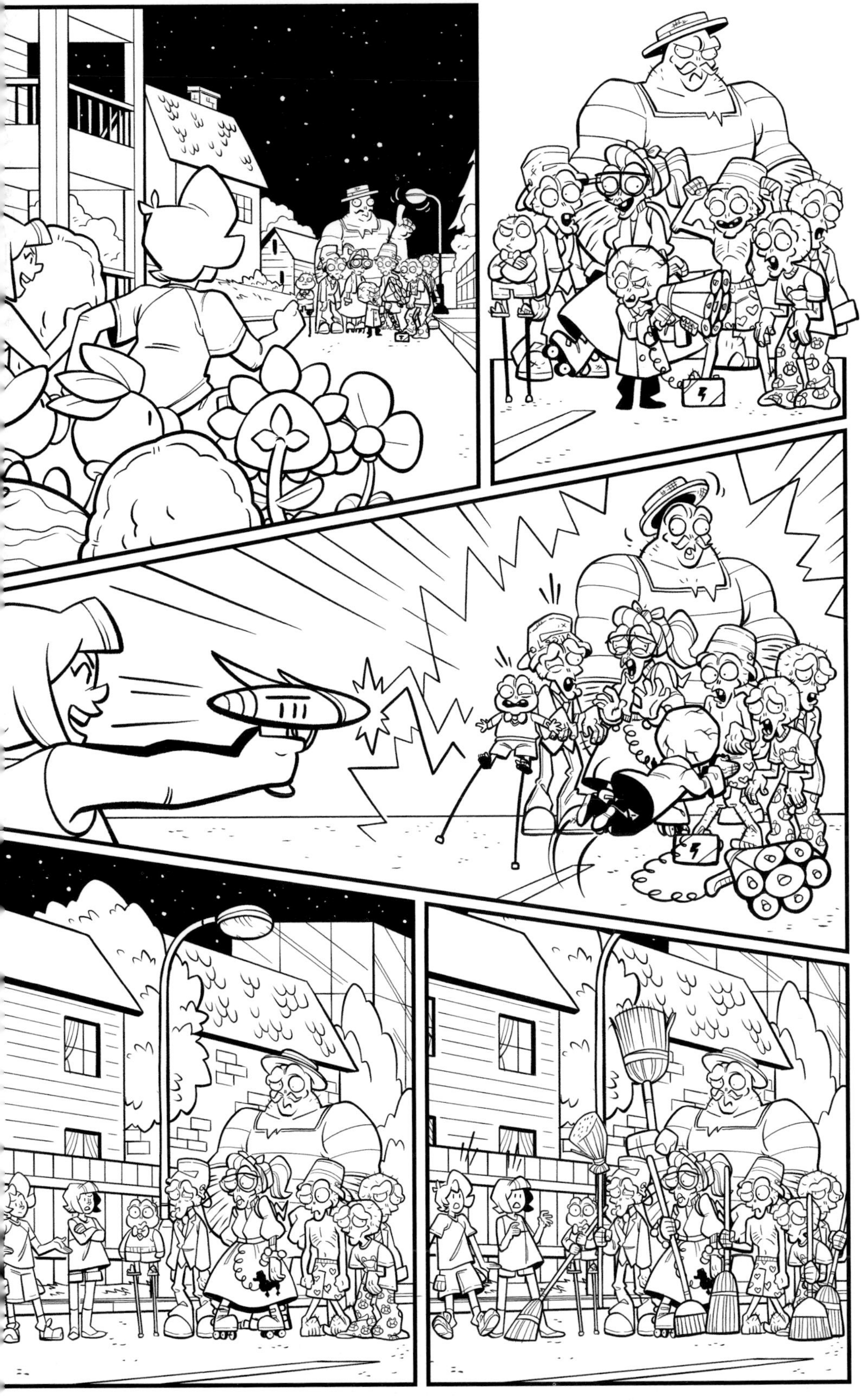

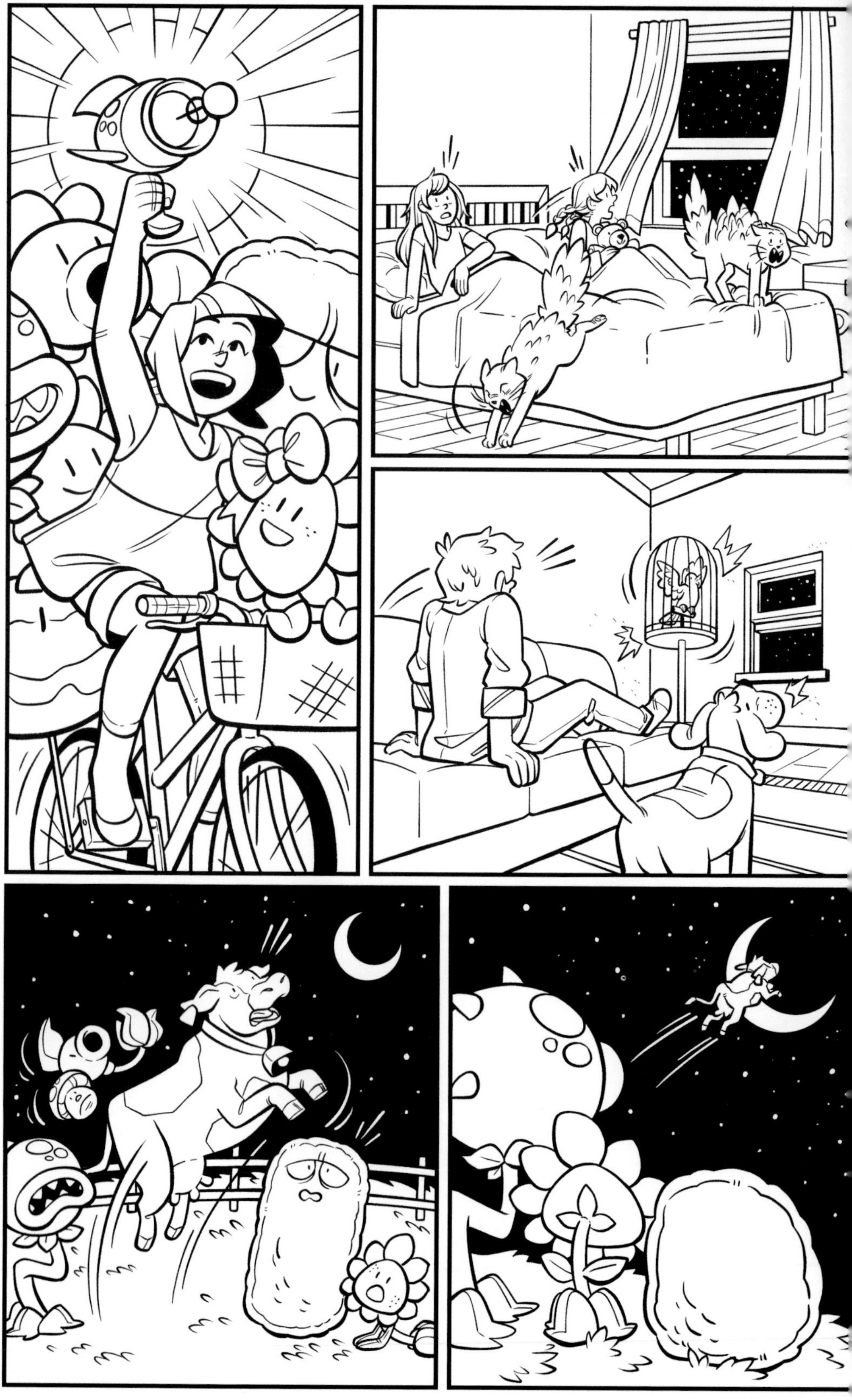

CREATOR BIOS

Paul Tobin

PAUL TOBIN is a 12th level writer and a 15th level cookie eater. He begins each morning in the manner we all do, by battling those zombies that have strayed too close to his pillow fort. Between writing all the *Plants vs. Zombies* comics and taking four naps a day, he's also found time to write the *Genius Factor* series of novels, the ape-filled *Banana Sunday* graphic novel, the award-winning *Bandette* series, the upcoming *Wrassle Castle* and *Earth Boy* graphic novels, and many other works. He has ridden a giant turtle and an elephant on purpose, and a tornado by accident.

Christianne
Gillenardo-Goudreau

CHRISTIANNE GILLENARDO-GOUDREAU is a comic artist and illustrator from Portland, Oregon. Her work has been featured in various anthologies and comics, including *Beyond: A Queer Sci-Fi And Fantasy Anthology*, *Plants vs. Zombies: Rumble at Lake Gumbo*, *Plants vs. Zombies: Better Homes and Guardens*, *Plants vs. Zombies: Multi-ball-istic*, *Harrow County*, and *Dept. H*. She is currently the interior artist for the series I *am Hexed*, by Kirsten Thompson. She lives with her wife, Donna, and their dumb cats, Hot Dog and Pancake.

Heather Breckel

HEATHER BRECKEL went to the Columbus College of Art and Design for animation. She decided animation wasn't for her, so she switched to comics. She's been working as a colorist for nearly ten years and has worked for nearly every major comics publisher out there. When she's not burning the midnight oil in a deadline crunch, she's either dying a bunch in videogames or telling her cats to stop running around at two in the morning.

Steve Dutro

STEVE DUTRO is a pinball fan and an Eisner Award-nominated comic book letterer from Redding, California, who can also drive a tractor. He graduated from the Kubert School and has been lettering comics since the days when foil-embossed covers were cool, working for Dark Horse (*The Fifth Beatle*, *I Am a Hero*, *StarCraft*, *Star Wars*, *Witcher*), Viz, Marvel, and DC Comics. He has submitted a request to the Department of Homeland Security that in the event of a zombie apocalypse he be put in charge of all digital freeway signs so citizens can be alerted to avoid nearby brain-eatings and the like. He finds the Plants vs. Zombies game to be a real stress-fest, but highly recommends the *Plants vs. Zombies* table on *Pinball FX2* for game-room hipsters.

ALSO AVAILABLE FROM DARK HORSE!

THE HIT VIDEO GAME CONTINUES ITS COMIC BOOK INVASION!

THE ART OF PLANTS VS. ZOMBIES
Part zombie memoir, part celebration of zombie triumphs, and part anti-plant screed, *The Art of Plants vs. Zombies* is a treasure trove of never-before-seen concept art, character sketches, and surprises from PopCap's popular *Plants vs. Zombies* games!

ISBN 978-1-61655-331-9 | $10.99

PLANTS VS. ZOMBIES: GARDEN WARFARE TRILOGY
Based on the hit video game series, these graphic novels tie in with the events in *Plants vs. Zombies: Garden Warfare 1* and *2* and *Plants vs. Zombies: Battle for Neighborville*!

VOLUME 1 ISBN 978-1-61655-946-5 | $10.99
VOLUME 2 ISBN 978-1-50670-548-4 | $10.99
VOLUME 3 ISBN 978-1-50670-837-9 | $10.99

PLANTS VS. ZOMBIES: LAWNMAGEDDON
Crazy Dave—the babbling-yet-brilliant inventor and top-notch neighborhood defender—helps young adventurer Nate fend off a zombie invasion that threatens to overrun the peaceful town of Neighborville. Their only hope is a brave army of chomping, squashing, and pea-shooting plants!

ISBN 978-1-61655-192-6 | $10.99

PLANTS VS. ZOMBIES: TIMEPOCALYPSE
Dr. Zomboss attacks throughout different timelines, keeping Crazy Dave, Patrice, Nate, and their powerful plant army busy!

ISBN 978-1-61655-621-1 | $10.99

PLANTS VS. ZOMBIES: BULLY FOR YOU
Patrice and Nate are ready to investigate a strange college campus to keep the streets safe from zombies!

ISBN 978-1-61655-889-5 | $10.99

PLANTS VS. ZOMBIES: GROWN SWEET HOME
With newfound knowledge of humanity, Dr. Zomboss strikes at the heart of Neighborville . . . sparking a series of plant-versus-zombie brawls!

ISBN 978-1-61655-971-7 | $10.99

PLANTS VS. ZOMBIES: PETAL TO THE METAL
Crazy Dave takes on the tough *Don't Blink* video game—and challenges Dr. Zomboss to a race to determine the future of Neighborville!

ISBN 978-1-61655-999-1 | $10.99

PLANTS VS. ZOMBIES: BOOM BOOM MUSHROOM
The gang discover Zomboss' secret plan for swallowing the city of Neighborville whole! A rare mushroom must be found in order to save the humans aboveground!

ISBN 978-1-50670-037-3 | $10.99

PLANTS VS. ZOMBIES: BATTLE EXTRAVAGONZO
Zomboss is back, hoping to buy the same factory that Crazy Dave is eyeing! Will Crazy Dave and his intelligent plants beat Zomboss and his zombie army to the punch?

ISBN 978-1-50670-189-9 | $10.99

PLANTS VS. ZOMBIES: LAWN OF DOOM
With Zomboss filling everyone's yards with traps and special soldiers, will he and his zombie army turn Halloween into their zanier Lawn of Doom celebration?!

ISBN 978-1-50670-204-9 | $10.99

PLANTS VS. ZOMBIES: THE GREATEST SHOW UNEARTHED
Dr. Zomboss believes that all humans hold a secret desire to run away and join the circus, so he aims to use his "Big Z's Adequately Amazing Flytrap Circus" to lure Neighborville's citizens to their doom!

ISBN 978-1-50670-298-8 | $10.99

PLANTS VS. ZOMBIES: RUMBLE AT LAKE GUMBO
The battle for clean water begins! Nate, Patrice, and Crazy Dave spot trouble and grab all the Tangle Kelp and Party Crabs they can to quell another zombie attack!

ISBN 978-1-50670-497-5 | $10.99

PLANTS VS. ZOMBIES: WAR AND PEAS
When Dr. Zomboss and Crazy Dave find themselves members of the same book club, a literary war is inevitable! The position of leader of the book club opens up and Zomboss and Crazy Dave compete for the top spot in a scholarly scuffle for the ages!

ISBN 978-1-50670-677-1 | $10.99

PLANTS VS. ZOMBIES: DINO-MIGHT
Dr. Zomboss sets his sights on destroying the yards in town and rendering the plants homeless—and his plans include dogs, cats, rabbits, hammock sloths, and, somehow, dinosaurs . . . !

ISBN 978-1-50670-838-6 | $10.99

PLANTS VS. ZOMBIES: SNOW THANKS
Dr. Zomboss invents a Cold Crystal capable of freezing Neighborville, burying the town in snow and ice! It's up to the humans and the fieriest plants to save Neighborville—with the help of pirates!

ISBN 978-1-50670-839-3 | $10.99

PLANTS VS. ZOMBIES: A LITTLE PROBLEM
Will an invasion of teeny-tiny miniature zombies mean the party for Crazy Dave's two-hundred-year-old pants gets canceled?

ISBN 978-1-50670-840-9 | $10.99

PLANTS VS. ZOMBIES: BETTER HOMES AND GUARDENS
Nate and Patrice try thwarting zombie attacks by putting defending "Guardens" plants *inside* homes as well as in yards! But as soon as Dr. Zomboss finds out, he's determined to circumvent this plan with an epically evil one of his own . . .

ISBN 978-1-50671-305-2 | $10.99

PLANTS VS. ZOMBIES: THE GARDEN PATH
You get to decide the fate of Neighborville in this new *Plants vs. Zombies* choose-your-own-adventure with multiple endings!

ISBN 978-1-50671-306-9 | $10.99

PLANTS VS. ZOMBIES: MULTI-BALL-ISTIC
Dr. Zomboss turns the entirety of Neighborville into a giant, fully functional pinball machine! Nate, Patrice, and their plant posse must find a way to halt this uniquely horrifying zombie invasion.

ISBN 978-1-50671-307-6 | $10.99

PLANTS VS. ZOMBIES: CONSTRUCTIONARY TALES
A behind-the-scenes look at the secret schemes and craziest contraptions concocted by Zomboss, as he proudly leads around a film crew from the Zombie Broadcasting Network!

ISBN 978-1-50672-091-3 | $10.99

PLANTS VS. ZOMBIES: DREAM A LITTLE SCHEME
Dr. Zomboss invents a machine that allows him to enter the dreams of Neighborville's citizens!

ISBN 978-1-50672-092-0 | $10.99

PLANTS VS. ZOMBIES: FAULTY FABLES
Dr. Zomboss sets out to lull the town to sleep with strange-yet-tedious fables of his own creation!

ISBN 978-1-50672-846-9 | $10.99

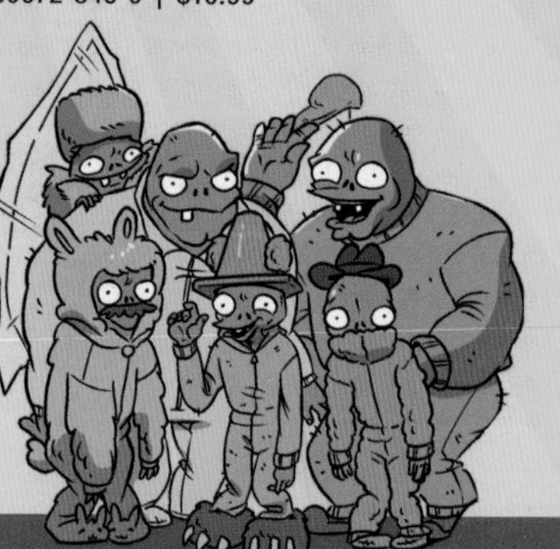

AVAILABLE AT YOUR LOCAL COMICS SHOP OR BOOKSTORE

To find a comics shop in your area, visit comicshoplocator.com. For more information or to order direct, visit **DarkHorse.com**

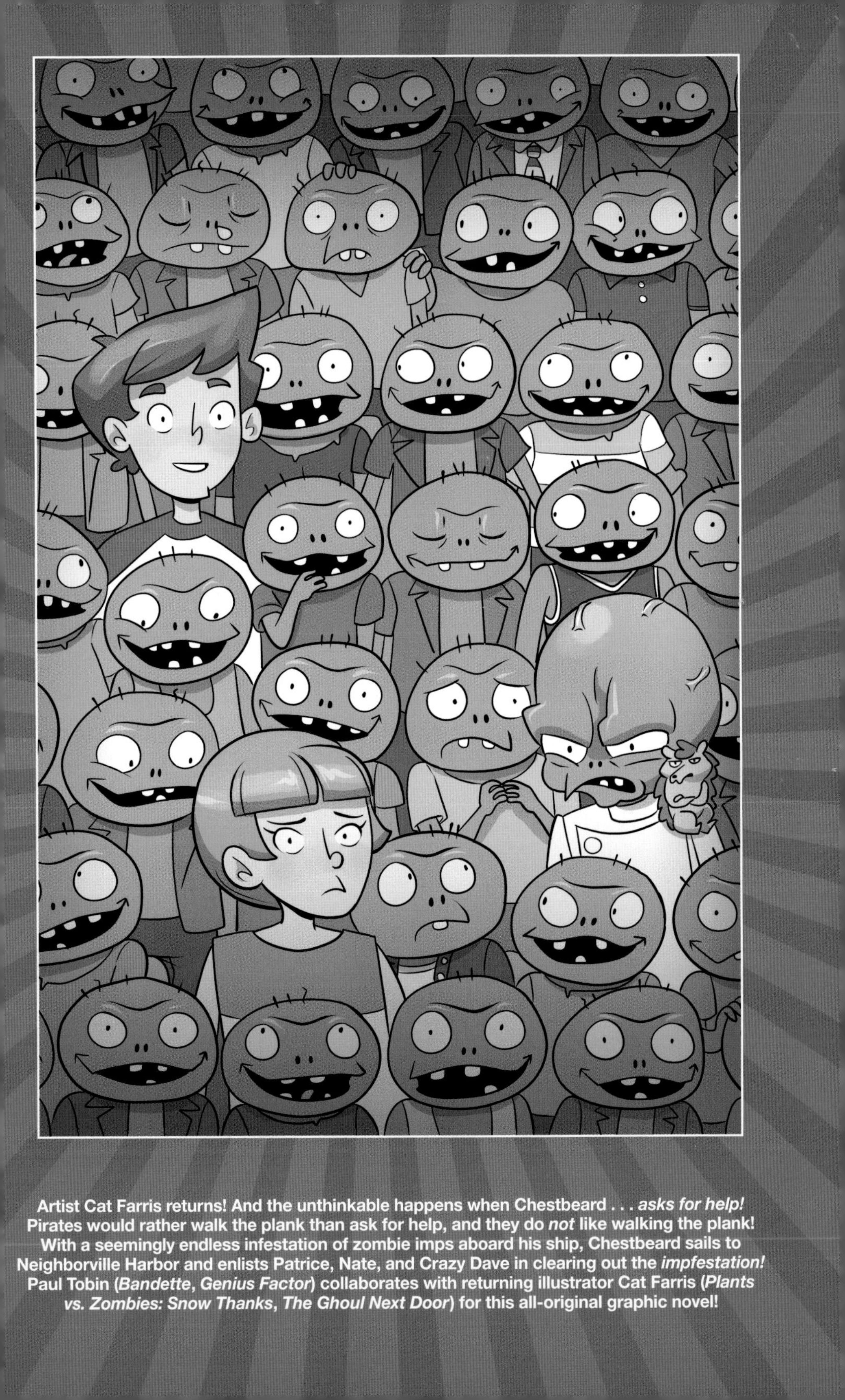

Artist Cat Farris returns! And the unthinkable happens when Chestbeard . . . *asks for help!* Pirates would rather walk the plank than ask for help, and they do *not* like walking the plank! With a seemingly endless infestation of zombie imps aboard his ship, Chestbeard sails to Neighborville Harbor and enlists Patrice, Nate, and Crazy Dave in clearing out the *impfestation!* Paul Tobin (*Bandette*, *Genius Factor*) collaborates with returning illustrator Cat Farris (*Plants vs. Zombies: Snow Thanks*, *The Ghoul Next Door*) for this all-original graphic novel!

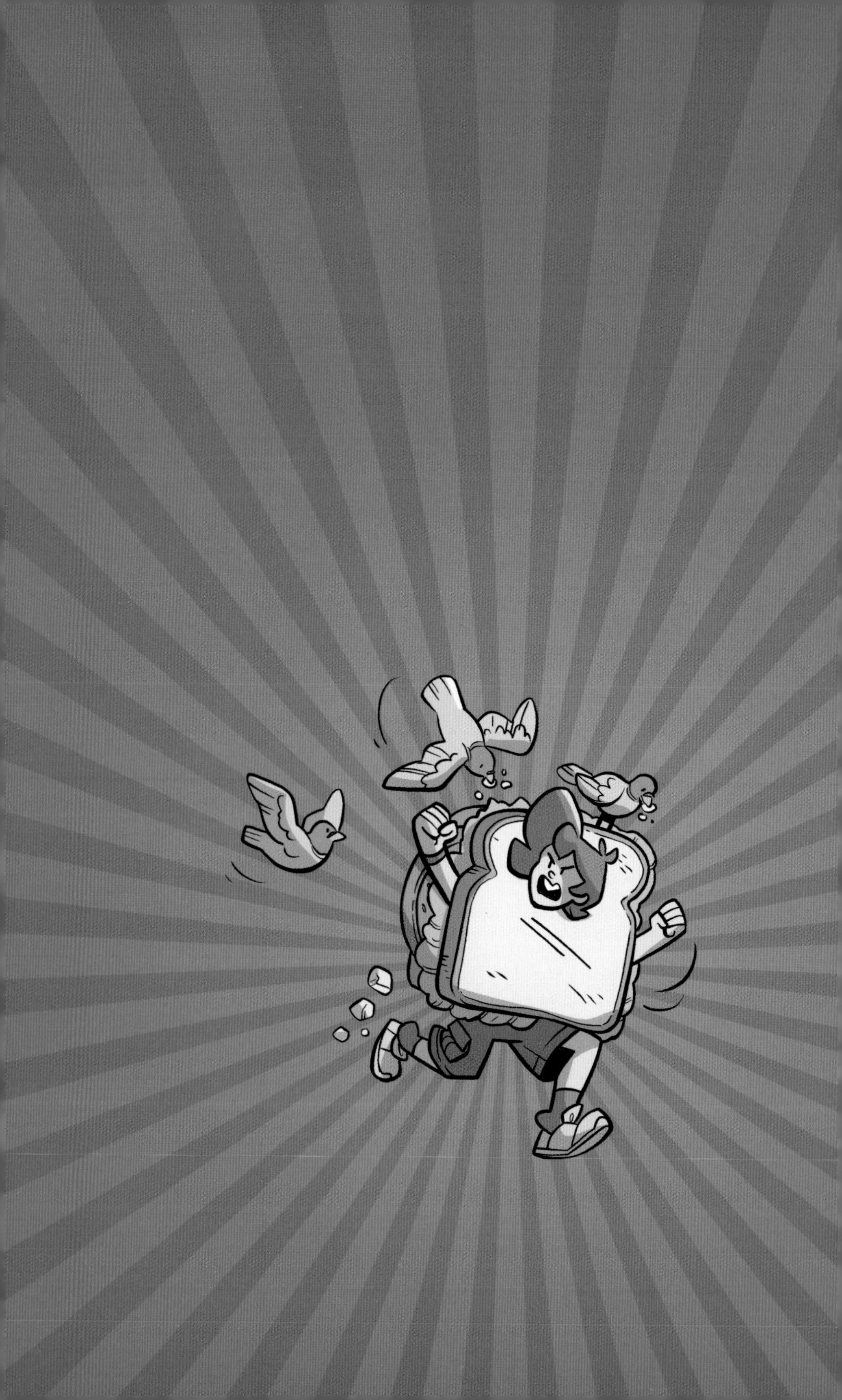

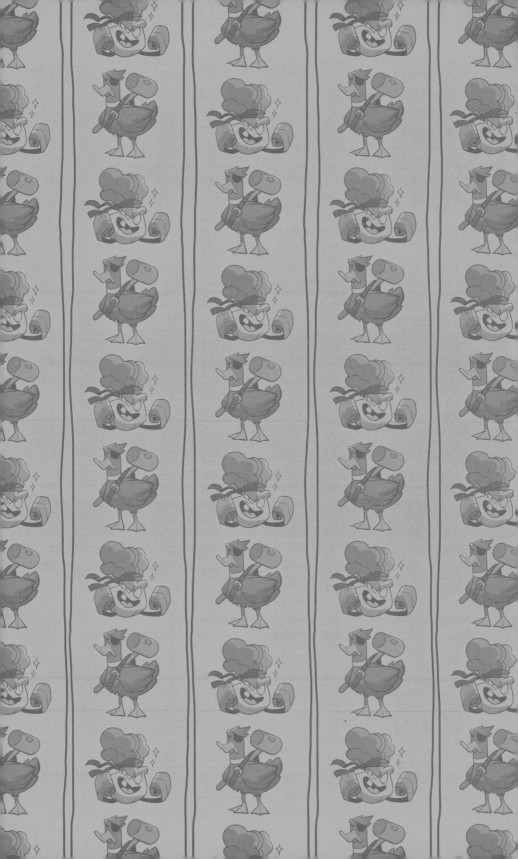